Book one of the RELATIVE series:

The Waking Hours

By Susan M. Nairn

ISBN-13: 9798694642736

Copyright © 2021 by Susan M. Nairn
All rights reserved.

This novel is a work of fiction. Names, characters, places, and incidents are either the product of the author's imagination or are used fictitiously. Any resemblance to actual events, locales, organizations, or persons living or dead is entirely coincidental and beyond the intent of the author.

The Waking Hours

Acknowledgements

I would be remiss if I did not first thank my family and my friends for their ongoing support. Feeling like I did not have to pressure you to read this novel before it was published means the world to me and inspired me to continue writing.

And to the many characters in my head, thank your for sharing your stories. Without you, this book would never have been written.

Cover Design: Agnesa Mahalla-Meha

Chapter 1

If Jack Brandon never slept again it would be a welcome change from facing the terrors that consumed him in his sleep each night. A new dream lurked behind the setting sun and the air was foul with the stench of his intense fear. His nerves were frayed, and his liver had been taking the brunt of his stress.

He looked at himself in the mirror for the third time. Dark circles were etched deep into his pallid skin and each wrinkle was a constant reminder of time marching across his face. He pulled his gaze from the mirror and glanced around his modest apartment. The collection of antique and clay figurines looked familiar but seemed vaguely out of place. He could not put a finger on it, but something was about to explode in his world and the acid in his stomach began to percolate, knowing he was about to endure another bad night.

He moved to the dry sink and poured himself a glass of red wine, subconsciously turning the glass three times before he picked it up. He padded through the thick carpet and sank into his favorite recliner. Although the condo was tastefully decorated, the recliner stuck out like a sore thumb. The remainder of the chocolate brown corduroy on the arms hung in tatters and foam spewed from the gaping holes but Jack refused to part with it. The chair had become his only comfort in a world where he felt like he was slowly going crazy. It was the one thing that grounded him and gave him the reassurance he still retained some of his sanity.

Since his vivid dreams had been slowly evolving into nightmares, he was happy he lived alone. Not only did he not have to disclose his physical reactions to his night terrors, but his other idiosyncrasies also never needed an explanation when he was by himself. He spun the remote control for the blinds three times before allowing himself to push the button to raise them to the top of the window. Taking three small sips from his wine glass, he woefully watched as the day commenced its journey into night. The sun lowered itself gradually, snuggled into the tree line and pulled up the blanket of the horizon.

As dusk inched its way into darkness, he remained listless in his chair. Blackness swept through the apartment and he was awash in a cascade of shadows and jagged streaks of moonlight. Although the solitude did have a serene quality, he could not shake the sense the darkness was preparing for a full-scale attack. After two more glasses of wine, he was feeling the effects and sleep crept methodically into the corners of his eyes, gently pulling down his eyelids. As his breathing became heavy and rhythmic, the black canvas of his dreamscape was brushed clean and anxiously awaited a new splash of color.

~~

Hours later, he emerged from his sleep to a tirade of rasping coughs and shallow breaths. In the few seconds it took for him to discern the sounds, Jack realized they were coming from him and beads of sweat rolled from his brow. His hands cut through the air in an arcing motion, reaching out for an invisible attacker. He worked at calming himself as he gasped large quantities of air. His dreams were no longer pleasant, and mornings were now a constant source of recollection and interpretation.

The fragments of his latest dream shimmered in his memory. The lingering image of a woman plagued his brain, but he could not retain any of the dream and she vanished. Pausing for a moment to collect himself, he rose unsteadily from the chair and tried to shake the fragments of sleep from his head. Shadows danced in the corners of the apartment and teased his eyes. He stumbled to the bathroom, having lost his equilibrium and he tripped over the furniture. After turning the doorknob three times he stepped into the bathroom, cranked on the hot water, and stripped out of his clothes.

The heated beads of water stung his skin, but he welcomed the pressure of the jet streams. Perhaps the pounding shower would help cleanse his growing sense of failure. His real estate career was going down the toilet and his reality suddenly slapped him in the face, leaving a giant handprint on his ego.

The Waking Hours

Although he was not ready to leave the shower, his hand involuntarily reached down to shut off the flow of water. He stared, completely puzzled by what he saw. The showerhead and faucet were different than he remembered. He tried to recall if the landlord had mentioned any upgrades, but nothing came to mind. He turned off the new faucets and threw open the shower curtain. Steam shrouded his vision as he toweled himself dry. As the mist began to clear, Jack stepped out from the shower and felt a plush bathmat under his feet. He did not own a bathmat. He reached to his left to wipe the mirror three times, but his arm only moved once. He had little control of his own body. He opened the bathroom door to let the fog escape and, after the last of the steam dissipated, his mouth fell open, gaping in utter disbelief at the bathroom that surrounded him. He was positive he had passed out in his own living room, but this was not his bathroom at all.

His body jerked unexpectedly and, as he slowly peered out of the bathroom door, the plaster surrounding the doorway exploded and showered him in chunks of debris. He was thrown to the floor, hands involuntarily covering his head as he listened to the second and third shots embedding themselves into the drywall behind him.

Chapter 2

Charlotte woke up with a hangman's knot tightening in her stomach. Her unsettled nerves twitched like onions in hot oil and she had no idea why she was feeling such irrational fear. As she waited for the kettle to boil, she crossed the hardwood floor in her living room and gazed out the open window. The morning promised nothing but gloom as the mottled gray clouds rolled through the sky, opening enough to allow tiny drops of rain to leak from them. The dank smell of wet pavement gradually intensified as the rain fell harder and it rose to greet her at the window. As the smell permeated the apartment, she pushed the window shut just as the kettle whistled its shrill cry. She sighed heavily as she crossed the floor to begin her morning routine. She could only hope the day would come when she would not be plagued by boredom and the impression that life had essentially passed her by.

After looking through her expansive collection of books, she chose a title she had not read in a while, got ready for work, and left the apartment. As she slid the key into the deadbolt lock, she could have sworn she heard the faint whisper of a man's voice behind her. She could not make out what he said but the hair on the back of her neck stood at full attention. Momentarily losing her balance, she staggered backwards and reached for the wall to help regain her composure. A swell of bile rose in the back of her throat and she wrestled with the acid, swallowing several times before it retreated to her stomach. As quickly as the feeling came, it passed, and the voice was silent. Were it not for the beads of perspiration on her forehead, she would not have believed what had just transpired. Her fingers fluttered slightly as she wiped the sweat from her brow. She glanced over her shoulder to make sure she was alone and continued her way to the antique shop.

The rain had stopped but the haze still hung in the distance. Her intuition made her extremely wary of her surroundings and it was an absurd feeling. She had traveled this route every day for the past five years. It was usually such a lovely walk through the park, but today the foreshadowing of the weather was lending itself to the gnawing in the pit of her stomach. She hunched her shoulders forward and trudged through the lingering puddles, constantly looking over her shoulder to make sure she was not being followed.

She continued her solitary journey through the remnants of the passing storm, realizing she had never felt more alone. Her parents had been dead for over five years, her brother for more than seventeen years, and Alzheimer's had ensured her only living relative did not know who she was. Once a week she dutifully spent a lonely hour with her grandmother and sat at the end of her bed, a stranger.

She followed the path through the park and eventually emerged on the other side. The traffic was beginning to build, and the din of the city reverberated in her eardrums. The pedestrian traffic grew denser as well and she found herself herded into the crowd. She passed an apartment building with a handsome man in the doorway, and something about his melancholy look caught and held her attention. Charlotte's frame was too small to fight the surge of the crowd and, as hard as she jockeyed for an escape, the crowd had her and would not let her go. The handsome stranger disappeared from her peripheral vision and she gave in to the flow of the crowd. Although she would most likely never see him again, the thought of him made her smile for the first time in a long time.

With her bout of vertigo and the strange whisper distant memory, she began her workday with a more cheerful outlook. The antique store was unusually busy for a Tuesday, and before long she had forgotten all about the episode and the man who had so easily captured her attention.

A slight breeze wound its way through the store and tickled the wind chimes just enough to make her look up. The man she had seen earlier was leaning against the store window. His face was pressed to the pane of glass and his hands were cupped around his eyes as if he were searching for someone. She felt a hot fire on her cheeks. She could neither explain her sudden adolescent reaction nor could she understand it; she only knew she had to control it. She spun to face the back of the store and put her hands to her cheeks, suddenly giddy. Lowering her hands, she slowly turned back to find the man had gone. She went to the window to look for him, but he had left no trace of being there.

She stood at the window in the front of the store for several minutes, willing him to come back, but hers was the only face she could see reflected in the glass. The clamor of activity in the space behind her increased until she was drawn back into reality. Before she stepped away from the window, she was overwhelmed by a juvenile urge. She put her face as close to the glass as possible without touching it and exhaled heavily onto the window, letting her breath settle on the glass in a small circle. With her index finger, she slowly traced the outline of a heart in the vapor. She smiled, but the smile faded as she watched the moisture evaporate and the heart disappear. With a slight hesitation, she turned around to engage with her customers. Although she loved antiques, she knew this store was a steppingstone in the path of her life and she was anxious to see what the next chapter of her life had in store for her.

When the traffic in the store had dissipated, Charlotte opened her laptop to pick up where she had left off in her online course. Her previous degree in Science allowed her to pursue a Master's degree in Library Science and she was eager to combine her passion for science with her love for reading and research.

Out of the corner of her eye, she could see the pattern of shadows change on the floor and she knew the sun was moving into its late afternoon position. Traffic on the sidewalk was now congested, which could only mean she was nearing the end of her workday.

Closing time came and was marked by the chiming of several grandfather clocks. She checked all the locks on the doors and windows, set the alarm and left the store to follow her familiar route home. The park beckoned and her walk home was much more pleasant than her hurried walk to work. She leisurely strolled the paths, breathing in the fresh early evening air and watched the leaves dance as they were tickled by the wind.

Chapter 3

Face down on the ground and hands still covering his head, Jack quickly tried to assess his situation. He was in a strange apartment, he had little control over his body, and he had been the intended target of a bullet or three. The click of the cylinder brought his attention flooding back to reality and his heart pumped blood through his veins at an alarmingly fast rate. As Jack concluded the shooter no longer had a loaded gun, the intruder sprinted for the front door and Jack crudely recovered from his dive to the floor to throw on his clothes and follow.

On his way through the living room, he realized the rest of the apartment was unrecognizable. Rushing through the unfamiliar room, he wondered if his eyes were playing tricks on him. He remembered comfortably losing consciousness in his favorite recliner but a quick glance around the living room assured him it was not there. With a twinge of fear and an inexplicable urge to look in the mirror, Jack glanced at himself on the way to the front door. He could see familiar parts of himself, but his appearance was different, almost like a hologram. From the hallway, he glanced back at the shattered drywall outside of the bathroom. The bullet holes were certainly real and so was the smell of intense fear. The sound of the gun shots moments ago must have startled the neighbors. Wailing sirens could be heard in the distance and Jack knew they were headed in his direction. He was pulled out of the unfamiliar apartment and awkwardly ran after the stranger who was probably halfway down the stairs.

Jack reached the apartment lobby and headed for the revolving door after the shooter but stopped when the security guard hollered at him.

"Hey Dave," the guard said. "You shouldn't be down here. Didn't you hear the gunshots?"

He stared at the guard for a moment before he responded.

"Yeah, they were a little too close for comfort."

The words the guard heard were not the words Jack spoke, nor was it Jack's voice that came out of his mouth.

Jack was happy to be pulled away from any further conversation with the security guard and exited the lobby. He stood at the top of the concrete stairs, watching the crowd move along the sidewalk. He spotted her in the middle of the mass. His breath caught in his throat and he kept his focus on her for as long as he could. She was the face from his previous dreams, the face that lingered for only seconds after he awoke, and the face he could never truly remember. Frozen in his place, he eventually lost sight of her, but the contours of her face were now imprinted in his brain. When he was at last able to take his eyes from the spot she had been, he glanced around the street. Nothing was familiar at all. This was not his neighborhood. These streets had rows of trees between them and smaller shops lined the streets. Where the hell was he? Who the hell was Dave? Was this all just a very lucid dream that he had yet to wake from?

He walked down the steps to the sidewalk and stumbled aimlessly, unsure of what he was looking for anymore. He suspected the mystery man was long gone but he moved to the window of a little antique shop for a closer look, thinking the man he was looking for may have taken refuge in one of these shops. The sun had been fighting its way through the clouds and the reflection was making it difficult to see. He cupped his hands around his eyes and peered into the store. His attention was immediately drawn to the back of the store and it took a few seconds for him to make out the contour of her face. The woman he saw on the street moments ago was only a few feet away. As he focused on her face, she turned away.

A sudden movement over his shoulder caught his attention and he turned his head. The gunman knew he had been spotted and took off at a fast pace. Although his desire to catch up to this guy was overwhelming, Jack wanted to see the woman's face again, but his body was jerked away from the window and he sprinted clumsily along the sidewalk. As he ran, Jack glanced at the street signs hoping they would give him a clue as to where he was. Nothing was familiar. He continued his pursuit for several blocks until he could not run any more. The streets seemed unnaturally silent. As he tried to catch his breath, Jack let his gaze travel around the unfamiliar streets and tried to quiet his panting. He knew he would not hear the guy he was looking for, but he did not want to draw any unnecessary attention to himself. Dark clouds smothered the sun's rays, and the threat of rain was imminent. Jack continued to search the side streets. The stranger had obviously been well-versed in losing a tail because, once they entered this new part of town, Jack lost sight of him and was convinced he was now the rodent in this crazy cat and mouse game. He cautiously wandered the alleys and tried to keep his wits sharp. He was so interested in the muffled sounds of the outdoor market business; he did not hear the footsteps coming out of the alley.

The guttural voice reverberated in his ears, "Fucking amateurs. Three times some jackass has tried to get rid of you. They should have just hired me in the first place."

Jack felt a stinging sensation in his upper arm and white-hot pain. Everything in his line of vision blurred and gradually disappeared.

~~

Jack slowly regained consciousness and strained to listen to the sounds of the muted voices around him. Blindfolded, the world beyond his mind remained dark. The deep burning in his wrists urged him to sit as still as possible so the ropes did not cut further into his skin. He was able to distinguish only a few words, so the gist of the full conversation was indecipherable. He had an acerbic taste in his mouth, probably from whatever it was that had been injected into his arm, and his bladder had expanded to twice its size. Now that he had time to reflect on the events of the day, Jack decided the most intelligent course of action would have been to dial 911, but there were too many answers he would not have had to the questions he knew the police would ask. How he had become involved in this situation and why he had no control over his body were still the most important questions at the top of his own list.

Time passed slowly and Jack struggled to hear the fragments of conversation that eluded him. Incomprehensible noises moved in and out like the ebb and flow of a tide. The lingering effect of the drug and the undulating sounds around him weakened Jack's strength. He began to lose consciousness and was startled awake by a gunshot. Moments later, his blindfold was removed and after rapidly blinking away the stark transition from dark to light, Jack was confronted by the silhouette of a man. He

wrestled with the bonds on his wrists and only irritated the abrasions. A hoarse laugh escaped the man in front of him. Jack's eyes adjusted to the low light in the room and his focus became riveted on the man's right hand, so he did not see the crumpled body of the other man in the corner. The man in front of him slowly raised the pistol and pointed it at Jacks' temple.
"Goodbye, David. Enjoy the darkness."

Jack never heard the shot before the bullet pierced his skull and everything turned black.

Chapter 4

Black. There was something about black that had always fascinated Victor. He would sit in his apartment for hours amidst the sparse furnishings in relative darkness. Intriguing images would dance in the shadows and Victor was convinced the phantom rituals were performed to entertain him. The dark never frightened him. When his mother had punished him by sending him to the root cellar as a child, she had done him a favor. He thrived in that cellar.

"She never knew." He spoke to himself in the voice of a petulant child.

The sound of his voice pulled him from his trance, and he focused on the barbed slivers of light filtering through the shadows. His apartment was on the twenty-first floor of a high-security building. Victor believed the higher the apartment, the more status you were understood to have achieved. He never worked at a real job. Terminating life had always been a great hobby of his and he had managed to turn it into a very lucrative career. He was good at what he did, and he was rewarded handsomely for his discretion and expertise. He had been all over the world, killing for many people and many purposes but, after the job was completed, he preferred the darkness and solitude of his apartment. He felt comfortable and safe there. He had never been prosecuted for his murderous habits, not even his mother's death, nor had any law enforcement descended on his sanctuary during any investigations. Victor felt he was invincible, above the laws of man. The darkness within him made him special.

He lifted himself from the tiled floor and crossed the room to stare out over the city. He fully opened the curtains to discover twilight had snuck up on the high rises. Victor welcomed the dusk. Streetlights sputtered as they tried to defend the sun's light in its absence and Victor was amused by their feeble attempts to cast out the murkiness. The obscurity of the dark was extremely powerful. Feeling a sudden kinship with the evening, Victor prepared to join the other creatures of the night. He pulled on his black

Levis and black hooded sweatshirt. He tucked his Glock 9mm into his shoulder holster and pulled his black jacket over the weapon. He chose the Glock because it was a gun designed to be easy to conceal.

He quietly left the apartment and took the elevator down to the lobby. Joe was on shift and greeted Victor with his usual exuberance. Looking up from his tabloid magazine, he nodded and went back to his article. Joe was not known for his conversation skills and it was one of the qualities Victor admired most about him. He left the building without incident and entered the night.

Startling only a few birds who were bathing themselves in the puddles, he meandered along the pavement. Unsure of his destination, he knew he would eventually be drawn in the right direction. He always was. His predatory instinct had always been acutely sensitive, and he was depending on it again tonight. Killing for a living was a great career but killing for sport was what Victor enjoyed most. The look of surrender that washed over the face of a person the moment death seized them was a gift for only Victor's eyes and that was where his strength came from. He first realized this truth at the tender age of fourteen when his mother had become his first victim. It was not a sad moment when he took her life. She had bestowed upon him the greatest gift he had ever received, the darkness, and for that he would be eternally grateful. But she had been holding him back and he had desperately needed to move on.

After the police ruled her death an accident, Victor was sent to live with his Godmother. He was enrolled in a high school he would never set foot in, but he was grateful to be in a more populated place. This new place was what Victor called a 'target-rich environment'. Although his Godmother noticed Victor was a loner, she had convinced herself he must have made some friends since he was going out every night. Since he had just lost his mother, she did not want to pry and left him to grieve as he wanted to grieve.

But Victor did not grieve, he hunted. He walked the streets at night to avoid confrontation. He never chose a target, the target was always presented to him, like an unwrapped gift. Even at the age of fifteen, Victor was careful about how long he spent watching his prey. He did not kill again for a couple years after his mother's death, not because his urges had disappeared but because he was smart, and once he had killed his second victim, there was no turning back.

Shaking the reverie from his mind, Victor realized he was at the edge of the park. He did not recall the route he took to get there but he put his faith in the power that guided him. There was a purpose for him being here. Joggers and dog walkers crowded the paths of the park, and in the glow of artificial light, the glorious bushes of floral combinations created a spectral portrait.

Although Victor preferred darkness, he was able to appreciate beauty. He stopped to let the rainbow of colors dance for him and when he looked up from the flowers she was there. Her long brown hair hung in waves half the length of her back and swayed ever so slightly in the breeze. If Victor were like other men, he might find her attractive. She had a serene quality that was quite endearing. But Victor saw only the darkness in her, the black oasis that was meant solely for him.

Evening had fully settled on the park and the blackness of the night enveloped her, caressed her. Victor stood with his hands at his side not wanting to move and startle the woman standing near him. She had an air of innocence and youth about her and she began to playfully kick the leaves in her path, not noticing the imminent danger. Victor lifted his nose to the air and inhaled a deep breath. The slight scents of Lavender and Eucalyptus penetrated his nostrils and the smell lingered with his refusal to exhale.

Victor took a step sideways to hide himself deeper in the shadows and remain out of her line of vision. She seemed to be lost in a memory and gazing at a mural into the past. As Victor took one more precautionary step, the sound of the cracking branch was deafening. He stumbled further into the bush. Like a deer in the wilderness, her shock and keen awareness registered immediately. Her reverie vanished and was replaced by fear. She walked along the path with the speed and grace of a jungle cat. Victor silently cursed himself for being so distracted and letting himself become careless. She streaked by Victor's hiding spot and continued along the path out of the park. She was smart and she stuck as close to the lights as possible. Victor would have emerged from his hole in the darkness to follow her were it not for the young couple approaching hand in hand. He moved back into the recess of the shadows and tried to visually follow the girl. She reached the edge of the park and disappeared into the night. Victor cursed under his breath again. The darkness was supposed to be his ally and tonight it conspired against him.

His anger swelled in his belly, rising like a tidal wave. The surge of emotion coursed through his veins and something inside him sprang open. Stealthily, Victor crept from his lair. His calculated movements allowed him to circle around the couple and surface from the dense brush. The couple was shocked to see him stumbling from the bush, distraught and on the verge of tears. Victor took shallow breaths and did his best to appear upset.

"Could you please help me?" His voice came in staccato bursts. "The kitten. My girlfriend. Asked me to look after it while she was away. I have to find it."

Victor absorbed the details of the young man. He looked like Opie from the Andy Griffith Show and thankfully had the same disposition. Without a moment's hesitation, the boy had convinced his girlfriend it would only take a few minutes. They left the path and joined Victor by the tree line.

Victor suddenly spoke in an octave much lower than his panicked plea.

"It is pretty dark in here. How do you feel about darkness?"

Chapter 5

As she had the previous morning, Charlotte awoke with an overwhelming sense of dread. This time it was self-inflicted as she reflected on her walk through the park the previous night. She chastised herself for staying out so late on her own, but the night was so fresh and the memory of the man she had seen earlier in the day had finally made her feel alive.

She smiled at the memory of him as she got out of bed and made her way to the kitchen. She plugged in the kettle and abruptly the smile vanished as she recalled the feeling of being watched in the park. The loud cracking in the bush had covered her smooth skin in goosebumps as she took heed of her inner voice and left the park as quickly as she could. Her body shook violently as the memory of her fear sent shockwaves through her temporal lobe.

She crossed the living room and turned on the television to watch the morning news. The lead story drained the color from her face. Police were investigating a double homicide that had occurred in the park the previous night. Charlotte's body swayed and the room began to spin but she remained in her place. The news anchor was describing the brutal nature of the crime as scenes of the park flashed across the screen. The two bodies, shrouded by cloth, lay listless on the ground. Charlotte recognized the spot immediately.

"I was right there." It was barely a whisper.

The kettle screamed and sent a dagger into Charlotte's chest, making her heart skip a beat. Unable to watch the rest of the broadcast, Charlotte turned away from the television and returned to the kitchen to stifle the screeching whistle of the kettle. The gooseflesh on her arms tingled and she could not suppress the urge to gag. With the kettle finally silent, Charlotte pressed her hands against the counter and closed her eyes. Being still and closing out the periphery calmed her slightly, but her imagination betrayed her. Behind her closed eyelids, emergency beacons began to flash, and she could only think of what might have happened to her in the park if she had not been frightened enough to leave as quickly as possible. Her eyes blinked open and she made herself a cup of tea. The memory of the man in the apartment building was vague, but it seemed to be the only thought she could maintain that gave her a sense of peace. She had only seen him for a moment, but his face was vividly ingrained in her mind. She desperately hoped their paths would cross again.

 The lights of the police cars were still flashing on the screen. She turned the television off and opted for a more pleasant scene that lay just outside of her window. The heat from the cup of tea seeped into her hands and she willed that warmth travel through her body. She was hoping it would magically assuage the chill she still felt realizing she was so close to danger last night.

 She dragged herself from the window and began the morning ritual of getting ready for work but, as she crossed the living room, she glanced over her shoulder to check the deadbolt and chain lock were firmly in place. She was unsure if the killer had even seen her but, if he had, she figured he would never give her a second thought. Her inner voice continued to nag until she walked to the door, unbolted, and bolted the lock three times and rattled the chain to make sure they were secure. Satisfied the door was impenetrable, she headed to the bathroom and turned on the hot water. The hiss from the tap startled her and she fell back onto the sink stand. Water slowly began to fight the air in the faucet and the water won.

 Charlotte was still hanging on the edge of the cabinet when she noticed shadows in her bedroom moving across the carpet. She stifled a scream until she remembered she had left the bedroom window open and the curtains were blowing in the wind. The shadows were performing an eerie dance on the floor and she was hoping their movement was not premonitory.

 The shower worked its magic and sluiced some of her weariness. Charlotte put her irrational fear aside and tried to recall anything of importance from the incident at the park the previous night. Perhaps her information could help the investigation, even if only in the slightest way. She replayed the walk home in her head. She remembered the feeling of freedom as she kicked the leaves on the path, and she tried to recall precisely where she had been when she had the feeling she was being watched. She committed herself to stop and speak to the investigators on her way to work to see if she could give them any insight into the case.

The Waking Hours

The tea did not have the calming effect she had hoped for and she promised herself she would put Anna in charge of the shop for the afternoon and she would leave early to avoid coming home in any sort of darkness.

Chapter 6

'Enjoy the darkness'. The words hovered over Jack's head in a cartoon dialogue balloon only he could see. He stirred from what seemed like one of his worst dreams yet. The pressure at his forehead was intense and his arms were precariously twisted behind his back. Beads of sweat trickled down his brow as he began to recall portions of his dream. The vividness of this dream was much stronger than any he had experienced before. He struggled to retrieve his limbs and all his muscles screamed as he returned his arms into a normal position. He noticed the dried blood on his wrists as the tenderness in his body became more apparent. Jack blinked repeatedly to focus and discovered he was back in his home and it showed no signs of a struggle. The clay figurines were all placed precisely in the locations they had been earlier in the evening. Jack glanced to his left and noted the lock and latch were both still engaged on the front door. His glass of red wine still secured its position on the table beside his chair and contained the remnants of the wine he had been drinking what felt like days ago but should only have been last night.

He lifted himself to a standing position and buoyed with a small bout of vertigo, which landed him back in his recliner. His head spun and his stomach screamed for permission to throw up. The symptoms did not feel at all like the flu and he could not ascertain how he felt. He sat for a moment to let the dizziness pass and focused on the details of the dream he could remember. He vaguely recalled a single light bulb on a chain, a chair, and a tiny room. The shadow of a man lurked behind his vision, but he could not put a face to him at all. He knew he had been shorter in stature and, as the pieces began to form segments of the puzzle, he recalled the voice. The low, gravelly voice reverberated in his brain, making his blood run cold. It was a haunting sound and one he recalled with great clarity. Jack tried to bring back more details of the dream, but the voice overshadowed all other thoughts and he reluctantly began to tremble.

The Waking Hours

Three times his hands went to his forehead and it was the third time he discovered the circular wound. He had not fallen, or at least not that he could remember, but his forehead certainly presented signs of trauma as his fingers gingerly moved around the laceration. From his sense of touch, he assumed the mark was round but, until he reached the mirror, nothing was sure. Once he saw his reflection, Jack was stunned to see the circular burn on his temple. His gaze fell to his wrists and his flesh was raw and inflamed. His eyes returned to the image in the mirror and his finger slowly circled the mark on his forehead three times. Jack had watched enough Criminal Minds reruns to know what a bullet hole looked like, or at least a crime drama facsimile of a bullet hole. What he could not comprehend was how his dream could be vivid enough for him to self-inflict lingering wounds in his sleep without waking himself up.

Jack had previously decided to go into the office today, but how the Hell could he possibly explain lacerated wrists and what looked like a bullet hole in his forehead? He called the office and made up some bogus story for his absence. He was sure by now they were beginning to keep a running log of his creative excuses for not being there.

Now that he was back in his own apartment, Jack went to his medicine cabinet and found his antiseptic cream. He applied it liberally to his wrists and forehead and took a couple of pills to ease the pounding at his temples. Although his dreams had become much more intense lately, Jack had never shown any physical injuries after waking from them until today.

When he was finished cleaning himself up, he headed back to the living room. Fragments of his dream played a game of tag in his brain and he subconsciously looked over his shoulder at the door frame to the bathroom. He was not sure exactly what he was looking for but there was absolutely nothing there that would trigger a memory. His dry sink stood to his left and, although it was still considered early, he poured himself a shot of whiskey. It was five PM somewhere. He let the alcohol linger in his mouth and enjoyed the slow burn as it slid down his throat.

Jack had only been awake for a short time, but he was exhausted. He knew his body needed rest, but he was too paranoid to let himself consciously go to sleep. After several more shots of whiskey, he walked zombie-like across his living room and sank into the welcoming recliner. He did his best to fight off the need to close his eyes, but his fatigue mixed with the pain killers and whiskey was too potent a combination and he fell into a chemically induced slumber.

Chapter 7

The brightness of the day was still strong when Charlotte left the shop for the day. Anna was exceedingly capable of minding the shop for the remainder of the afternoon and Charlotte wanted to be hyper-vigilant about getting home safely and not feeling like a victim as she had the previous evening.

Her path home was much more direct than usual, but she did not want to make herself a target to any predator who may still be lingering in the park. With her quickened steps, she did not take the time to inhale the smells of the park. She continued along the most congested parts of the paths so she would blend in with the crowds, and soon her apartment building was in sight. She left the throngs of people behind and was a few meters away from the entrance when she heard a man whisper the name "Charlie". She stopped in her tracks and turned to follow the direction she thought the sound came from. Nobody was behind her. The phantom voice seemed to have materialized out of thin air. The crowd she had so happily lost herself in had continued moving without her, leaving her standing alone in front of her apartment building hearing voices that were arguably non-existent.

She could not bring herself to go inside, not yet. Why had she heard the name Charlie? If it was meant for her, nobody had called her Charlie since her brother Max had disappeared seventeen years ago. He was the only person who refused to call her Charlotte. Hearing that name had taken her back and a melancholy smile made its way to her lips as she thought about her brother.

Her smile quickly turned sour as she weighed the reality of her situation. She was standing alone on a set of concrete steps, hearing voices, and running from the stranger in the park she felt had been targeting her. Truthfully, she could have just been in the wrong place at the wrong time, but in her gut, she knew she was the intended target. It was an irrational thought, but one she believed in with every ounce of her being.

She climbed to the top step but turned to seek the source of the strange whisper once again. There was nobody remotely close to her who could have uttered that name. Even the birds had gone silent. Charlotte knew when the forest goes silent there is a predator among the innocent, and they silence themselves to stay alive.

She opened the door to her building and made sure it locked behind her. She could not bring herself to go to her apartment just yet. She lingered in the lobby, silently watching the front of the building to see if anyone would come out of hiding. She knew she was grasping at the smallest of hopes, but she did not see another option.

The streetlamps began to ignite, and one by one the lights began to hum and coat the street with an eerie candescent light. As much as she knew it would be getting dark soon and her chance of seeing anything out of the reach of the lights would be impossible, she was riveted to her place. Other tenants returned home from their day of work, mumbling inaudibly as they passed, and Charlotte began to feel like the Wal-Mart greeter as her fake smile welcomed them into the lobby. She felt ridiculous and knew it was time to give up the spy session and go up to her apartment.

No sooner had she made the decision to leave, she thought she saw movement in one of the bushes. She pushed herself as far back as she could while maintaining her line of sight and continued to watch. Because the bush was between two streetlamps, it was difficult to see it directly. Shadows were dancing on the street and when she realized what the movement was, she rolled her eyes and came out from her hiding spot. The wind had picked up and was making the branches dance in the breeze. Charlotte had just spent the better part of an hour stalking a bush.

After making it back to her apartment, she settled into her chair with her old photo album. After hearing the name Charlie, she had become quite nostalgic and needed to see some old pictures of her brother. He had been so young when he disappeared. He was just sixteen years old, with his whole life ahead of him, and one day he vanished between his friend's house and their family home. Search parties scoured the neighborhood, his picture was plastered all over television news, billboards, phone poles and the internet, and slowly the search became less and less aggressive until the case finally went cold. Max was gone. Charlotte always held a small bit of hope that one day Max would magically walk back into her life, but that hope seemed infinitesimal after seventeen years.

    She had been so lost in her memories that Charlotte had not realized she had been crying. One teardrop glistened over a picture of Max and seemed to magnify the ring on his finger. She smiled when she saw the ring. Max was so convinced he would be getting a car for his sixteenth birthday, but instead he received this family heirloom proudly given to him by his dad. After Max got over the initial shock, he was proud to wear the family ring, but he would always refer to it as his Mustang.

    Charlotte closed the photo album and leaned her head back on her chair. She contemplated making dinner, but her body disobeyed every command to get up. She put the album on the floor, pulled the blanket off the headrest and allowed herself to drift off in her chair.

Chapter 8

There were no bullets whizzing by him, but when Jack woke up, he knew he was in danger. The musty smell combined with the fetid stench of stale body fluids that permeated his nose were glaring signs he was not in his recliner at home. He was seated. It was dark. But those are the only two things that vaguely resembled what his surroundings looked like when he had fallen asleep.

Waking up in this dream was nothing like the last time. He still had a slight headache, but he was not sure if it was from the stress of trying to figure out the last dream episode or if it had been related to the shots of whiskey he had consumed before he passed out.

The shrill sound of an intercom almost made him topple sideways to the floor in the chair to which he now realized he was securely fastened. Suddenly, Jack found himself at the mercy of whoever's voice was on the other side of that intercom. A red light clicked on and Jack knew he was being recorded. The lights in the room went up slightly and a low voice crackled inside the grey box on the wall, "Peter, you pissed off a lot of people and they want to see you suffer."

The voice was raspy and sinister, and it oozed through the intercom. Every word the man spoke slithered from the box down the wall and snaked itself around Jack as he sat motionless in the chair. Jack, or Peter as the man had referred to him, knew trying to untie the binds around his wrists was futile. Jack's level of fear seemed to wane slightly as he inaudibly repeated the same phrase in his head. 'It's only a dream'. 'It's only a dream'. He only hoped Peter, whose body he seemed to be sharing, had the same means of mental escape.

The light became even brighter and, as if reading his mind, the invisible man said, "If this feels like a dream, you are dead wrong". As the last of his words still hung in the air, Jack heard the hissing noise before he saw the cloud of gas escape the vent into the room. The noxious fumes swirled in the light and he could see a rainbow of colors dancing a very macabre dance in front of him. Jack tried to hold his breath for as long as he could, which seemed to amuse his captor.

"Take a deep breath, Peter. The gas is not going anywhere, and neither are you". Jack could almost picture the man reclining in his chair to watch the final scene in this grisly stage performance.

Jack began to cough as soon as the chemicals filtered into his lungs. His immediate thought was to cover his mouth and nose and sheer panic set in as he remembered the awkward position his hands were currently in, bound together behind the chair. The coughing turned into a combination of choking and sobbing as he realized, even though he was still convinced it was a dream, he was going to suffer a very horrific death, right here, right now.

His body was racked with spasms and he thought he tasted blood. He was dying. Jack heard the buzz of the intercom again and he waited for the low voice to speak but what he heard was completely different. It was just a whisper. "*You need to find Charlie*". Jack was not sure if the voice was a part of his crossing over, but he hoped those words would follow him into the morning when he woke up to give him some sort of clue as to what was going on.

Jack's body began to thrash in the chair with Peter and they fell backwards onto the concrete. Peter instantly vomited and suffered a massive pulmonary aspiration of his stomach contents. Within seconds he was dead, but somehow Jack lingered for a few moments before the end of his dream allowed him to leave Peter's body as they both moved into alternate realms. The gas had dissipated slightly, and Jack stared at the grey box on the wall. The only word he could utter before his spirit left the small concrete tomb was "Charlie". It was only a whisper, but he knew the man on the other side of the wall had heard it. And then Jack was gone.

~~

Had he been able to watch himself sleep Jack would have known he was dreaming again. His body tossed and contorted in the chair and he mewled like a dying animal. The familiar perspiration coated his brow as he flailed about in the recliner. Pieces of foam, trying desperately to stay attached to the Mother Ship, haphazardly fell to the floor that flanked the sides of the recliner.

    Jack continued to thrash in the chair as if he were having a seizure. His arms pulled in and held his stomach as he mumbled indecipherable phrases. Just before his body went limp, there was nobody around to hear him clearly utter the name "Charlie".

Chapter 9

Victor put on his gas mask and entered the room to stand over his latest prey. He never questioned what people did, or said, in their last minutes of life. He was only there to do a job and nothing else mattered. The calls for his services remained frequent and he was happy to oblige. His focus on his career had afforded him the distraction from the "one who got away" as he liked to think of her, but the park still lingered in his mind and he was determined to find her.

He aimed his attention on the scene before him. This man, limp in the chair that had been knocked to the ground, had intrigued him. He knew about his background and he had great knowledge of what this guy had done to become his latest target, but the name "Charlie" seemed to strike a nerve in Victor. He was not sure why, but he felt it was significant.

He lingered over the body for longer than he ever had after a job was done. He knew he had to clean up the mess, but Victor could not take his eyes off the dead man. There was something almost familiar about him. He knew the familiarity was not just from the dossier of Peter's life that he had studied in detail, and it had nothing to do with the number of times Victor had followed Peter to learn his habits and his patterns. There was something about this guy, but Victor was not able to put his finger on it.

One last muscle contraction in Peter's dead body caused the corpse to move and Victor almost jumped out of his skin. Death had never bothered him, so his juvenile reaction to this part of the process shocked him. He left the room hoping he would never give Peter a second thought.

After cleaning up his mess, Victor wanted nothing more than to go back to his apartment. Usually, his appetite was enormous after taking a life, but he could not even think about food. He was not able to shake his uneasiness, and his lack of control was causing him concern. He would never pass up a satisfying dinner and a few beers after watching someone die, but his longing for food was non-existent and, for some reason, that scared the shit out of him.

After passing Joe at the security desk in the lobby, Victor got into the elevator and pressed the button for the top floor. The doors closed and the small metal box began its ascent. Victor felt comfort in the movement and the soft hum of the elevator passing each floor, and he was thankful he was able to take the ride alone. Small talk was never his forte and he was grateful for the silence.

When the bell sounded and the door opened, Victor walked down the hallway to his door and fumbled with his keys. He began to feel disoriented and paused briefly, eventually leaning into the door frame for support. He was not sure if there had been a pinhole in his gas mask and he inhaled some of the chemicals he had used to kill Peter, but he suddenly wanted to purge his body of every foreign substance. The level of his panic made his hands gnarl into useless stumps. He had never had such little control of his dexterity. His fingers clumsily fumbled with his keys and it felt like an eternity before he was able to get the key in the lock and disengage the deadbolt. Victor practically tripped into his foyer and only managed to save himself from falling by holding on to the door.

Once his front door had been closed and locked, Victor made his way to the living room and pried his fingers apart until his hands were back to normal. He massaged each finger until the blood flowed normally and he had full range of motion. His apartment was blissfully dark, and he lowered himself to the floor and lay on his back, arms stretched out to the full extension at his sides. He had seen his mother do this on many occasions when she wanted to relax, and Victor could think of nothing else to help him now. After several minutes lying on the floor, his breathing became heavier and he counted the seconds between breaths.

He could feel his heart rate slowing and, as he pictured what he looked like lying on his floor, he realized he mimicked Jesus on the cross. This made him smile. He had not died, but he would be resurrected from this temporary set-back. He was a man of power. He was not one to be riddled with weakness of any kind. He was a professional and this episode would not mar his reputation. Even if he could not explain what had just happened in his present, he would not let it have any effect on his future.

The Waking Hours

Pulling himself up to a sitting position, Victor let the darkness in his apartment pass through every membrane in his body. He breathed in the solitude, he bathed in the shadows and he was energized by the dark. His chest swelled as he inhaled the joy he got from the absence of light. His cells were regenerated, and his skin tingled with electricity.

He sat in that position on the floor for hours. He had effectually put himself into a trance and relived every second of the kill. He could see the gradual escape of the vapor from the box on the wall and, in what seemed like slow motion, he watched Peter's body react to the poison, convulsing and contorting until the movement ceased. Victor had remained for several hours watching the corpse after Peter had choked on his own vomit and now, sitting on the floor in his darkened apartment, he wondered why he had such a fascination with Peter. He never had the urge to do anything other than to check for a pulse to make sure there was never one present. What was it about Peter that was so different?

Since Victor had no hobbies and no friends, he had nothing more to do than think about his obsession with Peter. He could understand his constant thoughts about the girl in the park, but he could not comprehend why Peter was still on his mind. He tried to bring the image of the girl into his meditation, but Peter hovered in the foreground and refused to leave. He was a job, just like every other job, but this guy would not go away. The lines of his face, the timbre of his voice, and the color of his eyes were etched in Victor's memory.

Victor tried to concentrate on the darkness of his apartment to suppress the thoughts of Peter, but his mind was pulled away and he was no longer in his meditative state. He remembered Peter's eyes and was fascinated by the fact the pigmentation of each iris was different. One eye was blue, and one eye was green. Victor had always prided himself on remembering details and he could not understand how he overlooked this detail in the file. Peter had two different colored eyes and Victor had never seen that before.

He was unsure if he slept or just spent the night sitting on his living room floor, but as the daylight began to chase away the shadows, Victor got up and headed for the shower. Perhaps the start of a new day would end his obsession with Peter.

Chapter 10

Jack awoke with a throbbing pain in his abdomen. He gasped for breath and his ribs ached like he imagined they would if he had been used as Mohammed Ali's practice bag. The taste in his mouth was unlike anything he could describe, and the rancid stench of his own breath hung in front of him, making him want to gag.

He had awoken in the fetal position on his bathroom floor. The cold tile had chilled him, and his body ached in places he did not know he could feel pain. He got up from the floor and looked in the mirror. His two different colored eyes stared back at him with a mixture of melancholy and déjà vu. He could no longer say he had any control in his life, whatsoever. These dreams, these trips to different locations as different people, were becoming more real to him than any semblance of the life he had been living for the past ten years. There had to be some explanation as to why he was having these out-of-body, in someone else's body, experiences.

Since he was already in the bathroom, he cranked on the water in his shower and stripped out of his clothes. The water was a welcome remedy for his discomfort, and the familiarity of his bathroom made him feel safe for the first time in days. He stayed in the shower until his skin glowed red from the hot water. Shaking off the excess beads of moisture, he toweled himself dry, pulled on his robe and enjoyed the fact his manly scent was no longer offensive.

He attempted to put together the pieces of his last few mornings and the subsequent injuries. He assumed he had been shot in his first dream and poisoned in his second dream. Each morning, he mentally catalogued his significant physical injuries that mimicked the horrific death he suffered in his dreams. He gingerly touched his ribs three times and made a mental note of the rawness of his throat. He also noticed that the lacerations on his wrists still existed but the bullet-sized bruise on his forehead had disappeared.

The Waking Hours

His stomach growled despite all the trauma that had happened to his body, but his hunger pangs went unanswered as Jack was distracted by the empty journal that sat in his grandfather's antique writing desk. Suddenly he wanted nothing more than to document his dreams. He made his way to the desk, pulled down the face of the desk that would create a table and sat down in the teak chair. The last time he sat at this desk, he was seventeen years old. He brushed his hand three times across the surface, clearing any dust or cobwebs that may have gathered inside. The journal was in the same place it had been when his grandfather had died. Jack had so many memories of his grandfather but the thing he missed the most was his grandfather's storytelling. He was known in many circles for his ability to adopt any dialect and have his audience in gales of laughter. Jack had his grandfathers' cassette tapes converted to digital recordings but could not bring himself to listen to them. They had a special bond, and his death was the one Jack had the most difficulty accepting.

He reached for the journal and opened it to the first page. The paper had yellowed somewhat over the years, but Jack was determined to tell his own story in this book, not knowing why it started and not knowing when or how it would end. There was something more honest about keeping his thoughts in this journal, this book that had belonged to his grandfather, rather than typing his thoughts into his laptop. At least if his laptop were hacked, this information would be stored safely. Nobody nowadays would think today to steal a journal.

Jack imagined what Bridget Jones felt like when she began her diary. He did not add his weight. And he did not add his daily cigarettes because he was not a smoker, but he did add the number of drinks he remembered consuming before falling asleep. He did not know if that would be relevant but, right now, any piece of information could help.

His entries into the journal were disjointed. He only remembered fragments of his dreams, so the bulk of his writing was about the physical injuries he seemed to have sustained during the dreams and the remnants of the abuse he felt after waking up. He wanted to start from the beginning, so he worked from the earlier lacerations on his wrists and the simulated bullet wound on his forehead. He wrote down the assumption he had been shot in the head. His brow furrowed as he tried to work his way backwards to see how much of his first dream he retained. There was a chase, and he unexpectedly remembered the exploding door frame as well as remembering the girl.

His hand trembled slightly as she hovered in his memory. He could not see her face, nor could he bring back any other information about her other than the fact he had seen her somewhere in his dream. He did not want to frustrate himself throughout his information recovery process, so he moved on to the second dream. He began with the resulting physical ailments of sore ribs, horrendous breath and waking up on his bathroom floor. Jack closed his eyes and tried to remember anything he could from the previous night. Since he was a Criminal Minds junkie, he tried to regress himself back into his dream, but he was unsuccessful. No memory would allow itself to be extricated and Jack was getting annoyed.

He got up from the writing chair and began to pace back and forth across his apartment. His fingers tapped on either side of his forehead three times. Suddenly, he spun around to look at the innocuous teak chair. Its unique wooden frame sparked a memory. He had been in a chair like this one last night in his dream. His wrists still showed signs of being bound and Jack now knew he had been tied to a chair just like this one. He hurried back to the desk and sat down to jot his memory on a piece of journal paper before it was gone. He had been unable to piece together any ideas, but every bit of recollection had to be important somehow. Jack strained to remember something else, anything else that he could add to his journal entry. He leaned back in the chair and let his head fall back. He closed his eyes and rubbed his hands together three times. The apartment was eerily silent since his neighbors were all at their day jobs. He thought about calling in to work but knew he was not really missed, so it was a moot point.

Jack stayed in that position for a while until his neck ached and his body vehemently argued about the discomfort of being in a wooden chair. He moved himself back to his recliner and let his body enjoy the contours of felt and foam. As he let his head hit the padded back of the chair, Jack clenched his eyes shut to try and force more memories from his brain. He was enjoying the kaleidoscope of colors behind his eyelids when his skin prickled like goose flesh. He immediately broke into a cold sweat as he remembered the voice from his dream. He moved back to the desk and wrote the word 'voice' in capital letters followed by several exclamation

The Waking Hours

points. He rubbed each arm three times to calm his anxiety and smooth the bumps back into his skin.

After a few more minutes at the desk, Jack knew he was not going to remember anything else. He closed the journal, closed the desk, and went to the kitchen to see if he even had anything to eat. He opened the fridge door and bent down to get a better look. As he reached for the pound of peameal bacon, the name Charlie was whispered into his ear. Jack bolted upright, hitting his head on the handle of the freezer door. His hand went to the rapidly growing goose egg on the top of his head, and he spun around in his kitchen to see where the voice had come from. He was alone. He ran into the living room, only to find it empty as well. The deadbolt was engaged, the patio door was locked, and Jack was stymied. Once again, he opened the writing desk, opened the journal, and wrote down the name 'Charlie' with three large question marks.

Chapter 11

During the night, Charlotte dreamed of Max. He was dressed in jeans and a football jersey, just like he was on the day he disappeared. They had eaten breakfast together that morning before they went to school and she had made plans with her friends, so he would be coming home by himself. Her dream portrayed a slightly different reality from what happened on the day he vanished.

In her dream, Max would not leave Charlie's side, but they never spoke. He attended her classes instead of his, he ate lunch with her at her cafeteria table and their journey home was taken together until they reached the door of their childhood home. Charlotte crossed the threshold into their home as Max stood on the porch, unable to come inside. Even in her dream, Charlotte knew Max not being able to enter their home had great significance. She went up to her bedroom and looked out the window to see Max, still fixed in his spot on the front porch, endlessly turning his ring, his Mustang, around on his finger and occasionally looking up at Charlotte's window.

Charlotte knew she was closer to being awake than being asleep and she tried to hang on to the dream for as long as possible. She felt like she had been with Max. She rolled over to look at the clock on her nightstand and it read 3:33 am. She usually had no trouble sleeping through the night, but now she rolled onto her back and stared at the ceiling. Her mouth was dry, and she got up to get a drink of water. The waning moon was casting a slight glow in her living room and, instead of getting the water, she unlocked her patio door and stood on her balcony. The night was slightly warm and, as silly as she knew it was, she looked down into the yard and thought she might see Max standing there. Of course, the notion was foolish. There was nothing but trees and benches, but Charlotte stood there for about ten minutes hoping Max would appear.

The Waking Hours

She inhaled some fresh air, forgot the water, and went back to bed. She thought she would be restless, and it would take longer for slumber to come but her dream was not finished, and it had waited for her to return.

She was once again in the bedroom of her childhood home, back in her dream at the exact place she was before she woke up. She went back to the window again to find Max standing on the porch with a strange man. Charlotte could not tell from her vantage point, but the man looked like he was soaking wet. Thinking Max may be in danger, Charlotte raced down the stairs and opened the front door. The man seemed no more menacing than Max. He shivered violently and Charlotte had been right, he was drenched. She went to the laundry room and returned with a dry towel.

Something about this man seemed familiar but Charlotte was sure she had never met him before. She silently motioned for him to come into the house to dry off but as he took one step forward, Max gently placed his hand on the strangers' arm and shook his head no. The man shrugged, nodded at Charlotte as if to say thank you and took the same step back. With no words shared between any of them, Charlotte handed the man the towel and felt compelled to close the door. She went back to her room and watched the exchange between the stranger and her brother, and then the man left as quickly as he had come. She had only turned her head for a second and he was gone, almost like a dream within her dream.

When she woke the next morning, Charlotte lay in bed for longer than normal. Never had she been able to pick up where she had left off in a dream. As she thought more about it, she knew she had seen this stranger somewhere before. Thinking about him was not going to make him materialize so she dragged herself out of bed and got ready to head across town.

The nursing home where her grandmother lived was a subway ride and two buses away. It took almost two hours to get there but Charlotte lived in a city with a plethora of public transit, so she felt no need to have the burden of car payments or insurance. The subway was surprisingly on-time and the traffic was minimal on the roads for the bus rides so Charlotte, even after stopping to pick up flowers, arrived earlier than anticipated. She signed in at the front desk and chatted briefly with the nurses about her grandmother's condition.

One of the nurses responded, "There has been no change in her cognitive situation, but she seemed quite chipper at breakfast this morning, and very chatty which was quite unusual."

The rest of the nurses nodded in agreement.

"Well, fingers crossed, maybe she'll remember me today," said Charlotte.

Charlotte left the desk and headed down the hall. Knowing that her grandmother probably would still have no clue who she was, at least she was in good spirits and that made Charlotte smile. She pushed the door open and her grandmother was propped up in her bed by about six pillows. Ottoline, or Tillie as she was called, smiled, as she would have done with any stranger, and Charlotte exchanged the new flowers for the ones she had brought last week. Tillie loved Hydrangeas so Charlotte made sure to buy one blue and one green every time she came to visit. She could never explain her need to buy one of each color, but her choice became a habit.

"Hi Grandma, I hear you are having a good morning."

Charlotte always started and pretty much carried on every conversation they had.

"I brought you some fresh flowers to brighten up your room, your favorites, hydrangeas."
"Mustang!" Tillie blurted out the single word as if her life depended on it.

Charlotte dropped the handful of wilting flowers on the floor and spun around to stare at her grandmother.

Tillie looked her straight in the eye and said, "Where's Max?"
Charlotte moved over to her grandma's bed and sat down, gently taking Tillie's hand in hers, "Gran, Max has been gone for seventeen years."
"That is impossible", whispered Tillie, "he was just here last night, Charlie."

The Waking Hours

The hair on the back of Charlotte's neck was standing perpendicular to her neckline. Their hands remained together until eventually Tillie turned to her side to gaze out the window. As she usually was during Charlotte's visits, Tillie became silent and unresponsive. Charlotte moved back to her chair and stared at her grandmother for what felt like an eternity. This was the first time in months that she had even remembered who Charlotte was and now she was calling her by a name she had never used and talking about Max. Tillie had over-spent her energy and her eyes closed. Her gentle breathing and slight snore made Charlotte smile. She looked so peaceful that Charlotte stayed for another hour just watching her grandmother sleep, still feeling the bond with Tillie she had lost so many years ago.

During the remaining time in her grandma's room, Charlotte's mind raced. Why now? Why would Tillie remember Max? And how in the world, through every piece of her life she had forgotten, could she remember the Mustang?

Charlotte's train of thought went back to her dream the previous night and to the voice that had whispered 'Charlie'. All these things seemed to be connected somehow but Charlotte was at a complete loss as to what the connection could be. Tillie continued to snore, and Charlotte quietly put on her coat, grabbed her bag, and left the room. She avoided the nursing station completely because there was no way she would be able to explain what had just happened.

Her ride home took longer than the trip there and she realized she had no desire to cook. Charlotte stopped at her favorite boutique restaurant, ordered the Coq au Vin to go and waited on the bench inside the front of the restaurant for her dinner. She watched all the restaurant patrons enjoying their meals with friends or family and she felt the familiar pang of loneliness. She turned her body slightly to look out the front window and froze. His shorter frame held his extra weight well. She did not think she had ever seen him before, but every ounce of her blood turned into a cold gel just looking at him. All the features of his face and his body were harsh and unfair. If she could read auras, she knew his would be dark. He was dressed completely in black and thankfully was distracted by his cell phone ringing, so he did not see her duck away from the window.

The cashier arrived with her dinner to go but she no longer had an appetite and was afraid to leave the safety of the restaurant. She smiled as she grabbed the bag and asked to see Joey. The cashier nodded and went to find the manager.

"Charlotte, I haven't seen you in a while." Joey came out of his office with a smile.

"I know Joey, it has been a while. I need a favor." Charlotte was clearly shaken, and Joey gently grabbed her elbow.

"Whatever you need, sweetie." Joey was beginning to worry.

"I know I only live two blocks away but, could you walk me home?"

Never in the years that Joey had known Charlotte had he known her to be this timid in the city she loved. Without hesitation, Joey told the cashier he would be back in ten minutes and they left the restaurant together. The bells on the restaurant door rang as the door opened and closed. Charlotte jumped slightly and looked around to see if the man in black was still there but there was no sight of him. Joey noticed how skittish she was and asked if everything was okay.

"I am fine Joey, thank you. Sometimes you just get a bad feeling, you know. It's probably nothing."

Charlotte kissed him on the cheek when they reached the door to the lobby of her building. Joey stood on the sidewalk, watching until Charlotte was safely inside with the door locked and then made his way back to the restaurant. Charlotte did not turn to wave goodbye to Joey, so she missed the man in black as he slowly ambled past her building.

The Waking Hours

Chapter 12

The many shades of green and blue in the park were a welcome distraction for Victor. He had taken a few days after his last job to destress, and he was finally beginning to feel like himself again. So much so he felt the urge to find a target of his own, just for fun. He had not received any new calls lately, so he embraced the time he had to concentrate on his personal desires. Being in the park during the day was a strange feeling for him but felt like he was where he should be. His instinct always pulled him in the right direction and today it pulled him here.

The park was not its usual hub of activity. A few couples aimlessly strolled the paths, but nobody grabbed and held Victor's attention. He sat on a bench and noticed a few sideways glances from some of the people walking by. He also noticed they picked up their pace slightly as they went by him. He was used to that. When his mother was feeling particularly mean, she would always tell him he had the face for radio. One side of his mouth turned up into a slight smile as he remembered watching her die. As far as he was concerned, she deserved it and the world was better off without her negativity.

Victor sat for what felt like an eternity. The sky was still bright blue, the sun was slowly making its way from one horizon to the other and Victor enjoyed the warmth on his face. But he was not feeling a kinship with the park anymore. This was not where he was supposed to be. He left the bench and meandered out of the park, unsure of where he was going but determined he was going that way for a reason.

Victor did like the city. It was not over-populated in a noticeable way, and there was something for everyone. He continued to walk in random directions, eventually ending up in front of a bookstore. Victor hated books. He could not understand why people would spend hours reading about made-up lives instead of making their own life more exciting.

He had never owned a book or intentionally read a book. He had much better things to do with his time.

He stood on the concrete path and smelled the blend of ethnic foods wafting through the air, pushed out by the exhaust fans of several restaurants in the area. The only time Victor really enjoyed food was after a kill. His appetite was slightly offensive, so the staff always remembered him if he happened to frequent the same establishment. He realized he was standing across the street from his favorite little French bistro when his cell phone vibrated in his pocket. That could only mean one thing. He answered on the first ring and his end of the conversation was very succinct. There was movement in the restaurant window, but he was too focused on the details of his phone call to pay attention. When the call was over, he opened the back of the phone, removed, and smashed the SIM card and threw the phone into the nearest garbage can.

He crossed the street and headed home to prepare for his next job. The couple ahead of him seemed to be in a hurry to get where they were going, maybe to enjoy the take-out meal she was carrying, but she was quick to get into the building and left the poor guy standing on the street. The man turned around and began heading back in Victor's direction, nodding at Victor as they passed. Victor glanced at the lobby of the woman's building, but it was empty.

He got back to his high-rise, signaled to Joe's replacement for the day, and headed to his apartment. He bolted the door and turned on the only lamp he had in the room. The sun was beginning to sink behind the trees and soon the night would be Victor's ally. This job did not allow him his usual time to prepare. This one had to be done immediately. He never knew his targets personally, but he believed the world was better off without them and he was more than happy to facilitate their departure.

Given Victor's small window of opportunity, he had no time to play with this one. The job had to be quick and extremely effective with no chance of this guy being found. Victor had not been to the river in a while and with the rising currents of late, he thought it was a perfect way to make this guy vanish. He took a moment to sit on his floor, cross-legged as always, and envision what he would do. He imagined taking control of this guy, subduing him, and throwing him in the trunk of his '76 Cadillac Deville. Although Victor was not really a car guy, he liked the space the

The Waking Hours

trunk afforded him. The car was stored in the basement of his building and he only took it out when he really needed it. Since Victor had no driver's license, no insurance and no registration, the fewer times the car was on the road, the better.

Victor changed his clothes into some appropriate garments for the task at hand and took the freight elevator down to the basement. The regular elevator stopped only at the lobby and anyone going to the basement had to switch elevators in the lobby. Victor did not want the hassle or the chance of running in to anyone else, so he used the key he had unlawfully obtained for the freight elevator. The dank smell of the basement reached his olfactory senses before he was even off the elevator. His car was in its usual spot, covered by a tan tarp that was covered in dust. It had been a while since he had taken the car for a spin and he hoped it was up for another challenge.

The first turn of the key was met with nothing but a clicking sound. Victor waited a few seconds, pumped the gas pedal, and tried again. The engine roared to life and plumes of smoke poured out of the muffler. Once the car had been given a chance to idle, the RPM meter dropped, and the car purred like an over-sized kitten. Victor put the car into reverse and carefully maneuvered his way out of his parking spot. As he pulled out the button to turn his headlights on, the settling dust danced in the beams of light. Victor paused for a moment and was amused by the performance. He pulled the gearshift down three notches into drive and headed out into the night.

The dossier of his latest target was tucked away in his messenger bag and all the tools he needed were already organized in his trunk. He always made sure to leave everything precisely as he would need it the next time. And since he had a camera constantly pointed at his car, he knew nobody had touched it since the last time he was in it. The gas tank was full, the oil was relatively fresh, and he was ready. The garage door argued loudly as it opened, and Victor drove out into the night.

The streets were relatively busy, as he knew they would be. Several guys at stop lights smiled and gave him the thumbs up as they appreciated the pristine quality of his Deville. Victor drove through the city and knew he was getting close. The more distance between the streetlights and the more rural the surrounding area became, the nearer he got to his target.

He pulled over on the side of the unfamiliar street to double-check the address. He was close. His boss told him that the man would be alone tonight expecting to be on a conference call for work and he had sent his wife out for dinner. Victor got back on the road and when he was close to the driveway, he extinguished his lights. He turned into the driveway, happy to see it was downhill, so he put the car in neutral and glided down the paved path. He shut the engine off when he felt certain the car could not be seen from the road. He was halfway between the house and the road, just as his boss said he would be. A solitary room was lit in the house and Victor assumed the man was in his office waiting for his phone call.

    He got out of the car, mindful to shut off the interior light before he opened the door. He carefully popped the trunk and made sure no light crept out of the cargo space. The tools he had in his car were the things he would need later. Victor needed nothing to subdue the man except his hands. He left the door to the trunk ajar to make it easier to dump the man into it when he got back. Victor put on his black leather gloves and strolled towards the house.

    As he suspected, he could see a man, same height and build as described, pacing back and forth in his office. Victor could almost smell the man's anxiety. His senses always became heightened when he was working. He studied the man for a few minutes, learning his gait and his speed. He thought it may take a bit more effort to put the man down since he seemed so wired, but Victor loved a challenge. Victor was told where the motion lights were, so he carefully stepped around in the dark to not alert the man to his presence. When he was at the back door, Victor pulled out his tool set, picked the lock and entered the kitchen. He knew there would be no alarm because his boss had electronically disconnected it earlier. Victor waited for a moment so he could adjust to the noises of the house. He could hear the man's shoes hitting the hardwood floor as he continued to pace. Precision and timing were everything to Victor and his boss had known that from the beginning. The details Victor received for each job were explicit and always remarkably accurate. As if on cue, the phone rang, and the man quickly snatched up the handset.

    Victor could hear him quickly trying to get a few words in, but he stopped talking when he realized he was just meant to listen. Victor was very stealthy for a man of his exaggerated girth and in a few seconds, he had silently made it from the kitchen to the office. He had taken off his belt as he walked down the driveway and now it hung at his side like a noose. The man had hung up the phone just as Victor emerged in the office doorway. He immediately caught Victor's reflection in the window and spun around to find Victor in his personal space. He was about to shout when Victor punched him in the throat. The man gasped and dropped to his knees, unable to get his breath and then Victor was behind him. The belt buckle was around his neck before he knew what was happening and his arms began to reach for the belt trying to loosen it as it constricted tighter around his airway.

 Victor had at least a hundred pounds on the guy, so it took no time at all for Victor to win the battle. Victor was somewhat sad that he had to be behind the man and was unable to receive his gift, but this was a quick job that paid a lot of money, so he had to make some sacrifices. Without effort, Victor swung the dead man over his shoulder in a fireman's carry and took him out to the waiting Deville. Victor dumped him in the trunk with no more regard than he would have had for a sack of potatoes. He started the car and headed to the river.

 The road was bumpier than Victor remembered, and his passenger was banging around in the trunk with each pothole that Victor encountered. When he finally arrived at his destination, Victor parked the car and lifted the trunk. The man's sightless stare was familiar. His brown eyes seemed slightly milky so there was nothing left for Victor to do except to weigh down the body and toss him into the churning current. He knew the area was abandoned but he worked quickly anyway. After putting as much weight on the body as he could, Victor looked into his eyes one last time. Looking back at him from the corpse was one blue eye and one green eye.

 Victor stumbled backwards and slowly inched closer to see if he had been seeing things. The different colored orbs, slightly bulging and framed with petechiae due to the strangulation, were there. He dragged the body to the bridge, lifted him over the railing and listened as his body splashed into the water. The weight dragged the man down far enough and the current did the rest. The body was gone.

 Victor could not move. He stood for a long time with his hands on the railing trying to figure out what those eyes could represent. As sure as Victor knew he was meant to be a killer, he knew those eyes were an unbelievably bad omen for him.

The Waking Hours

Chapter 13

Jack was exhausted but he could not think of a worse omen for him than wanting to fall asleep. His head ached from slamming it into the handle on the freezer door and the name Charlie kept going through his brain. He wanted to find some answers, but he was getting nothing. He poured a glass of wine and sat in his aging recliner. He made a mental note to pick up the pieces of foam that had exploded out of the chair during his last dream.

It was only 6:30 pm and Jack needed to stay awake. He looked at the glass of wine and realized the pseudo-barbiturate was not going to help him stay up. He took the wine into the kitchen and dumped the glass and the rest of the bottle down the sink. He found his Bodum coffee press and made a pot of strong coffee.

With a cup of steaming java in his hand, Jack sat back down on the wooden desk chair. The less comfortable he was, the more likely he would stay awake. The journal sat in front of him with the two words that plagued him the most, Voice and Charlie. His gut told him somehow the two things were connected, and he wanted desperately to know why. He took a few more sips of his coffee and was feeling the increase in his heartbeat in reaction to the caffeine surge. He enjoyed the alertness and he picked up the pen, hoping he would be inspired to add something to those two words. He had heard of ghostwriting and thought something like that would be extremely helpful right now, although he knew it meant something completely different.

But the pen did not move. It sat as motionless in his fingers as Jack did in his chair. He glanced around his apartment, hoping something would trigger a memory or even a snippet of a thought, but he got nothing. He knew something was happening in his dreams, so perhaps that was why there was not anything in his own apartment that could help him.

He had run out of ideas and had begun to doodle in the journal. He mindlessly moved the pen in small circles and, as he looked closer at the scribble, he realized it looked just like the mark on his forehead that had resembled a bullet hole. He wrote beside it 'first dream - shot in head?'. He drew a pair of hands beside the circle and scratched the pen on the surface of the paper to mimic the lacerations he had on his wrists. He could not remember the exact night he had that dream, so he wrote June tenth with a question mark. He hoped this journal would help him keep track of the things he could remember and try to find a pattern, if any, in his dreams.

On the next page he drew a facsimile of his desk chair with rope on the ground. He did not remember the rope, but he assumed there had been one to secure him to the chair. He wrote in detail about the pain in his abdomen and his horrible breath, not sure of the cause but certain it was important. He dated this entry June twelfth with another question mark. Jack was getting a positive feeling from putting his thoughts down in his journal. He warmed up his coffee with refills and squeezed his eyes shut to try to remember anything else. Once again, colors exploded like fireworks behind his eyelids and after the pyrotechnic display had disappeared, Jack was left with only darkness.

His eyes popped open and he could not write the word darkness fast enough. He circled the word and added several exclamation points. He knew it would become a pertinent piece of the puzzle.

Jack needed a break, so he took his coffee out onto his balcony. The night air was cool and filled with the scent of the blossoming trees. He inhaled deeply and suddenly began to cough. His hand went to his throat and he gasped for air. He wheezed as he tried to take air into his lungs and in a minute after the attack all the discomfort was gone, and Jack was breathing normally again.

He poured the rest of the coffee over his balcony thinking he had merely choked on a drop or two he had not swallowed properly. Jack went back into his apartment, locked and barred the patio door and got a glass of water. His laptop was on the dining room table, so he moved from one uncomfortable chair to the next and brought his computer to life. Avoiding sleep was going to be difficult but he thought YouTube might help. One video led to the next and, for the first time in a long time, Jack was laughing.

He had not realized how much time had lapsed and when he looked at the time, it was 2:45 in the morning. He was confident he could keep up this pace all night and cheat the sandman out of his nocturnal victim. James

The Waking Hours

Corden was hosting people in his Carpool Karaoke and Jack kept clicking on the videos but could feel his eyelids getting heavier. His posture leaned towards the table and the last thing Jack remembered seeing was the time of 3:33 am.

~~

The sound of fire trucks racing along the street outside awoke Jack with a start. He was still at his dining room table. As he jolted up from his sleeping position, his arm hit his laptop and brought the screen to life again. YouTube videos were still playing, and Jack was soaking wet. Clenched under his left arm was a towel that did not belong to him. The carpet below him had been catching the water dripping from his pant legs and the cushion on his dining room chair was saturated. Jack quickly ruled out the fact he may have peed his pants because every article of clothing he wore was drenched. He felt the chill from the damp clothes and stripped himself out of the wet gear.

He looked over the clothes to see if there was anything noteworthy on them and quickly threw them in his laundry basket. This time of year, it was usually too warm for his not-so-masculine fuzzy bathrobe, but he put it on to warm himself up, slid his feet into his slippers and made his way to the kitchen to make another pot of coffee.

Once his body temperature had returned to normal, Jack opened his bathrobe to examine himself. Apart from the sore throat from his earlier bout of choking, there was nothing out of the ordinary. Nothing, of course, except the fact he had woken up soaking wet, holding a towel that had no place being in his apartment. With a fresh cup of coffee in hand to warm himself from the inside, Jack found the towel and hoped it would provide some clues as to where he had been.

The towel was nothing special. It was forest green and a product any person could buy at any department store, but upon further investigation, Jack saw an embroidered letter B on the bottom right corner. That was no help, but he moved back to the writing desk to jot down the three pieces of his newest information. 'Woke up soaking wet, sore throat, strange towel with letter B.'

There was something else just at the edge of Jack's memory. He had never had this feeling of being so close to remembering a dream, but he had also not spent a night consuming too much coffee instead of too much wine and he was starting to see the relevance. He tapped the pen on the journal. There was something else there, like when you have a word on the tip of your tongue, but you cannot say it. The towel. Where did he get the towel?

He closed his eyes and images flashed like scenes in a movie theatre that appear seconds apart on a black screen. He was in the river. Black screen. The current swept him away. Black screen. He was on the front porch of a house with a young boy. Black screen. He was given a towel by a girl. Black screen.

The girl. He had only seen her face for a second, but he knew he had seen her somewhere. She was younger but her face was familiar. He jotted down the girl in his journal, knowing that she was going to play a big part in this somehow.

When he had finally exhausted himself and was unable to remember anything else, Jack changed into some jeans and a sweater and got ready to leave his apartment. He knew he should make an appearance at the office sometime soon, but a quick call and a story about a nasty stomach flu bought him a few more days. Instead, Jack headed to the pier to see if anything there triggered any more memories. The water from the river emptied into the lake at the pier and Jack felt a strong urge to be there.

Chapter 14

Carrick Doyle thought of himself as a hard ass. He was well suited for his job as a cop, but his intellect and his Detective's shield required that people respect him and, rather than earn it, he demanded it. He hated his birth name. When he was seven years old, he insisted he be called Gunner and did not give people an option to do otherwise. He would not answer to anything else.

He was logical and analytical to a fault and it served him well. He could not imagine another career in which he would be more apt to excel. Simple things that escaped the attention of others flashed like beacons in front of him. He never missed a detail. He liked to refer to his prowess as his second sight and nobody cared enough about him to question it. He liked to work alone, and the other detectives were only happy to oblige. They knew he was a great investigator, but his personality was abrasive, and he was simply an asshole.

Gunner scoured the first file that had been sent by his division. The other files were on their way. The bodies were accumulating, and Gunner was asked to be a one-man task force to combine the information. The Mayor's office wanted to keep the city under control, so the files were collected, and all the evidence was being sent to Gunner. His bulldog approach and his keen eye for the smallest of details made him the perfect set of eyes to find a pattern in the seemingly random attacks that had begun to plague the city. There had to be a connection. He felt it in every fiber of his being, but the other investigators had come up with squat. It was up to Gunner to connect the dots and he took his job very seriously.

He looked for his cup of coffee and realized he had left it in the microwave. Everyone in his office knew which direction to point when Gunner screamed "where's my effin' coffee?" He maneuvered his way through the desks, punched in another 20 seconds and pushed start. His patience was already worn thin and he turned to the microwave and yelled, "come on!"

He collected the moderately radiated cup of caffeine and made his way back to his office. He knew he would have the privacy he needed to look over the files because nobody understood his process and they left him alone to do what he needed to do.

The first case was the couple in the park. He took in each detail and tried to place himself in the path of the violence. He closed his eyes and pictured the light posts in their serpentine pattern along the paths. Luring one unsuspecting person into the shroud of the bushes was doable but getting two of them in there and being able to kill both and leave the park without drawing any attention went beyond that. This guy was skilled, practiced, and Gunner took it personally that this atrocity happened in his jurisdiction, although to Gunner the whole world was his jurisdiction.

The crime scene investigators had gingerly turned over leaves and moved twigs to uncover the tiniest shreds of evidence. After fully processing the scene, they had absolutely nothing to go on and Gunner was already convinced this was going to be an exceedingly difficult case.

In the photos, a crowd had gathered beyond the crime scene tape and were eagerly trying to get a glimpse of what was happening. The Medical Examiner established an approximate time of death and the two young bodies had been transported to the morgue for further examination. The cause of death had been blatantly obvious as each victim had a line carved across their throat from one ear to the other. If Gunner had any sense of humour, he would have called it the smile of death.

The ground was saturated with blood and the CSI unit took as many samples as they could to be tested at the lab. They bagged and tagged anything that looked out of place that may point to the killer, but there were not many things to exhume from the dense underbrush other than the lifeless bodies of the two victims and a lot of arterial blood spray.

A plain-clothed officer arrived with the other two files Gunner requested. The most recent murders in his city added up to the young couple in the park, whose file he had already seen, an unidentified male shot in the head and the most recent death of Peter Mahon. The officer dropped the files on Gunner's desk and left, not waiting for any questions because he knew Gunner would never ask any. All the information he needed was in the files.

The Waking Hours

The first file was an unidentified male, shot in the head, execution style. There were ligature marks on his wrists, suggesting he had been tied up. His body had been dumped so there was no scene to process and no cartridges to study, just one dead body which proved to have no identification and no indication as to why this had happened to this guy. Forensics gauged by the size of the hole in the man's forehead that he was shot with a Glock 9mm, but even that would not be a proven fact until the post-mortem had been completed and the bullet had been extracted from his skull.

Gunner moved on to the next file. Peter Mahon, five-foot eleven, brown hair, brown eyes, death by asphyxiation due to pulmonary aspiration. Peter had been reported missing by his girlfriend twenty-four hours before his body was found. Peter's girlfriend, according to the file, worked at a local strip club and Gunner got the feeling Peter had some skeletons in his closet. The coroner had made an annotation about the eyes being affected as well as his lungs and Gunner wrote 'Chlorine' under the coroner's note with a question mark. Until he had the full coroner's report, nothing would be ruled out.

The newest files made Gunner think he was investigating different cases. Where the victims in the park seemed to be casualties of a random attack, the next two files screamed targeted hit. If these deaths were connected, Gunner was going to have to polish his skills to find this guy. He was good, but Gunner was better. The two kids in the park did not fit in with anything else he had been looking at. The other two murders were singular in nature and executed with brutal efficiency. If these park murders had anything to do with the other two deaths, it would take Gunner some serious cop work to figure out why. But he was a goddamned professional and this guy was a twisted bastard.

The more he looked, the more he felt disappointed by the lack of a cohesive set of clues. The profile would have to wait until he had a chance to really wrap his brain around these murders. If there was a connection, he would find it. But that connection seemed so elusive at this point he knew it would take every bit of effort to connect those damn dots.

Gunner did not notice day had turned to night. The office lights burned brightly to fend off the darkness as he continually turned the pages, looking for any pieces of the puzzle he may have missed. He chose to put the reports of the park murders aside and concentrate on the two deaths that seemed more like professional hits. Maybe he had two different killers on his hands, and it would serve him better to find the one who was more confident and would keep going. When he looked up at the clock, it read 2:00 am. Gunner knew he would solve nothing more by reading the same things over again, so he packed the files into his messenger bag and headed home. Turning off the lights in his office, he paused and looked back. The darkness of his office taunted him. He had missed something in the transcripts. His gut never steered him wrong and it had now taken control of the wheel again. He shut his office door and quickly made his way home. It was going to be a long night going through the files to see what he had overlooked, but the freshly brewed coffee and Italian biscotti would help him push through until he either found a connection or woke up face down on the table in his kitchen.

Chapter 15

Victor was unable to leave his apartment for a week after throwing the body in the river. His level of unease after seeing the two different colored eyes had increased so much his appetite had become non-existent. He chose to reflect on what had been happening. He had no desire to kill and that worried him. Since his work phone had been silent, he was able to cocoon himself in his living room and pretend the outside world no longer existed.

He wanted nothing resembling color or light in his apartment, so he pulled down the blackout blinds, dressed in his black sweatpants and hoodie and unplugged his refrigerator so no ambient light spilled onto the dark hardwood floor of his living room. He felt like he was back in the root cellar and as much as he tried to extinguish any glimpse of light on the color spectrum, he could not rid his mind of the green and blue of the eyes that seemed to follow him.

Victor ruminated on the past few days. The couple in the park had been a huge disappointment. He had wanted the girl. He had never wanted something so much in his life. He had no idea why she became his sole focus, but he began to worry that she could cloud his judgment and influence his professional life. His obsession was alarming.

And the eyes. What was the significance of the green and blue eyes? He had looked at Peter's eyes before killing him and they had been brown. Now that he really thought about it, so had the eyes of his latest victim who was now at the bottom of Lake Ontario feeding schools of unidentified fish. But when Victor had last looked at him, the eyes he saw were green and blue. It had to mean something and just thinking about it made Victor's heart pump blood through his veins at a rapid pace.

For the past thirty-six hours, Victor had not slept. He replayed the scenes of the last two murders over in his head trying to find an explanation for the eyes and he had drawn a blank. But after spending thirty-six hours wide awake and tense, his appetite had returned and so had his urges. It was time. He had spent too many hours trying to control things he could not, and it was time to move on. He was starving now, and he needed to fuel his over-sized body.

He checked his phone for the time. Because the blackout blinds were still down and the backlighting on his phone was dimmed, he had no idea if the time was 6:45 in the morning or the evening. He peered behind one of the blinds and was welcomed by the promises of the light grey sky of dusk. Victor smiled. With a full stomach and a whole night ahead of him to find new prey, his day and his mood were about to get much better.

After passing by Joe and exiting the lobby of his high rise, Victor stopped outside to embrace the sounds of the city at night. Car horns honked, traffic rushed by and people carried on mindless conversations as they brushed past Victor standing on the front steps of his building. He needed food, and he needed it fast. He had not eaten in a week and he would have to settle for a restaurant that was close.

Victor remembered the Chinese buffet that was two blocks away and headed in that direction. He was going to get his money's worth tonight and his mouth began to salivate thinking of all the things he was going to consume. He could see the layout of the restaurant and, in his mind, he strategically went from one station to the other, sampling the wonderful array of Canadian-Asian food they had to offer. When he arrived at the restaurant, he paid upfront for two buffet dinners since he knew he would eat more than his fair share and began to gorge himself.

Victor was putting the last bite of his first Eggroll in his mouth when he spotted the young man. Usually his preference was for women, but something about this boy drew and captivated his attention. Victor pushed pieces of food around on his plate as he stared at him. His face was nothing out of the ordinary. He had strawberry-blond hair and, from what Victor could see from a distance, a few freckles on his face. His smile was nothing extraordinary, but Victor could not avert his eyes.

The young man got up from his table to revisit the buffet and Victor followed. Victor went to the opposite side of the food station and the two inevitably met at the fried rice dish when they both reached the end of the island. Victor said nothing, nor did the young man. When he looked up at Victor, his one blue eye and one green eye met with Victor's eyes and they stared at each other for a moment. The young man nodded and continued back to his table, but Victor was unable to move. He stood for what seemed like an eternity before a server came to ask if everything was okay. Victor attempted at a laugh and squeaked out, "food coma" and made his way back to his table. He was having trouble catching his breath.

Victor's food had turned cold and was congealed on his plate but every time the server came to the table, Victor waved him off. He had to wait until the young man was ready to leave. The kid finally asked for the check and he and his buddies left the restaurant. Victor was sure people could see his rapid heartbeat through his shirt. He reached into his pocket, dumped some change on the table as a tip and left the restaurant. He shoved his sweaty hands into his jacket pockets and followed behind the group at a distance that would not be considered out of the ordinary.

After maintaining that safe distance but keeping a visual on the kid, Victor noticed the rest of the group went one way and his target went in the other direction. In his head, Victor had heard the phrase 'things happen for a reason' and thought there might be something to it. The streetlights became more prominent in the last of the daylight and each block cast more shadows than the previous block. Victor was feeling at home. The light grey sky had eased its way beyond charcoal and was moving rapidly into black. If they had not been in the city, Victor imagined there would be several stars dotting the night sky and maybe even a slice of the moon. As it was, the lights of the city killed any romance that may exist in the sky, but Victor was only interested in one thing and that thing had just veered off the sidewalk towards a tiny house with one low bulb burning on the porch.

Victor had kept his distance, but he slowly closed the gap between the two of them. The young man seemed to be fumbling with his keys and finally disengaged the lock on the front door. Victor found slight cover behind a bush and, although it was only four feet high and Victor was five feet ten inches, he tried to blend as well as he could.

It was not long before the freckle-faced boy emerged from the house, locked the door, and moved quickly down the path. Victor had no time to think. He rounded the corner and dropped to his knees, groaning in pain with his hand clutching his chest. The young man rushed to his aid, helping lift Victor from the sidewalk. A look of recognition registered in the boys' eyes the moment he saw Victor's face. Victor quickly spun the kid around, pulled the knife from the front pocket of his coat and cut the kid's neck from ear to ear. The carotid artery sprayed blood in a stream and Victor let the boy's body drop to the pavement, watching him lay still as the blood slowly began to pool around his corpse.

    Victor walked away quickly and left the boy to bleed out. He thought he would feel a greater sense of satisfaction after taking the boy's life, but he felt nothing. Victor knew more now than ever that the God's were conspiring against him, and he was losing his focus.

The Waking Hours

Chapter 16

Gunner opened his eyes and his kitchen slowly came into focus. His mouth was dry, his back hurt and he had deep indentations in his cheek from the file folders he had used as pillows. The shrill sound of his old rotary phone pulled him into reality, and he grabbed the handset off the wall. "Doyle."

The day sergeant from his division spoke quickly. "We got a report of a missing male. Ted Baines was not home when his wife returned from dinner last night and their kitchen door was wide open. His car is in the garage and she has not heard a word from him."

"Text me the address," Gunner said and hung up.

Wiping the drool from his mouth and the crust from his eyes, Gunner listened as his cell phone chimed with the address of the latest murder. He did not care if his clothes were three days old and he had not brushed his teeth since yesterday, people were dead and that was more important than his personal hygiene habits. He left the files on his kitchen table, microwaved the cup of coffee that had been there since yesterday and headed to the suburbs with his steaming mug of day-old coffee.

The house was remote. There were neighbors but, although they were close enough to borrow sugar from, they were far enough that they were not in your day-to-day business. Gunner pulled into the driveway and parked in between the forensics van and a few squad cars. He clambered up the stairs to the entrance of the house and knocked on the front door. A very distraught blonde woman, who Gunner guessed to be in her mid-forties, answered the door.

"Gunner, ma'am. How do you do?"

He put his right hand forward to shake hers, but she was too far gone to make small talk. She burst into tears and pushed the front door open for him to come in. The forensics team had already been there for several hours dusting for prints and looking for clues but had come up empty so far. There were still a few of their team lingering in the man's office, which seemed to be the focal point of their investigation.

One of the crime scene investigators saw Gunner and said, "The wife says he was supposed to be on a conference call, so she went out to dinner with friends. When she got home at 9:30, the house was empty, the kitchen door was open and there was no sign of her husband. His car is still in the garage and his wallet was in the desk drawer. It is now in an evidence bag."

Gunner was curious, "Was there any sign of a struggle?"

"No struggle, sir. The lock on the kitchen door was picked but there is no blood, nothing broken, it's like the guy walked out the door and vanished."

"Or somebody helped him vanish, "Gunner's last thought was muttered under his breath.

He stayed long after the forensics team had finished. Alice Baines had gone to stay with her sister, so Gunner was given full access to their home. Once the place had cleared out, he sat in the man's office chair and pretended to be on a conference call. He put his feet up on the desk, then he paced the room with the phony call on mock speaker phone and pretended to be distracted by the phone call. What Gunner could not ignore was the wall of windows in front of him. How could a man be so distracted by a phone call as to not see a stranger either outside his windows or in the reflection of his windows?

Gunner leafed through the files on Mr. Baines' desk. Nothing set off any alarm bells in his mind. He opened desk drawers, leafed through reams of papers in a stack of trays and everything was perfect, too perfect. Gunner's Spidey senses were tingling, and he knew he had to keep looking. He did not know what he was looking for, but he would gamble his salary on the fact there was some valuable information in this room.

He did a full three hundred and sixty degree turn before his eyes settled on the portrait. It was Eighteenth Century, perhaps a memento of a

The Waking Hours

long-dead family member, or maybe just a flea market purchase to cover up a wall safe. Gunner moved closer to see what he was dealing with. Instead of being hung on the wall, the picture opened to the left and behind it lay a locked and combination-protected wall safe. Gunner wanted answers and he had to find a way to get in.

As he was searching for a tool to chip away at the drywall surrounding the safe, his cell phone rang.

"Sir, we have something you might be interested in. A young man was just found with his throat cut. Not sure if it is connected but we thought you should know. The coroner just arrived on the scene. I texted you the address." The line went dead.

Gunner had to get to that crime scene. Although these two cases were worlds apart, he knew they were connected. Gunner knew that as deeply as he knew his name was really Carrick Doyle. He spent a few last moments taking cell phone photos of the wall safe and the office and he was on his way to a block of university houses many kilometers away.

After what seemed like an eternity, Gunner pulled his car over beside the flashing lights of the squad cars. Caution tape surrounded the house and, after showing his credentials, Gunner ducked under the tape. Officers were everywhere and the crime scene investigators were busy gathering whatever samples they thought were relevant.

The deceased lay on the sidewalk in a pool of blood. The closer he got to the body; Gunner realized the victim had a deep cut in his throat that went from ear to ear. Gunner tried to stifle a smile and noticed a few sideways glances from the team collecting samples, so he put his stern face back on and surveyed the scene. Maybe it was a connection, a potential lead. This guy was going to eventually make a mistake and Gunner was going to be there to catch him. The original feeling he had about the park murders not being connected was cast aside and he began to believe that he was looking for the same un-sub, he just could not explain why at this point.

Gunner squatted down next to the body. The kid could not have been more than twenty-two years old. His eyes stared sightlessly at the sky and, although the pupils had become slightly dilated and the iris had become milky with death, Gunner could tell the kid had one green eye and one blue eye. If the difference in color was still noticeable, he had not been dead that long. He did not know if the difference in the eye color was significant, but

Gunner pulled out the tiny notebook from his pocket and began to jot a few things down. He put the eye color at the top of the list with an asterisk beside it. He also made a note in capital letters about the cause of death. He had seen many victims who had their throat slashed but it was rare to see a cut go ear to ear.

The younger beat cops had been going door to door to ask if any of the neighbors had seen or heard anything. The response was the same from every house. Nobody saw a thing.

There was not much more Gunner could do at the crime scene, so he told the cops at the scene to call him if they found anything significant. He ducked back under the crime scene tape and pointed his sedan in the direction of home. It was going to be another long night of trying to find a connection or just a clue that would help him find the killer or killers. Pretty soon the city would start to panic, and he needed to have one or two answers to all the questions he knew the residents would have.

The files were just where he had left them, and he noticed the stains on the top files where he had drooled on them in his sleep. Gunner stripped off his coat and threw it over the kitchen chair. He headed to the coffee maker but quickly turned towards the fridge. He had a long night coming up and a beer or two would make his brain a little more accepting of some far-fetched ideas. He rolled the giant white board out of his office and started scribbling notes along the top about each of the murders with the dry erase markers. He wrote the names of the victims, if he had them, the date and time of death, where the body was located and how they died. If there was a connection, this always helped him find it.

He sat down and stared at the board. Apart from the kids in the park and now the kid with the different colored eyes, he would have sworn these other two murders were a professional hit. With Ted Baines in the wind, Gunner wondered when his body would show up to be added to his list. He felt sympathy for Alice Baines. He knew the chance of her husband returning home alive was very slim, but he let her hang on to her optimism as she left the house with the officer who would drive her to her sister's house.

Gunner got up and paced in his kitchen. It was early in the investigation, but time was ticking, and he knew he would have the higher-ups breathing down his neck for something, an idea, a profile, an arrest. But the information in front of him made no sense. Although the park murders and the most recent murder both seemed to be done with precision, Gunner just could not see how they could be connected to the man shot at point blank range and the man who was asphyxiated. And was Ted Baines related to these cases, or did he just skip out on his wife and make it look like he was kidnapped?

His phone remained silent as he leafed through the files. For the first time in a long time, Gunner could not immediately see the pieces of the puzzle that he usually saw without even trying. This just might be the first time that Gunner had ever felt stumped and he fucking hated it.

Chapter 17

Feeling slightly embarrassed after asking for an escort home from the restaurant, Charlotte ate what she could of her take-out dinner and mindlessly flipped through the TV channels. The Coq au Vin should have been delicious, but the taste was soured by her memory of the man across the street when she had been in the restaurant. Although she knew she could count on Joey to get her home safely, she still remembered feeling like a victim when she saw the strange man and she had no idea why she felt that way.

She left the dining room table to take her dishes to the kitchen and was still listening to the news channel she had been on for the six o'clock news. The anchor had begun reporting on a murder that had just happened near the university. Charlotte dropped her plate in the sink and watched it break into three pieces. She could not handle any more murder stories, so she picked up the remote and turned the TV off. She tried to put all her uneasiness to the back of her mind and think about her grandmother but thinking about her did not bring any calmness to her situation.

Charlotte replayed their conversation about Max over in her head. Her grandmother had convinced herself that her long-dead grandson had come back to life and been to visit her last night. And, although she never remembered Charlotte on any of her visits, Tillie distinctly remembered the ring that Max wore that he called his Mustang and the fact that Max had referred to Charlotte as Charlie.

Charlotte wanted nothing more than to forget the day that had just transpired. She went into her bathroom, put the plug in her tub and drew herself a nice hot bath. She even opted for the scented bath beads that she was given for Christmas by her mom many years ago. She did not like to use them often because she dreaded the day when they would run out but today, she needed them.

The Waking Hours

The bath water fogged the mirror in her bathroom, so she knew it was ready. She grabbed the novel she had started three days ago, dipped one foot into the tub to test the temperature and eased her way in. The book had already begun to show the signs of being exposed to moisture, but it was of no consequence to her. All Charlotte wanted right now was a distraction.

The bath water felt sublime. Charlotte could already feel the stress of the day being eradicated from her body. She greedily turned the pages of the book and could feel it absorbing more moisture from her bath, but she did not care.

She had turned at least thirty pages in the book and could feel the temperature of the bath water cooling. She let out some of the cool water and ran the tap to replace it with hot water. Her fingers and toes had begun to prune but she was not concerned. This was the most contented she had felt in a long time, so she continued to enjoy her bath. She was going back to work tomorrow so she was going to enjoy this brief escape into a fantasy life for as long as she could.

Charlotte had read another ten pages in the book when she was startled by the sound of her TV coming on by itself. It was shortly after eight pm and the news should have been long over, but Charlotte could distinctly hear the story of the latest murder echoing through her living room. There were only a few details about the man who was killed since the next of kin had not been notified but they did share some of the details of the murder. The police had no suspects at the time but were warning residents of the city to be cautious if they were out on their own.

The water in the bath was still steaming from the addition of the hot water and the mirror in Charlotte's bathroom was covered in a thick layer of fog. She ignored her television and was about to put her nose back into her novel when she noticed the small letters that had surprisingly appeared in the bottom left corner of the mirror spelling the name Charlie. Charlotte dropped her book into the bath water.

Chapter 18

Jack stood back far enough so the spray from the lake meeting the concrete of the pier did not completely soak him. The wind had changed to push the waves directly at the pier, but Jack noticed the water from the river still bullied its way into the lake and created a small eddy where the lakes' power took charge. He had no idea why he had been drawn here and, now that he was standing here, he felt like an idiot for chasing an idea.

Jack cracked three of his knuckles and continued to stare across the lake. He watched the strong current of the river dissolve into the tidal motion of the lake. If the river thought it was Leon Spinks, the lake was Mohammed Ali. Anything coming out of that river would immediately become victim to the whim of the lake.

It was still early morning, and in the distance, Jack could see the sailboats enjoying the strong gusts that were propelling them across the top of the water. The sun had introduced itself to the horizon and, after they had shaken hands, found its place in the mid-morning sky. Jack stood for another thirty minutes hoping for some sort of sign as to why he felt the need to be here. Apart from enjoying the beautiful morning and watching the boats tacking as their sails gracefully caught the next gust of air, Jack was at a loss.

He glanced to his right and saw the familiar flat stones he remembered from his childhood. He made his way across the pier, picked up three of the rocks and headed back to the end of the pier. Although the lake was still choppy, Jack grasped one of the rocks and waited for a calm period. Mother Nature acquiesced and the wind was slightly subdued for a moment. Jack side-armed the rock into the lake and watched it skip six times across the surface of the water. He smiled thinking about how his dad had taught him to skip rocks when he was a child.

The lake seemed to be enjoying Jack's reverie and remained calm enough so he could throw the other two rocks he had picked up. The third

The Waking Hours

time was a charm and Jack watched his rock skip nine times before its weight was pulled under the water. If this were the only reason for Jack to be at the lake today, he would take this moment and enjoy it.

He left the pier with a smile and had just reached his car when a piece of Ted Baines' trousers buoyed slightly in the current. Jack drove away without even seeing it.

He went to the grocery store on the way home and cooked himself a healthy dinner. He limited himself to two glasses of wine, wrote something in his journal about being at the pier and went to bed early. For the first time in what felt like forever, Jack slept without dreaming.

Chapter 19

The wind had picked up and Victor pulled his coat closer around his neck to avoid the draft. The wind itself was not particularly cold but some of the bursts of air felt like cold talons picking at his flesh. He knew the scene around the boy's body would be littered with people and he had enough of a head start that he was not concerned about being too close. Victor was more concerned by the fact that he did not feel the usual high he felt after taking a life. Usually, he would be ravenous and eat two or three entrees, plus a few appetizers, a few beer and a couple of desserts.

As he walked aimlessly along the sidewalk, Victor felt nothing more than nauseated. He had no appetite whatsoever and he now had no clue what to do with himself. Normally, this is the time he would spend in a restaurant, eating his way through his euphoria and allowing his pulse to return to a normal rate until he was calm enough to go home. Victor tried his best to serpentine through the side streets to avoid being seen on the main streets. He spotted what he was looking for and threw his switchblade into a dumpster he found in a back alley. His fingerprints were not in any database, but he wiped the knife clean, just in case.

Victor had nowhere left to go but home. He wanted nothing more than to sit in the darkness of his living room and try to figure out what the Hell was happening to him. He did not make eye contact with Joe as he moved through the lobby to the elevator and Joe continued reading his book.

Victor closed his apartment door and, for the first time since he had lived here, used the chain lock as well as the deadbolt. His paranoia was really starting to get to him. The blackout blinds were already closed, and Victor's apartment was as dark as it could be. He stripped out of his clothes, leaving a trail of them in his hallway as he made his way to the center of his living room. He sat cross-legged on his floor and began breathing deeply to center himself. He failed to notice he had been rocking himself back and forth.

The Waking Hours

Victor closed his eyes and let himself go back to that dark root cellar from his childhood. He could smell the earth and hear the movement of the creatures who shared his space. He was never afraid of them, but he knew they were terrified of him. His swaying motion had stopped, and he sat in a trance-like state. His pulse was slow and moderate, and he felt like himself again. Taking himself to that cellar always gave him strength. His body spent hours sitting naked on his laminate floor, but Victor's spirit was somewhere else, somewhere transcendent, and he began to mewl like an animal.

He inhaled deeply and slowly brought his head up. Victor opened his eyes and was only met with more blackness. He smiled, feeling he had regained his power and his appetite. He turned on a small lamp with a 40-watt bulb. The weak glow of light was all Victor needed. He found his cell phone and ordered take-out. It was enough food to feed four adults, but Victor knew there would not be many leftovers.

The dull light guided him to the closet, and he dressed in sweatpants and a black sweater. He found his wallet and got enough cash to cover his bill. He paced the floor waiting for the delivery person and he finally heard the buzz through his intercom. The exchange was always the same. The delivery person would knock, Victor would pass the cash through the mail slot on his door and the bags of food would be left outside Victor's door. Nobody ever questioned it because Victor was always generous with delivery tips. He appreciated the discretion.

Victor waited until he heard the elevator beep its arrival and the door had opened and closed. He released the chain lock, turned the deadbolt, and grabbed his order. Once the deadbolt had been re-engaged, Victor paused, staring at the chain lock. Although he felt much stronger than he had when he arrived home, Victor still slid the chain lock back into its housing. He took the food to the dining room table and let the carnage begin. There were no plates used, no utensils and no napkins. Victor just began to satiate himself like a tiger eating its latest quarry.

He was three quarters of his way through the meals when his cell phone rang. Victor wiped his hands on his sweatpants and picked it up. His greeting was always the same, so the caller knew they had the right person on the other end.

"Go." Victor's simple word allowed the caller to proceed.

He did not recognize the voice on the other end of the line but, if the guy had Victor's number, he got it from a reliable source. Victor's number changed with every new disposable cell phone he had so he could avoid being tracked and he only ever gave his number to one guy.

The voice on the phone was succinct and explicit. Victor began jotting down the information in his journal and was having trouble keeping up.

"We do NOT want this to look like an accident. We want the body on display in a very public place, so the media eats it up. We do not want it done quickly, we want it done right and we have heard from many reliable sources that you are the best. We are sending a particularly important message."

Victor waited until the man had stopped talking to speak, "My fee is $750,000.00. It needs to be wired to my offshore account and it needs to be there before I even start making a plan."

Victor gave the man the account number, instructions on how to wire the funds and he hung up. He lied about not making plans before the money was wired. He was excited about this one. A public display - the possibilities were endless. Victor collected the rest of the food and threw it in his fridge. He had an appetite for something else now.

He turned on his laptop, got onto his secure server and began to do a little research about his next victim. The internet was overrun with stories of this guy and Victor began to understand why the public display was necessary. This guy was a waste of human flesh. Everything he did was corrupt. Victor knew that he himself was no saint, but this guy was a complete asshole in every aspect of his life. He abused his wife, he ran shady businesses and swindled innocent families out of their life savings. It did not take Victor long to formulate the plan, but it would take some time to figure out how to do it properly.

Victor got notice of an incoming email and the wire transfer was done. These guys wanted this guy gone, and they wanted to make a grand statement. Victor made a quick phone call to the only person who really knew he existed. After a short conversation, Victor knew an envelope of cash would be couriered to him no later than tomorrow. The business deal was done, now the fun began.

Chapter 20

Gunner's phoned beeped with an incoming text message telling him to check his email. He pushed the files aside and opened his laptop. The officer investigating the latest murder had sent Gunner some information about the kid that had just been killed. His name was Adam Whatley, he was twenty-three years old and about to graduate university. He had been at the Chinese Buffet with some friends and left them to head to the pub while he went home for his inhaler. Some of his friends had come back to the house to see what was taking Adam so long since he was not answering his cell phone and they arrived to flashing lights and police tape.

Gunner made a mental note to go to the restaurant to see if any of the staff had noticed anyone or anything suspicious. For now, he added Adam's name to his white board and listed the limited things he knew about this case.

He sat back down at the kitchen table and leaned back, interlocking his hands behind his head. Where Gunner could usually see a pattern, the only two connections he had right now were the similarities between the park murders and Adam Whatley. And Gunner could not even say for certain those were connected. Adam Whatley's murder could have been a copycat since the details of the park murders were broadcast ad nauseum all over the news media, a fledgling killer trying to get his or her ten minutes of fame.

Gunner went back to the first murder. John Doe had been shot at point blank range. Gunner was still waiting for forensics to send him any information as to who this guy was. There were no fingerprints in the system, and they had taken a mold of his teeth to see if they could identify him through dental records. John Doe was found tucked behind a tiny makeshift store front. The owner had been disturbed by an odd smell and finally began to tear the place apart when it got to be so bad that he could not stand

The Waking Hours

to stay in his store. Gunner figured John Doe had been there for several days.

He skipped over the park murders and went to Peter Mahon's file. Peter had been poisoned by an undetermined gas that Gunner would have bet was Chlorine. His body had been found in a ravine just outside the city. Since the land there was barren, Gunner knew Peter had been killed elsewhere and dumped like a piece of garbage.

Gunner had left a few rookie cops in charge of acquiring details about Peter's life and he was waiting to hear what they had found. He assumed Peter Mahon and John Doe both had a few skeletons in their closets and the sooner Gunner knew what they were, perhaps the easier it would be to make a connection between these two corpses if there was a connection.

Two professional hits, or so it seemed. Both men were killed quickly and efficiently. Both bodies had been dumped far from any crime scene in opposite ends of the city. And both corpses were trying to tell him something, but he was not getting the message.

Gunner looked at the clock on the wall. Somehow, he had not even noticed that the early evening had turned into the middle of the night. He had consumed two beers for dinner and figured he should pack it in for the night and start fresh in the morning. He left the files as they were, extinguished the kitchen lights and headed for the couch. He wanted to be close to the white board in case something came to him in the night.

He woke up just before the sunrise and his brain was just as stumped as it was the previous night, which pissed him off. Gunner had a hot shower, checked for any emails or text messages, and headed to the office. He wanted to see if anyone had made any headway. The office was empty at that hour in the morning, so he rifled through a few files on the desks. They were just as full of nothing as Gunner's files were. He poured a cup of coffee and took a donut from yesterday's Tim Horton's run. It was stale, but it tasted better than the shitty cup of six-hour old coffee. As terrible as it was, Gunner took a few gulps and refilled his mug. He made a mental note to talk to the waiter at the Chinese Buffet. The office began to buzz with life and the investigating officers met in the conference room to share any leads they may have found.

It was a waste of time, as far as Gunner was concerned, and he left before the meeting was over. He hopped in a squad car and headed for the restaurant. He wanted to chat with the waiter before the lunch rush started.

Mike was eighteen years old and taking a year off to make money before he went to university. He seemed like an intelligent kid and he had a good eye for detail. He remembered Adam and his friends that night. They all gave Mike a hard time because he asked them all for ID before he would serve them any alcohol. They busted his chops for a while but nothing out of the ordinary happened and they left him a good tip. They all left the restaurant together and told Mike they were going to get wasted at the pub. Adam was wheezing a little when he left.

Gunner took down a few notes. The wheezing made sense since the kid went home to get his inhaler. Gunner asked Mike if anyone else stood out, if it seemed like anyone was paying more attention to Adam.

Mike thought for a few minutes and could not think of anything out of the ordinary. Gunner asked him to close his eyes and go back to that night.

"Keep your eyes closed and look around the room. Who do you see?", Gunner was hoping Mike would remember something.

With his eyes still closed, Mike moved his head back and forth as if he were scanning the tables. He recalled a family of four in another section of the restaurant with two bratty kids, Adam and his friends, a few older couples, and the big man at a table by himself.

"Don't open your eyes. Now tell me about the man," Gunner said.

"He has been at the restaurant before. He is big, like overweight big, always wears black and has a really deep voice, like horror movie deep." Mike opened his eyes again.

Gunner wanted more, "Do you know anything about this guy?"

Mike wanted to help but the only thing he could think to say was, "I'd say he was about five foot ten and looks like he is pregnant. Everyone remembers him because he always pays for two meals, eats a ton of food and leaves a really shitty tip."

Gunner thanked Mike for the information and left the restaurant. He was not in a rush to get back to the office, so he meandered his way up the street in the direction that the boys had taken the other night. Three of the four boys had veered right halfway up the hill to head to the university pub and Adam continued another two blocks up the hill to their rental house. The boys were all roommates and, according to the other three, Adam was liked by everyone. He did not have a mean bone in his body, and everyone wanted to say they were friends with the guy with two different colored eyes.

Gunner noticed a few pieces of police tape on the bush in front of the house. He moved around it to pick it off and guessed that the bush could have given some sort of cover to someone who did not want to be seen. But Adam was not supposed to be home. It was pub night and, had he not forgotten his inhaler, he should have been at the bar with his friends. If someone knew his schedule, they should have been waiting for him much later than they were.

Gunner's thoughts went back to the big guy in the restaurant. He pulled out his pad of paper and made a note to ask Adam's friends if the large man in black contacted any of them throughout dinner. Gunner was feeling the niggling of a hunch, but he could not put a finger on what that hunch could be.

Chapter 21

Victor felt invigorated. Between the meditation, the large dinner, the new job, and the immense deposit to his bank account, he felt his power had returned. Shortly after 11:00 am, Victor's intercom buzzed with Joe informing him of a courier delivery. Victor gave the same explicit instructions to the courier as he had given to the take-out delivery guy and moments later there was a knock on the door and the package was left outside of Victor's apartment.

Looking through the peep hole, Victor saw the Purolator driver getting back onto the elevator and the doors closing. After he had confirmed the hallway was empty, Victor disengaged his locks and grabbed the parcel. Because of the strange hours he kept, Victor did not ever see many of the other tenants in his building and he wanted it to stay that way. He was not trying to hide, but he was not about to throw a neighborhood party any time soon. He engaged the deadbolt and let the chain lock dangle free.

Victor opened the package and leafed through the wad of cash tucked inside. The rainbow of bills flashed brilliantly and, although Victor hated these new plastic-coated Canadian bills, the colors made it easy to recognize the denominations immediately. He pulled out ten of the brown ones and put the thousand dollars in his wallet. He closed the courier enveloped and opened his wall safe, stashing the rest of the cash for his shopping once he had a firm plan in place for his next job.

They wanted him to take his time and to make a statement. This hit would be a little more challenging for Victor since he was usually a man who got things done quickly. But he was up for the challenge. Who said no to a little creative freedom in their job? That was something Victor did not usually get.

He sat down at his laptop and began to dig deeper into this newest target. Victor jotted down many notes and, with each new story of what this guy had done, Victor knew he deserved a horrible death. But this death also

The Waking Hours

had to send a message and Victor was unsure how to do that just yet. His one page of notes turned into two and Victor began to highlight the similarities in his notes. This man was heartless and turned a blind eye to everyone but himself. He was narcissistic and Victor knew he was going to enjoy ridding the world of this douche bag.

After several more hours of painstaking research, Victor was pleased with the idea he had come up with. It was bold, it would be very public, it would certainly send the necessary message and the media would be tripping over themselves to see if they could get any photos for their stories. To pull it off, Victor's plan would have to be executed with precision down to the last detail. One misstep and things could go horribly wrong. This plan would be like creating an intense domino display. If one tile fell out of place, the rest of the show was over.

Victor began to make a list of all the things he would need. He was not too keen on having to go back to his warehouse so soon after Peter's death, but almost everything he needed to make this plan work was in his shop. There were a few things he would have to buy but that is why he had the money sent to him. Victor did not have a local bank account, nor did he have any identification to open one if he had the desire, which he did not. For all intents and purposes, Victor did not exist, and he liked it that way. Anonymity was Victor's closest ally.

Victor went to the fridge and pulled out the rest of his take-out. He stood at the kitchen counter polishing off the cold remnants of his earlier dinner. He knew he was going to have to be at the top of his game to pull this off and he imagined how much more he could charge for his services if this worked. It was going to be one for the history books.

Chapter 22

Jack awoke to a light breeze coming in through his bedroom window. He was shocked to see that he was in his own bed, sleeping on his own pillow and his body showed no signs of anything other than latent wrinkles from being wrapped up in his sheets.

He could not tell if he was happy to be safe at home or disappointed that he would have nothing to enter in his journal today. He still had enough money stashed away to not have to be too concerned about going into the office any time soon. Jack knew that even if a client came in looking to buy a home, he would not be able to concentrate enough to be the best choice for a realtor. He was doing them a public service, really, by not going to work.

Fresh coffee made and a steaming cup in his hand, Jack turned the lock three times, opened the sliding door to his balcony and sat outside to enjoy his first morning of not having to catalogue his injuries. There were still a few muscles that disagreed with some of Jack's movements but, for the most part, he felt rather good. The late spring air was warm, and he could hear the faint sounds of the highway traffic in the distance. The streets around his building were unusually quiet so Jack enjoyed his coffee in peace.

After getting up to refill his cup, Jack took a moment to glance down into the courtyard below. It was usually empty this time of day, so Jack did not expect to see anything other than the flowering bushes that had been planted a few years ago. As he scanned the small park, he noticed a scruffy blond dog lying on one of the benches. Jack looked around to see if any humans were close to where the dog was, but the dog seemed to be on its own.

The Waking Hours

Jack brought his second cup of coffee back out onto his balcony and moved his chair to the railing so he could watch the dog. As far as Jack could tell, the dog was asleep on the bench. After watching for about five more minutes, the dog lifted its head, sat up and stared back at Jack. He was unsure how he knew the dog was staring at him and not something else, but Jack felt like they had locked eyes. The dog chuffed at Jack and seemed to enjoy their staring contest. Jack was almost convinced he had seen the dog smile and then it yawned and jumped off the bench. It slowly looked over its shoulder, took one last look at Jack and meandered its way out of the park.

Many of his neighbors walked their dogs in the courtyard, but Jack had no memory of ever seeing this mutt before. And he certainly had never seen a dog alone in the park. He did not think the dog had any relevance, but he wrote it down in his journal, just in case.

Jack decided to use his time wisely. He dressed in some old jeans, long-sleeved shirt and baseball cap and headed to the public library. He was spinning his wheels on the internet and wanted to find some literature that he could take home to learn more about lucid dreaming. The librarians were always willing to share their knowledge and eager to help people who still took the time to use their services. They were not just about books; they were a wealth of information about research.

Jack did not bother making up a story, he simply went to the counter and asked if the library had books on lucid dreaming. Jack imagined these ladies had been asked for information on just about everything, so his request did not seem to faze them. He was led to a section in the library and shown the rows of books on dreams. He avoided the books about analyzing dreams and found a few that would have more pertinent information for him. He took the books back to the counter, pulled out his library card and headed home with his volumes of information.

Jack had no idea that the study of dreams was so prominent. He was mesmerized by the vast quantity of analysts who spent their time studying what happens to people when they dream. He had been so consumed by his research that he had not realized the day had morphed into early evening. He put the books down and listened to the sound of his hunger pangs. If he were going to keep going, he would have to eat.

Jack quickly fried two eggs and found a piece of ham in his fridge that he warmed in the same pan. He poured a glass of wine and went back to the table to continue reading. After another couple of hours, Jack could feel his eyes getting heavy, but he fought it with every bit of strength he could muster. He put his elbow on the table and used his hand to hold up his head. The words in the book were beginning to blur and his head began to feel like it weighed thirty pounds. Jack put his arm on the table and used it as a pillow, still holding up the page he was now trying to read sideways. His eyes would close as he was reading, and he would blink them open again. Before long, Jack was asleep, ironically on top of a book about lucid dreaming.

~~

When Jack started to come around, he thought he had left his windows open and a strong breeze was whipping through his apartment. But the moment Jack felt the chugging motion of a roller coaster, he knew something was horribly wrong. His eyes stung as the wind picked at his pupils. He tried to close his eyes, or even to blink, and it was impossible. The roller coaster continued to hurtle along the track and Jack could do nothing but stare into the rushing air, but no tears were running down his cheeks. He was given a slight reprieve as the coaster leveled out and began its ascent up to the next part of the ride.

Jack took that moment to take stock of what was going on. It was dawn. He could see the pink lining on the horizon as the sun struggled to get out of bed. The amusement park was closed and, as far as he could tell, the body he now found himself in was the only one on the ride.

Jack could taste rubber in his mouth. His eyes were propped open by some antiquated wire device that made it impossible for him to close his eyes. His shirt was wide open, and the immense pain Jack felt in his chest made him feel like he was having a massive coronary. As the car of the roller coaster lurched closer to the top of the hill, Jack glanced down and noticed the gaping hole in the chest of the man's body he was occupying. That hole was all that remained of the place where the man's heart had once been, and the rest of his torso was covered in blood and small, jagged pieces of flesh.

Jack felt the urge to vomit, but knew it was impossible. This body was already dead, and Jack was just along for the ride, literally. Jack could not tell which car he was in, but he knew the train was ready to crest the hill and continue its terrifying descent into the next chain of loops.

Jack had never been on a roller coaster and now he knew why. Who in their right mind would purposely put themselves through this circle of Hell? The train had gone through a set of three loops and Jack fervently hoped that this was the end of the ride. The train slowed as it pulled into the gate where old riders could make their wobbly exits and excited new riders could enter the cars for the next ride. Jack was content to stay in this man's body for as long as he had to if the ride was over. But after sitting for only a few minutes, the cars chugged forward, and the ride began again.

Jack must have done four turns around the track before the security team realized the ride was running on its own. They waited until the cars pulled into the gate again and overrode the switch, bringing the train to a permanent halt. Jack knew if he, or somebody, was going to figure out what was happening to him, he would have to leave some sort of clue. Since the hands he had access to were duct taped to the bar at the wrists, Jack, stretched the index finger of his right hand as far as he could and tried to make a cut in the left hand. He was happy he had not cut his fingernails lately and, remarkably, he was able to leave an inch-long slice in the dead man's skin. Even though Jack was not physically connected to this body, he could leave a physical sign. He made two more cuts in a row, leaving behind three scratches resembling the number 111. At least Jack knew he was still more of himself than the dead man. His obsessive-compulsive nature to do thing in threes had followed him into his dream.

He heard the voices of the guards get louder and more panicked as they discovered the dead man in the middle of the roller coaster. Jack felt like he was being pulled away from the dead man's body and only hoped it was back to the safety of his bed. Before he was completely gone, Jack made a mental note of the name of the ride he had just been on - The Grifter.

Chapter 23

With his plan firmly in place, Victor set himself in motion. He was proud of his inventiveness and knew the staging of this murder would get the intended notoriety that his client demanded. This would be splashed all over papers, television news and the internet and Victor could only hope that the symbolism of his methods would be understood by many. He knew the body would not be shown on the news, but the media loved sensationalism and those details would not be left out of the lead story on the six o'clock news or on any social media sites.

He had gathered everything he needed and set up the back room in his warehouse. The ceiling, the walls and the floor had been covered in plastic. The ten-by-ten room had a single chair set in the middle of the room and the microphones had been positioned to make sure that they would pick up every wretched sound the man made as his body was mutilated. Victor's new client wanted to make sure that this man suffered a very painful death, and they were not afraid to hear his tortured screams to know the job had been done sufficiently.

But that was only phase one. Victor had done some leg work at the amusement park to learn how to program The Grifter to run continually until it was discovered by security. He had seen how lax the overnight guards were so he knew the discovery would not be made until they finally did their rounds a few hours prior to the park opening. It paid to be a creature of the night. Victor had only one thing left to do and that was to acquire Mr. Keston.

Victor's plan, although solid, was not foolproof. There was always room for error and Victor knew that this was the most delicate part of the plan. Although Victor liked driving his Cadillac, this job would require the limousine that was stored in the larger part of the warehouse. The canvas cover had kept the limo free of dust and, since Victor had left it clean and in pristine condition, all it required was the turn of a key.

The Waking Hours

Victor listened to the engine roar to life and settle into a gentle hum. He adjusted the mirrors and tested the privacy window between the driver's area and the passenger's seating. The power windows worked, the radio was clear, and the windshield wipers thumped back and forth with precision. Victor left the engine idling and did an outside tour of the car to make sure the lights were all working. Everything was in order and the tinted windows preserved the privacy of the occupants of the car.

He was almost ready. Victor shut the car off and crossed the concrete floor to a set of lockers. Inside the end locker was a black suit, white shirt, black tie, black shoes, and black hat. He changed to look the part and went back into his office for the final piece of the puzzle.

Victor had been out early that morning and placed a device in Mr. Keston's personal limo that would allow Victor to disable the engine with the use of a remote control. Victor had to be within 30 meters of Keston's car, but if his information was right, Victor would be in the precise spot he needed to be when Keston came out of the gala he was attending.

Victor jockeyed for his position in the row of cars and was directly behind Keston's usual driver. When Keston came out, Victor pushed the button on his remote and smoke began to billow from under the hood of Keston's limousine. The driver jumped out of the car after releasing the lock on the hood and desperately tried to find the cause of the plumes. Keston looked nothing short of annoyed and moved towards Victor's car.

Victor lowered the passenger side window and said, "Need a ride, sir? That looks like a bit of a problem."

Keston did not even speak to Victor before he opened the back door and let himself in to the car. He belched out an address and Victor pulled the car out of the line before Keston could change his mind or his regular driver would even realize that Keston was gone.

Victor did not want to make small talk, nor would Keston lower himself to respond, so they drove in silence. Keston was so immersed in his iPhone that he did not realize Victor had missed the correct exit from the expressway to get Keston home. When he finally took the time to look up and pay attention to where they were, Keston hollered up to the front of the car.

"Hey, you idiot, you missed the turn." Keston was pissed.

Victor pushed the button allowing him to close the privacy window. The second button he pushed released gas into the passenger compartment and, after a few seconds of yelling and pounding his fist on the privacy glass, Keston had slumped back in his seat and was unconscious.

Victor got off the expressway and made his way through several prominent neighborhoods. Seeing a limousine in these blocks was like seeing a Robin in the spring, they were everywhere. Victor knew it would not be out of the ordinary to see a limo in these parts so he drove through as many of these neighborhoods as he could rather than an isolated stretch of the expressway where he would stand out. He eventually got back on the highway to reach his warehouse. Keston was out like a light but nowhere near dead. Phase one had gone much better than anticipated and the next phase was the one in which Victor excelled. He knew tonight's victory dinner was going to be enough to feed at least five people based on his current appetite.

Victor pushed the button on the garage door opener and watched as it gracefully opened to welcome him home. Instead of parking where he had been before, Victor drove to the back of the warehouse and shut down the engine. The small room was waiting for Mr. Keston and Victor effortlessly lifted the man out of the back seat and took him to his destination. Victor propped Keston up in the chair and bound his wrists and ankles. Keston had slumped forward in the chair so Victor retrieved some rope and propped him up although his head still hung down, resting on his chest.

Victor left Keston alone and made his way back to the lockers. He hung up the suit and shirt, polished the shoes and placed the cap on the top shelf. He closed the door of that locker and opened the door at the far end. Inside the new locker was a hazmat suit. Victor put on the running shoes that were on the bottom shelf, climbed into the jumpsuit and zipped it up to his neck. The hood and the mask dangled from his shoulders, but he did not need those yet. Victor had a spring in his step as he made his way back to Keston.

The gas in the limo was not a long-acting gas so Keston was coming to as Victor entered the room. Keston saw Victor in the hazmat suit and

The Waking Hours

immediately began to thrash around in the chair. Victor's throaty laugh echoed off the walls and Keston stopped moving. His head was still free of restraints so Keston pivoted his line of sight to see the table with duct tape, what looked like a red plastic heart, a wire speculum, and a large hole saw. Keston wet himself.

After watching the man's pants become saturated with urine, Victor pulled up the hood of his hazmat suite and put on his goggles and mask. He reached for one wire speculum at a time and struggled with the thrashing body as he used them to prop open Keston's eyes. Since this piece of shit had turned a blind eye to everyone he destroyed, Victor wanted him to witness as much of his own death as he could stand. Keston began to scream. Victor let him wail for about thirty seconds for the recording, then took the rubber heart and shoved it into Keston's mouth, securing it safely with duct tape. Keston's not-so-public phrase to the families he had left destitute was 'Eat your heart out' and Victor could only describe this as very apropos.

Keston began to whimper and Victor moved on to the next step. He reached for the hole saw and turned it on. Victor made sure everything of importance was covered, including himself, and he moved the hole saw to within an inch of Keston's chest. Keston passed out and, although his eyes were propped open, he missed the moment that the hole saw began tearing at his flesh and cut a hole five inches in diameter into his sternum.

Keston's body convulsed in reaction to the drill that was boring into his chest. If he could have been awakened from his unconscious state by the sounds of his death, his blood loss made sure he missed the main event. Keston was already dead and bleeding out when Victor had uttered the phrase 'you are a heartless bastard' and surgically removed Keston's heart from his body.

~~

For Victor, getting the body to the amusement park was easier than making sure Keston got into the limo in the first place. Victor knew the security guards were watching reruns of Seinfeld and he had already rewired the security video to loop a tape of an empty parking lot, so Victor had no fears of these two guys coming out of their office any time soon. Although most of his blood was in the warehouse, Keston was wrapped in plastic in the trunk of the Cadillac.

Victor tossed the body over his shoulder and made his way to The Grifter. He chose that roller coaster because its name was synonymous for cheater. Again, apropos. Victor unwrapped Keston and propped him up in the middle of the roller coaster. He used the duct tape to fasten Keston to the bar and used many strands of more duct tape to secure his midsection to the back of the chair. He had no idea how bumpy the ride would be, but he was confident in the amount of tape he used and knew Keston would make it through the ride. Victor could only imagine the whistle of the rushing wind as it entered the gaping hole in Keston's chest.

Victor looked at the body one last time. He knew lingering over the dead body was a bad idea, but he looked into Keston's eyes and saw only two, slightly cloudy, hazel orbs staring sightlessly. Victor switched the ride to ON. He stepped back to survey what might have been his finest hour yet. Keston's body jerked with the motion of the train and it was on its way to experience his last ride. He watched briefly as Keston and the roller coaster rolled along the tracks.

Chapter 24

Charlotte picked the saturated book from the bath water and threw it in the sink. She got out of the tub, fumbled for her bathrobe, and ran to find her cell phone. She wanted to take a picture of the mirror to prove to herself that the name Charlie was written in the bottom corner. She found her phone in her purse and got the camera ready. The name was still etched in the dewy remnants of her bath. She took a few shots and opened the pictures to see what she had captured.

The only thing visible in the photos was her fog covered mirror and the corner of her bathroom counter. The name Charlie was not visible at all and by the time Charlotte realized it was not in the photograph, the fog on the mirror had dissipated and the name was gone. Frustrated, she threw her phone on the floor of the bathroom and heard the screen crack. The sound of the TV in the background became very grating and Charlotte left the bathroom to extinguish the noise.

She did not sleep well at all that night. She tossed and turned, paced her apartment trying to pull answers out of thin air and make any sort of sense of what had been happening. Ever since she saw the man in the doorway of the apartment building, her life seemed to have been turned upside down. She had not given him much thought lately, but the contours of his face were still etched in her mind. She lay in bed thinking about him.

Charlotte was sure she had just fallen asleep when the chiming of her alarm woke her. She did not feel like going to work today but the antique store was not going to open itself and she needed the steady source of income. Since she had spent so much time in the bath the previous night, Charlotte felt she could skip her shower this morning. Besides, she did not want to see what other things may appear on her bathroom mirror if it fogged up again. She dressed, put her hair up in a ponytail, put on some mascara and left the apartment. She was going to treat herself this morning and get her tea and a croissant at the patisserie down the street from her shop.

The croissant was still warm. If she had not been holding her tea in the other hand she would have reached into the bag and eaten it on her way. When she reached the store, Charlotte tucked the tea in the crook of her elbow and fished the shop keys out of her pocket. As she was fumbling for the right key, Charlotte noticed the dog sitting on the sidewalk at the corner of her building. It seemed to be looking across the street and paying no attention to her. Charlotte finally found the right key, unlocked the deadbolt, and opened the door. As she was trying to key in the code for the alarm, the dog snuck past her and went into the store setting off a series of loud bells since Charlotte had not finished entering the passcode. She punched in the numbers again and silenced the alarm.

She hurried across the shop to call the alarm company to confirm it was a false alarm before they sent the police. When she finished the call, Charlotte took off her coat and found the dog lying in a patch of sunlight in the middle of the store. It seemed quite content to be there and did not mind that Charlotte tentatively pet its head. The dog had a collar and a name tag that said Norman but there was no contact phone number or vet information.

Charlotte looked at Norman for a few minutes and the dog seemed to have drifted into sleep, snoring slightly. She went back around to the other side of the shop counter and took the lid off her tea. She sat on her stool and watched the dog's rhythmic breathing as she sipped her tea and allowed the still-warm croissant to melt in her mouth. Norman's legs twitched a few times as he slept.

Charlotte assumed Norman must live in the neighborhood, so she waited to see if anyone came looking for him. Customers came in to browse and Norman welcomed everyone with the same enthusiasm Charlotte did. She laughed to herself thinking she might have to put him on the payroll as she watched him maneuver people through the store. He was more responsible for her sales that day than she was.

When nobody had come to inquire about Norman, Charlotte called the local animal rescue shelter to see if anyone had reported a missing dog. They had nothing matching his description at all. Charlotte asked about the possibility of dropping him off at the shelter and quickly changed her mind when she heard about their euthanasia policy when dogs were not claimed

The Waking Hours

within a short time frame. Charlotte hung up the phone and stared at the dog. He returned her stare. Norman chuffed at her and Charlotte could have sworn he was smiling.

She spoke to Norman as if he would understand, "This isn't a permanent solution, you know. This is just until we find out where you belong."

When the shop was closed for the day, Norman waited patiently on the sidewalk for Charlotte to set the alarm and lock the door. Once the shop gate had been secured as well, Charlotte and Norman set off down the sidewalk. They walked for a few blocks, Norman never leaving her side, and she suddenly realized she was going to have to feed him. They made a quick detour into the nearest pet store where she asked a few questions and left, confident she had the right food for Norman.

When they entered the park, Charlotte was sure Norman would run around like any other dog off his leash. Norman proved her wrong and stayed right beside her through the length of the park and until they reached the stairs to her apartment building. His ears pricked up slightly as he sniffed the air. She thought he was going to take off, but he strolled over to the bush in front of the building, lifted his leg and marked his territory. Satisfied that he had ably defended his new home, Norman once again joined Charlotte and waited to be shown inside.

When they reached her apartment, Norman pushed past Charlotte and, like a sentinel, checked every room for intruders. Satisfied that they were alone, Norman sat by the doorway to the kitchen and Charlotte realized he was probably hungry. She had never been a dog person so she hoped Norman would forgive her inability to immediately understand his needs. She filled a bowl with water which he lapped at right away and she found a small bowl for his food. The sound of the kibble hitting the stainless-steel bowl seemed to make Norman happy and he wagged his tail in approval.

He did not inhale the bowl of food, but instead gracefully picked up a few pieces at a time and seemed to savor his meal. Once finished, Norman sat in front of the sliding door to the balcony and kept watch. Charlotte thought he wanted to go out on the balcony, so she unlocked the door and slid it open. Norman maintained his position as guard and Charlotte closed the door. She made her dinner without being bothered by a begging dog. She sat at the dining room table while Norman stayed steadfast in his position by the sliding door. Later in the evening, Charlotte took Norman out to do his business and the two of them went to bed for the night, Charlotte tucked under the covers and Norman sleeping in the doorway to the bedroom.

Chapter 25

Gunner's sleep was not restful. As quickly as he would drift off, his brain would process another clue and he would be wide awake. He was in one of his more sleep-filled moments when his cell phone rang.

He could hear the commotion in the background as the detective barked into the phone, "Get to the amusement park, now!"

The clock read 6:02 am. He jumped out of bed, threw on whatever clothes were hanging over the end of his bed and left his apartment. With his flashing lights on and the relatively light traffic before rush hour, he made it to the amusement park in good time. There were media vans everywhere and reporters tried to get Gunner to make some sort of statement before he even knew what was going on.

He pushed past the reporters with his usual 'no comment' and was ushered through the security gate as he flashed his credentials. He was led to the middle of the park where The Grifter sat with its lone rider. The park was crawling with cops and the two security guards were being grilled about what had happened. Their faces had drained of color when they discovered the body and none of their pigment had returned. They both looked like ghosts.

He ducked under the police tape to get a closer look. Although his face was distorted by the wire speculum and the duct tape, Gunner knew this guy was no John Doe. He could not come up with his name off the top of his head, but this guy would be easy to identify. His eyes travelled down to the cavernous hole in the man's chest. Gunner was no doctor, but he could safely say the man's heart had been removed and from the remnants of flesh and blood on the man's clothing, that hole was not created post-mortem.

The forensics team had not allowed anyone to get close to the body until they were sure they had not missed any evidence. Gunner was the first one to be allowed to step onto the car to get a better look at the body. This was either another hit or some whack job trying to get some recognition. But a whack job would not have been this meticulous about the details. There was a lot of planning required to pull this off. This was a hit.

Gunner was careful not to touch anything but catalogued as much to memory as he could as well as taking several pictures with his cell phone. When the examiners came back, Gunner had asked if they could remove the duct tape from his mouth. The gloved hand of the lead examiner gently pulled back the tape to reveal the small rubber heart in the man's mouth. The phrase 'eat your heart out' flashed like a beacon in Gunner's mind and he said, "I think this is Gord Keston."

Gunner took a few more minutes to look over the dead body and saw three strange lines on Keston's hand. He flagged down the forensics guys and asked them if they had swabbed the cuts for DNA. The cuts had been catalogued and swabbed so Gunner took a picture of the marks with his phone and left the team to do their job.

This was a spectacular scene meant to draw attention. The media were practically frothing at the mouth to get any details that they could send out into the viewing world. They thrived on mass hysteria and this latest murder would have them creating their own theories about a serial killer. This city was about to explode, and Gunner had to find the connection fast or all Hell was going to break loose.

He knew he needed to get to his white board. Gord Keston was a big name in the media and once they got confirmation that Gord was the victim of this massacre, it was going to be splashed across every broadcast for at least the next forty-eight hours. The identification of his body would have to go through the proper process, but Gunner knew it was Keston. Once he got back to his house, he Googled Keston and the resemblance, although slightly altered, was confirmation enough for Gunner to add Keston's name to his growing list of murder victims.

Under Keston's name, Gunner detailed what had been done to his body. He also made a special note about the three cuts on Keston's hand. For the first time since these murders had begun, Gunner felt like he had found a significant piece of the puzzle. If it was a number, what did one hundred and eleven mean? Was it a street address? A safety deposit box? The possibilities were endless, but Gunner knew somehow it would become an important clue that he would eventually understand.

Chapter 26

Jack could detect the familiar scents of his apartment before he even opened his eyes. He felt nauseous and assumed any sudden movement was going to make him vomit. He knew he was upright and sitting in his desk chair simply because of the discomfort he felt from his shoulders to his thighs. He tried to move but felt like he was fastened to the chair.

He opened one eye to survey the situation and when he realized he was, indeed, back in the safety of his living room he allowed the other eyelid to flutter open. He stretched his back and moved his head from side to side to loosen his neck muscles. Over his shoulder, Jack could see the book on lucid dreaming that he had been reading at the dining room table when he fell asleep. He cracked three knuckles on each hand and attempted to stand up.

The quick rise from the chair was too sudden and Jack fell back into a seated position. The pain in his chest was excruciating and he had a horrible taste in his mouth. He rubbed his eyes for a few seconds and longed for some soothing eye drops. The sockets of his eyes were dry and rubbing them felt like he was scratching them with sandpaper.

His journal sat at the open writing desk and almost begged for Jack to go the mirror to see what harm had come to him in this latest dream. He slowly pushed himself up from the chair and made his way to the bathroom mirror.

The bruising around Jack's eyes made it look like he was wearing a sleep mask. His chest had a band of slight bruising from side to side and his wrists were red and raw, but the worst of the abrasions was in the middle of his chest. The deeply bruised circle was about four inches in diameter and a

The Waking Hours

dark shade of purple. It was tender to the touch, so Jack left it alone. He retrieved his cell phone from the dining room table and took pictures of the trauma his body had suffered in this last dream. If the torture got any worse in the dreams to come, Jack feared he would simply not wake up.

    He put a pot of coffee on and struggled to recall anything about his dream last night. He downloaded the pictures he had taken of his battered body onto a USB stick and made a mental note to print them and add them to his journal entry today. His body argued with every movement he made. Every muscle screamed in discord over every step Jack took. With a fresh coffee in hand, Jack put a blanket on the desk chair to give it some padding and tried to take himself back into the latest dream.

    The only thing he could remember was the wind. It seemed to batter him like hurricane winds did to tall trees. It still hurt to breathe, and he was honestly hoping he would not remember what happened to create this large, circular bruise on his chest. Thankfully, he was feeling slightly less nauseous than he had when he first woke up, so he pushed himself up out of the chair and stared out across the park. There was no wind that Jack could see so he turned the lock three times on the sliding door and went out on his balcony for some fresh air.

    The lounge chair was much more comfortable than his desk chair and he settled into the comfort of its foam. He could hear the movement of the city in the distance while enjoying his peaceful oasis on the balcony. He glanced sideways at the courtyard wondering if the fuzzy stray dog was back, but the bench was empty, and the paths were deserted. Jack sipped his coffee and waited for the dull throb in his chest to dissipate.

    He desperately tried to remember something from the previous dream. Frustrated, Jack began to drum the fingers of his right hand on the arm of the chair. He could feel something under the nail on his right index finger and brought it closer for inspection. There was something wedged under his nail and if it could be of any help to jog his memory, Jack wanted to know what it was. He went to the bathroom and found his mom's old train case. Nobody today would even know what a train case was, but Jack was unable to part with it or any of its contents. He retrieved her old nail file and ran it under his nail three times to scrape whatever was wedged under his nail onto a piece of toilet paper.

Jack went back to the desk, sat, and inspected the object on the toilet paper. To Jack it just looked like something he had picked from his nose but, if it had relevance, he wanted to hang on to it in the hopes that it meant something. He neatly folded the toilet paper and put it in the back of his journal.

His brain was tired. His body felt like it had been at the wrong end of a battering ram and he felt so detached from reality that he could not remember what day it was. The laptop did not take long to come to life and Jack found the shortcut to the local newspaper to see what he had missed.

The headline of the morning paper was about a body that had been found at the city's largest amusement park and Jack absent-mindedly dropped his coffee mug on the floor. The hand that once held the mug immediately went to the wound on his chest. No details were released through the media, but he had a chilling feeling he would find those details familiar if they were ever made public. After he read the entire article, Jack went back through the news from the past few days and found a small article about a university student murdered outside of his house. He read about Adam and was extremely drawn to the fact that Adam had one blue eye and one green eye as well. He was not sure why that was important enough to be included in the details of Adam's untimely death, but whoever was investigating his death obviously felt it was important.

He shut down the laptop and stood in the middle of his living room. He knew he could not ignore his career for the rest of his life, so he made the decision to get dressed and go into the office. He was sure there would be some questions about the bruising around his eyes, but Jack had concocted a story that would explain the blackened hue of his skin and he felt confident it was believable.

He dressed in khakis and a long-sleeved shirt to cover the abrasions on his wrists and made his way out of the apartment, turning the key three times in the lock as he left. The elevator was empty, and the lobby deserted as Jack left his apartment building, this time of his own volition. He walked two blocks to the bus station and waited for the next bus that would take him downtown. The man sitting on the bench beside him was consumed by the day's paper and Jack saw the headline about the murder at the amusement park.

The Waking Hours

The man looked up briefly and made eye contact with Jack. As soon as he noticed the dark rings around Jack's eyes, the man buried himself in the paper and avoided any possible conversation. Jack stood up and waited outside of the bus shelter, giving the man the freedom Jack was sure he was wishing for.

The bus arrived and Jack sat directly behind the driver, avoiding any more unwanted glances by not having to walk down the aisle. He pulled the chain and the bus let him off a block from his office. He wished it had been a sunny day so he could hide behind his sunglasses.

When he entered the office, Jack could not discern whether the stares were due to the bruised mask on his face or the fact that he had not set foot in the office for so long. He nodded briefly at his office mates and quickly made his way to his desk. Nobody cared enough about him to ask any questions. There were a few messages, nothing pertinent, and Jack spent as much time as he deemed necessary pushing piles of papers from one side of his desk to other to make it look like he had done some work.

Only a few hours later, he watched a few other agents packing up for the day and he mirrored their movements. In mere moments, Jack was following a few of them out the door and headed back to the station to wait for the bus home. The bus arrived early and, just as Jack was about to board, he recognized the dog he saw in the courtyard. He was dutifully walking beside a woman who Jack could have sworn he had seen before. He hesitated on the bottom stair of the bus and heard the agitated voices behind him asking him to keep moving. In the time it took for Jack to look back at the crowd behind him and then back to the girl and the dog, they were gone.

Chapter 27

After leaving the scene of his triumphant murder at the amusement park, Victor went home and thought about the girl. His last job had consumed him so much he had almost forgotten about her but now the scent of her perfume filled his memory and, even though he needed time to recharge his batteries, he had a strong desire to find her.

The park was the only place he had ever seen her, and he knew if he were patient, he would see her there again. With his recent assignment being so financially lucrative, Victor could afford to turn down a few jobs, so she became his sole focus. His thoughts were about her. His meditation became about her and his drive to kill revolved solely around her. If he had to sit in the park every day for a month to find her, that is what he would do.

Daylight enveloped the apartment building, but Victor sat in darkness with the help of his blackout blinds. He was sitting on his living room floor in his meditation pose, reflecting on the death of Mr. Keston. Victor was quite proud of the way he had incorporated all the man's misgivings into one mortal finale. In his recollection, he could see the paparazzi clambering over each other to get any sort of statement from local officials. It was a media feeding frenzy and the news piranhas had begun to nibble on anyone in their peripheral vision.

His elation slowly turned to fascination as his thoughts went back to the girl. He was admittedly obsessed, and he knew he had to kill her. The mantra he had planned for this morning was replaced by a slow incantation about this elusive woman. His upper body moved in circles as he chanted repeated phrases, all the while picturing her death in his mind. She had become his muse and his sole ambition.

When he had completed his meditation, Victor pulled the blind slightly to see that it was late afternoon. He had spent much more time ruminating than he realized, and he knew he had to dress quickly to get to

The Waking Hours

the park on time if he had any chance of seeing her. He was going to keep vigil until he saw her again and it was going to start today.

Victor had arrived at the park just as the foot traffic began to increase. He picked a bench with a great view of all the paths, close to the entrance from the art district, and just waited. He knew if she were anywhere in that park, he would feel her before he saw her. Many people passed by the bench Victor occupied. Some glanced at him and picked up their pace and many just ignored him. Victor sat and waited.

When the daylight began to wane, Victor knew he would not see her tonight. He could have sworn he had detected the slight scent of Eucalyptus in the air, but just as quickly as it found his olfactory senses it was gone. He was not sure if he was conjuring the odour from his memory, but the scent lingered in his nose. He left the park and meandered along the sidewalks, following the smells from the restaurants during their dinner rush. Victor's stomach growled as the combined smells of barbeque, Italian and Asian foods triggered his hunger and he knew he had to eat. He stopped in front of the apartment building where he had seen the two people the other night. He looked up at the column of balconies, unsure of why he felt compelled to stop.

The smell of food slowly quelled his curiosity. Victor had taken a few steps towards the Texas BBQ joint a few blocks down when he felt the vibration of his cell phone ringing in his pocket. He had set it to vibrate while he was in the park so the noise of a call would not draw attention to him. Because he knew it was a call for another job, he answered in his usual fashion.

"Go."

The dog barking on one of the balconies above made it difficult for him to hear the voice on the other end of the phone so he continued to walk as he listened. Victor did not see the girl standing on the balcony four floors above him trying to figure out why her dog was acting so crazy.

Chapter 28

After another day at the shop watching Norman win the hearts of her customers, Charlotte closed the store for the day and Norman waited patiently as she set the alarm. There had been no calls from the animal shelter about anyone looking for a lost dog so Charlotte just assumed she would have Norman as a roommate for another night or two.

They headed along the sidewalk that led to the park and Norman suddenly became agitated. He stopped in his tracks and turned in a few circles. Charlotte had no idea what was happening and bent down on one knee to see if she could comfort him. Norman was panting and his eyes looked huge. He whimpered almost inaudibly and started off in a direction away from the park. Charlotte was concerned he was having some sort of seizure, so she followed Norman down some side streets she was familiar with but had never travelled.

The further they got from the park the more Norman seemed to relax. Before she could calculate where they were, they entered the main street from an alley she knew was two blocks from her apartment building. Norman had fully regained his composure, and when they reached the front of her building, he marked his territory by befouling the bush in front of the stairs to the lobby.

Norman sat down and wagged his tail as Charlotte stared at him. She was mentally going through reasons why he was so nervous about going through the park on their way home today. They had walked her usual route the previous night and again this morning and Norman did not seem to have a care in the world. His nose lifted each time he caught a new scent that seemed to intrigue him and walked happily alongside of her, wordlessly greeting others as they passed them on the path. But the only way she could describe his behavior tonight would be that he had been spooked by something or someone. Charlotte had not known him that long, but Norman was easy to read so far so she did not think her diagnosis was too far off.

The Waking Hours

They entered the building and, while Charlotte checked her mail slot, Norman moved around behind the security desk to greet the afternoon guard. After a few scratches behind the ears, Norman rejoined Charlotte and the two boarded the elevator.

Once inside the apartment, Norman did his usual security check of all the rooms and when he was satisfied, they were alone, he sat at the door to the kitchen. Charlotte was happy for the reminder that it was Norman's dinner time. Having never had a dog, she would have forgotten to feed him had he not been so direct with his message.

While Norman gracefully ate his dinner, Charlotte called the nursing home to check on her grandmother. The nurses responded with their familiar report and Tillie's status remained unchanged. Charlotte was afraid to ask if her grandma mentioned Charlie or Max again, but she figured the nurses would have said something if anything in Tillie's routine was out of the ordinary.

When Charlotte hung up the phone, she noticed Norman sitting beside her coffee table. He gently placed his chin on the side of the table beside the photo album that Charlotte had been looking at a few days ago, the album with all of Max's childhood photos. Charlotte sat down on the couch and stroked Norman's head. While he seemed to enjoy the attention, he was more focused on the photo album. He stared at the book and was almost willing Charlotte to open it. His message was loud and clear, and Charlotte turned to the first page of photos of Max as a baby.

Norman seemed content to examine the album as Charlotte slowly turned the pages. He sat quietly as she flipped from page to page, each taking the time to look at the pictures. Charlotte was nearing the end of the album when Norman unexpectedly barked. Charlotte was so startled she jumped back on the couch, staring at the dog with a confused look. If a dog could stare, Norman remained fixated on the album. Charlotte regained her composure and tried to turn the last page but Norman moved closer to the album and placed his chin on the book so Charlotte could not turn the page. She had no idea why Norman was acting this way, but she moved in closer to the photos to see what had captured his attention.

This page near the end of the album held pictures Charlotte had taken of Max while he was playing with his band. Max used to go down to his friend Danny's house, and they would jam in his garage until almost midnight every night, much to the chagrin of Danny's neighbors. Charlotte followed Max on that night and took a few Polaroid pictures of Max and his friends doing what they love. She stayed to listen to the first song and realized they were not half-bad. If they practiced enough, they may really find a groove. As the sun began its descent Charlotte left the boys to their music and headed home just as it was getting dark. The night Charlotte took those pictures was the last night Max had been seen. He left Danny's house about 11:30 pm, according to his friends, and somewhere in the three blocks that separated Danny's house from Charlotte's house, Max had vanished into thin air.

Charlotte traced the outside of the photos with her finger and Norman lifted his head from the book. His nose went up in the air, as if he had caught a scent of something, and he moved quickly to the sliding glass door that opened to the balcony. He paced the short length of the glass silently asking Charlotte to come and open the door. She obliged and Norman began to bark incessantly, staring down at the front of the building near the bush that Norman had claimed as his own.

Charlotte went out on the balcony to silence the dog, knowing her neighbors would not be thrilled. She leaned over the balcony to see what was causing the commotion and only saw a faint shadow of a body entering the next block. With Norman finally quiet, the two went back into her apartment and locked the sliding door. Charlotte did not know why but she went to the front door and double-checked the door was bolted and chained. Norman had made Charlotte a little fearful something was out there and somehow; she knew the dog would understand if she did not take him out for a late-night outing.

Charlotte made some poached eggs and enjoyed her light dinner while Norman snored softly on the floor beside her. She stared at her furry companion, thinking how remarkable he was for a stray dog, if he even was a stray dog. He seemed to be very tuned in to human emotion and Charlotte assumed that could only happen if he had been living in somebody's home.

She made a mental note to call the animal shelter again tomorrow, but she was beginning to feel like she was becoming extremely attached to Norman very quickly. Maybe that phone call would have to wait a day or two.

The Waking Hours

Chapter 29

Gunner's notes on the white board were getting too crowded and messy for his liking. He called the station and asked for another board to be delivered to his house immediately.

"Like, 'hit the noise and the cherries' immediately."

He could not comprehend why he referred to the flashing police lights and sirens like he was a young beat cop in the seventies, but they got the message. Within ten minutes a cruiser appeared in his driveway. They had been smart enough to silence the sirens and turn off the lights before they pulled into Gunner's driveway. The last guy who forgot to do that had been reassigned to being a bicycle cop and was still peddling the streets of the city, now three years later.

Gunner mumbled some form of thank you and ushered them out as quickly as they had come. He slammed the door and got back to work. He could not decide whether to split the boards into random murders and possible hits, but he wanted the timeline to flow so he kept the killings in the order in which they happened. Gunner had his own collection of dry erase markers, so he used a different color for each murder to help him focus on the individual cases.

He was fixated on making sure each case had the same details in the same order - name, date of death and cause of death followed by the analysis and notes from the crime scene investigators. Since the two murders, the body dumps that Gunner was convinced were hits, had no crime scene to analyze there was a gaping white space at the bottom of those cases.

He got the red marker out of the case and began with the name Gord Keston. Since Gunner always trusted his intuition, he knew this case was important and warranted the color to make it stand out. The date of death was June seventeenth. The cause of death had not been officially ruled by

The Waking Hours

the Medical Examiner until the body was fully examined so Gunner just wrote 'mutilated' as the cause until he received the official word.

Gunner's first note in the details was the strange mark on Keston's hand, 111. He could not fathom why the killer would take the time to leave a calling card unless it had some sort of significance. Gunner opened his laptop and Googled 111. The first link he saw referred to it as Angel numbers, powerful numbers of manifestation. The guy who killed Keston was certainly no Angel and, after briefly scrolling down the first Google page, Gunner knew he was grasping at straws. He was not going to find the meaning of this strange message by using an internet search engine.

He leafed through the files and used some Scotch Tape he found in the drawer to attach photos of the bodies and the crime scenes to the top of each of the squares on the board. He sat down at this table and leaned back, moving his head back and forth as he looked for any connections, any little thing that could help him link these murders. He got nothing. He was now starting to believe that he had two or more killers on the loose in his city since these murders seemed to have no connection whatsoever.

His stomach rumbled and his concentration was broken. He tried to remember the last real meal he had while his body was gently reminding him it had been a while. He picked up his cell phone and entered his usual request to an online ordering system for the pizza joint a couple of blocks from his house and ordered the meat lover's deluxe. They had his credit card on file so all he had to do was confirm his password and wait. He paced in his kitchen, still staring at the number 111. What the Hell did it mean?

Within fifteen minutes, Gunner's front doorbell sounded, and his dinner had arrived. He opened the door, handed the delivery kid five bucks, and closed the door, locking it behind him. He stopped in his living room and stared at the pizza box. The irony of his dinner choice dawned on him as he saw the phone number on the box 967-1111. The number 111 was going to haunt him.

As Gunner paced the kitchen eating his pizza, he realized he had forgotten to add Ted Baines to the list. Although Ted had not turned up dead, Gunner figured it was only a matter of time before his body appeared somewhere. As he moved onto his second slice, Gunner called the office to see if Alice Baines had received any word from her husband or any ransom calls. There had been no contact at all. Gunner knew Ted was dead but right now there was no way of telling how or why. Beside Ted's name on the board, Gunner wrote the word body, followed by a big question mark.

Gunner opted for a third slice of pizza and sat back to look at all the information he had just organized. For the first time in his career as a cop, Gunner felt discouraged and it was pissing him off. Apart from all these people being dead, Gunner could not see a pattern. The two kids in the park and Adam Whatley only shared their relatively youthful ages. When the investigators examined their backgrounds, nothing with these kids overlapped. They went to different schools, lived in different parts of the city, and had probably never crossed paths. This was a large city, so it was possible to live only four blocks apart and never run into each other.

Gunner chalked those up to random murders and moved his attention back to the more professional kills. There was an element of arrogance to planning and executing a homicide and this guy had skill. This was not his first rodeo. Gunner scoured over the three files that had any sort of detail, but his brain was now spinning in circles. John Doe, Peter Mahon and Gord Keston had all been executed in an extremely specific manner. The first two were body dumps but Keston was put on display. Gunner could understand that Keston's death was meant to send a message. Keston lived his life in the eye of the media and the things he got away with were outrageous. He made the wrong people mad, that was for sure, and they paid him back by having his murder become just as public as his heinous behavior had been.

Five murders had occurred in a span of a couple of weeks. Since the two body dumps had been found and dealt with quickly, the media had not gotten a whiff of the scent of their deaths. That was buying Gunner a small amount of time to formulate a theory. Once the newsies got involved, the city would be in state of a panic and Gunner would be under scrutiny until he found out what was happening.

Chapter 30

Jack was basically pushed up the stairs on to the bus by the crowd behind him waiting to board. He grabbed the first seat behind the driver again and strained his neck to see if the girl and the dog were anywhere to be seen. They were too far out of his sight and the bus pulled away from the sidewalk. The energy on the bus was palpable and he tried to drown out the noise.

Putting his hand on his chest, Jack was still trying to pull some memory out of the vault in his brain to indicate what had happened to him in his last dream. The only solid thing he could remember was the wind. He tenderly felt the bruising around his eyes, but his thoughts were interrupted by the guy who had taken the seat next to him as he turned and spoke to Jack.

"What does the other guy look like?" The guy beside had assumed Jack had been in a fight.

"I can open my eyes, he can't." Jack lied, following along with the guy's theory.

Before Jack was forced to make conversation, the driver's voice was heard over the intercom advising people that his route had been changed due to a large structure fire several blocks away. Many of the roads had been closed to allow fire fighters access from all sides and the bus was given an alternate route to take. The driver pulled over to the curb to allow passengers the option to disembark and take another means of transportation home. Jack was in no rush to get anywhere so he stayed on the bus to see where the detour would take him.

Since Jack never went out much, there were a great many parts of the city that he had never seen. He enjoyed the architecture of the buildings he passed, and he could see the paths leading into the park he had never taken the time to visit. As the bus made another turn, Jack's breath caught in his throat. He had never been in this part of the city before, but something was familiar. This quiet street that paralleled the main road they should have been on could be a scene from a romantic movie. The two traffic lanes were separated by a row of trees and the presence of the foliage made Jack feel like he had left the city completely.

Art shops lined the streets, there were a few family style restaurants, bakeries, and collectible stores. Jack's head swiveled from one side to the other, taking in all the interesting things, and then he saw the antique store. He knew he had never been there before but something about it was recognizable. When the bus went through the intersection, Jack found a scrap piece of paper in his pocket and quickly jotted down the street names, knowing that somehow this was one of the many pieces of his puzzle that he was missing.

The bus ride continued for another thirty minutes before Jack was close enough to walk the rest of the distance home. Although the days were getting longer, the night sky was battling the reds and oranges of the sunset and the darkness was winning. Jack could hear the streetlamps sputtering to life and he knew it would be dark soon. Passing by a local burger joint, he stopped and ordered a cheeseburger with no onions and an order of French fries to go. Since the dinner hour had passed, the burger place was practically empty and, in a few minutes, Jack had his takeout and headed home.

The lone elevator was being used to move in a new tenant, so Jack took the stairs. He figured the small workout would do him good before his greasy dinner. He knew he was out of shape, although round was a shape, but Jack had long forgotten how out of shape he was until he reached the top of the fourth flight of stairs and realized how much he was panting. A few other tenants who had opted for the stairs passed Jack, glancing back tentatively to make sure he was alright.

He made it to his apartment and the workout had made him ravenous. He took one big bite of his burger and, before he had finished chewing, shoved the burger in for a quick second bite. The taste of the raw onion hit him immediately. Jack lifted the top bun and spotted the culprit amid all the other toppings. He had asked for no onions and figured the request would not be impossible given the lack of customers. Jack picked the rest of the onions off the burger and threw them in the bag. He crammed a few French fries in his mouth and started back on the burger. The burger was good but sadly Jack's dining pleasure had been marred by the lingering aftertaste of raw, red onion. He knew the protest from his stomach would begin soon. Its objection to having to digest the small amount of onion he ate was implied and he could already hear the faint rumbling sound he knew so well.

Once he had finished his dinner and cleaned up, Jack poured a glass of red wine and sat back at his writing desk. He wanted to jot down as many details of the art district as he could while it was still fresh in his memory, especially the antique store. He detailed the streets, lined with the beautiful foliage of the birch trees and he noted a few things about the display window at the antique store. The bus had already been halfway past the store when Jack saw it, so he did not have a chance to see the sign with the name of the shop. Jack fumbled in his pocket for the piece of paper on which he recorded the street names at the intersection. With his hands quickly going to each of his pockets, Jack came up empty. The piece of paper was nowhere to be found. He checked his jacket and even pulled the take-out bag from the garbage to see if it had somehow fallen in the bag. It was gone. The rest of the particulars from his detour seemed irrelevant so Jack closed the desk and sat on his balcony enjoying a few more glasses of wine.

The workout on the stairs was harder on his body than Jack realized. He had been enjoying his wine and the symphony of sounds from his digestive tract when his chin came to rest on his chest and his mouth fell open. Jack curled his body to one side and was sound asleep on his balcony.

~~

Jack awoke and knew immediately that he had lost his sense of balance. It was night and he could smell the fishy odour of the lake. It took him a few minutes to discern he was at some sort of marina or yacht club and he was standing on a boat. The waves had been coming in off the lake causing the rocking motion and his moderate feeling of sea sickness.

As Jack took in his surroundings, he realized the body he was in was still very much alive and seemed to be in no danger whatsoever. Jack, who was unwittingly along for the ride in this stranger's body, moved with the man as he put his boat to bed for the night. The sails had been secured, the boat moored to the dock and the cabin below was well lit, allowing Jack a small glimpse of the living space. He was decidedly enjoying this part of the dream. The calming motion of the water soon began to soothe Jack and he no longer detected any feeling of nausea. The only ill-effect he had currently was the lingering taste of raw onion in his mouth and he wondered if his host was able to taste that as well.

The captain of the boat moved below deck and poured himself a single-malt scotch, sat back and put his feet up. There was a fat cigar sitting on the small table beside him begging to be lit. Jack had never smoked a cigar in his life and waited to see if this was going to be his first. Before the cigar came close to being lit, the man moved towards the bathroom. Jack had never anticipated this being part of the scenario and was glad to know that not every part of his body was attached to this stranger, so Jack was able to keep his hands to himself as the man gave his bladder the relief it needed.

Jack was comforted by the fact the man had some decency and he washed his hands before heading back to his drink. The scotch was topped up and the cigar was lit. Jack and his new body sat back, put their feet up and drew deeply on the cigar, exhaling the smoke before any of it got into their lungs. Jack had not realized a cigar could have such a smooth taste and the smoke was not meant to be inhaled.

While the captain enjoyed his vices, Jack's eyes travelled around the small space. He had been familiar with boats as a kid, but it had been so long since he had been on one, he had forgotten all the sailing terms. There were charts on the walls, rules for steering through channels, and symbols that were aids to navigation. Jack was trying to read all the symbols when the captain abruptly got out of his chair. They stood for a moment with their heads slightly cocked as they listened intently to the noises around them. The captain could hear something on the deck that sounded like hail stones bouncing across the bow of his boat.

They slowly went up the stairs and on to the deck. There were two small rocks that had landed on the bow that were not there when they had gone below. Apart from the waves lapping the boat and the dock, the silence was unnerving. The captain looked around, saw nothing, and was about to go back to his scotch.

The Waking Hours

There was a quick sound of a rushing burst of air and Jack felt like his stomach was on fire. The stinging sensation was intense, and his hands moved with the captain's hands to feel the harpoon on either side of his abdomen. The captain dropped to his knees and Jack went down with him. The body twisted, turning to its side and fell to the deck. The blood had begun to pool, and Jack could feel the captain's heartbeat weakening. His eyes were still open, but his breath slowed to a stop. He was dead.

Jack assumed he would wake up at home soon, but he seemed to linger in this body for longer than he had in the others. Even though Jack felt that no harm could come to him personally, the sound of the footsteps was still disconcerting. Whoever was standing at the side of the boat stayed out of Jack's peripheral and, once he was satisfied the captain was dead, he started to walk away. Had the killer examined the body more closely, he would have seen the two different colored eyes staring sightlessly as Jack lay helpless in the dead man's body. His parting remark chilled Jack to the bone, not because of the message but because of the voice.

"Enjoy your place in Hell. You deserve it."

Jack was paralyzed by the sound of the voice. He feared that voice and wanted nothing more than to be back in the safety of his apartment. He was willing himself to leave but realized he could move his arms and was somehow able to feel the physical touch of the things that surrounded him. Dipping his finger in the captain's blood, Jack drew three diamonds on the deck of the boat, far enough from the pooling blood that they would not be covered. If the cops were going to find this psychopath with the terrifying voice, Jack was going to do everything in his power to help them catch this guy.

Chapter 31

Victor was proud that he had removed another piece of human scum from the earth. He had never been fishing but now had a modicum of understanding of what it would be like to harpoon a whale. Once he had determined the man was dead, gauging from the amount of blood he had lost, Victor immediately began to think about the girl again. He was moderately perturbed she had not been in the park. His instincts were always right but she had evaded him again.

Victor was about four-hundred yards from the boat when he realized he had forgotten to look in the man's eyes. He had left too quickly and abandoned his gift. He was becoming so obsessed with this girl that he had denied himself that true moment of death and he berated himself as he walked away. It was too late to go back now. Victor was unsure if any of the other boats had been occupied and he was not going to get close enough to find out.

Now, more than ever, he wanted her. He could not put a finger on what it was that drew him to her, but he was going to enjoy torturing her several times before letting her die. If he were an artist, he would liken her to his Mona Lisa. Sure, he had dabbled in the past and would continue to do so for as long as he could, but this girl would be his masterpiece.

Victor was two blocks from his apartment before he noticed how far he had walked. He was consumed by thoughts of her and, in his mind, he had transported himself to his warehouse as he walked. He thought of all the things he wanted to do to her and pictured all the tools he would use to do them. The thought of that made him smile.

Nodding at Joe in the lobby, Victor went to his apartment. He took off his clothes, put them in a garbage bag and threw them down the garbage chute. He was always careful not to have any evidence in his apartment if the worst-case scenario happened and he was caught. He knew that was ridiculous because he would never get caught, but one could not be too careful.

He should have been hungry, but Victor had no appetite. His apartment was dark, and he could vaguely smell the wet earth odor from his boots, instantly triggering memories of his mother's cellar. He had spent a great deal of time in there. Victor became himself in that space. He gained his power from that dank room and he had developed a lucrative career with that power.

He thought about his mother and her subsequent death. Child Protective Services had removed Victor from the home and placed him with his Godmother. He had spent three years waiting until his eighteenth birthday so he could move out of the wretched home in which he had been placed. After years of being told there was something wrong with him, Victor finally gained his freedom. For a large boy, he could be very stealthy in his movements and in a matter of minutes had been through any wallets and money stashes he could find, thrown his duffle bag out his second story window and climbed down the trellis to find the life he knew was waiting for him.

He saved the cash to buy food and he found shelter under dense brush in the park. During the day, Victor would simply watch people. He studied their movements, he absorbed how they interacted, and he learned how to behave like he belonged among them. But Victor knew and they knew that he was an outcast. He would never be one of them. It was painstakingly obvious when the high school kids would pass him in the park. He could see them whispering, hear their snickers and every so often the phrase 'I think he killed his mom' would float on the breeze and land on Victor's ears. He never minded. He did not want to be part of them and the more he listened to them, the more he knew his adolescent urge had returned and he was going to kill one of them.

With his desire bubbling within, the young Victor had to change his tactics. He could not be that kid in the park who just watched people. He would only draw unnecessary attention to himself. He had to become a creature of the night and observe people when they thought they were safe and were not being watched. Since his murderous desires had been born out of darkness, it only made sense for to him to thrive in the place he felt most comfortable.

Victor became very adept at following people without them having any knowledge of being followed. Shadows became his allies, and the night became his friend. He went to a thrift store and purchased a new wardrobe, all black, making it easier to blend into the night. He then spent months honing his skills, practicing his self-control, and becoming the master of his own mind. When he returned to the park in the early morning hours, Victor taught himself how to meditate so he could better control his urges. His cover under in the park bushes made it virtually impossible for anyone to see him as they passed by and, as Victor soon realized, most people were too self-absorbed to notice anything other than themselves and the group of friends they were with.

When Victor felt that he had full control of himself, he would venture out at night into the neighborhoods that surrounded the park. Some homes left their curtains open so Victor would catch a glimpse of their lives. He could see the random patterns of light moving on the walls, so he knew the television was on in the room. He stopped briefly to watch family members enter and leave the room. At each home where Victor stopped to observe a family, he wondered if one of these people would be his first victim. He knew nothing about them and who they were meant nothing to him.

Like a dormant volcano, Victor knew the lava was boiling inside him and he would soon erupt. Each night, he carefully chose a neighborhood that was a good distance from where he had been the previous night. He followed the sidewalks. He absorbed the details of the homes and the cars and he listened to the sounds of family life through any windows that remained open to enjoy the night air. Each neighborhood mirrored the next, and each night Victor felt like he was on repeat. Nothing grabbed his attention. Nobody had a neon sign above their head saying, 'kill me first' and Victor was not even sure what he was looking for. He just knew that when found it, he would feel it in his bones.

As he rounded the corner of the sidewalk, Victor was surprised to see a young girl out on her own. The day had just moved from dusk to dark and she was hurrying along the path to get home. Under the light of the streetlamp, Victor could see she held a Polaroid camera in one hand and a recently developed photo in the other hand. He stopped and let himself be partially shrouded by the large Oak tree on the corner. The girl was smiling

The Waking Hours

at the photo when the headlights of the approaching car made him move back into the shadows. The car paused at the stop sign and, when Victor was able to move out from behind the tree, the girl had vanished into one of the houses on the street.

Victor came out from behind the tree and stood there, waiting to see if he could see her in any of the windows. He seemed to have lost time and when he checked his watch, two hours had gone by while he had been looking for her. He eventually continued along the sidewalk and the sound of music got louder as he walked.

After a block and half, Victor heard the band booming from behind a garage door. He was surprised the neighbors were not outside protesting the sound since it was after 11:00 pm. The musicians must have read his thoughts because the music came to an end after one last guitar solo. Victor could hear the equipment being shuffled around after the amateur concert came to an end. The garage door was lifted electronically and slowly chugged into its open position. Victor once again found protection behind a large tree.

Four young guys stood inside the garage, each of them was drenched in sweat and holding a beer. After seeing the foursome, Victor knew he was ready to kill that night. He had seen these guys in the park. Of all the taunts and comments Victor had heard in the park, these guys had been the worst offenders. The nature of their comments went beyond vicious and Victor knew in his gut the time was now.

He waited as three of the four boy-band members had headed for their separate homes and he followed the cocky sonofabitch who was the mouthiest of the four. The kid even had a garish walk as he sauntered down the sidewalk.

Victor lingered behind until the kid was between streetlights and in front of an empty lot. He snuck up behind him and threw his arm around his neck, dragging him further into the shadows. The kid was flaccid at first, not yet reacting to the arm around his neck, but then he began to fight back. His elbow connected with Victor's sternum, almost knocking the wind out of him, but Victor's strength was overpowering, and the kid was being deprived of the oxygen he needed to fight.

After a short time, Victor could feel the kid's body becoming heavy in his grip as he fell into unconsciousness. Victor allowed gravity to pull the body to its knees, but he held his arm tight around the kid's neck for another thirty seconds. Victor knew without hesitation the kid was dead. He let the lifeless body fall to the ground and moved around him to get a better look at his eyes.

Victor used his foot to roll the kid onto his back. The dull color of his pupils was slowly becoming milky, but Victor was captivated by the fact that one eye was blue, and one eye was green. Staring death in the face made Victor feel more alive than he had since he had killed his mother. After three years of living in a house and feeling like he should not exist, Victor felt reborn. While staring at the dead teenager on the ground, Victor thanked him and made a quick plan to dispose of his body in a way that would guarantee it would never be found.

The investigation continued for months and the family searched for years after he had killed the band kid. He watched the news and knew the police were only trying to appease the family by maintaining their search until the case was eventually deemed cold. Victor was elated by his first success and mused at how ironic it would be if the family ever decided to have a funeral service and he could be in attendance.

~~

Victor was jolted from his meditation pose when the name 'Charlie' came to mind. He immediately snapped out of his recollection of the band kid and back into reality. He was intrigued by the interruption. The name had been important enough to pull him from his memory, so it had to mean something significant. Victor received lots of messages through his meditation but none of the messages had ever been so compelling.

Although he enjoyed his stroll down memory lane, Victor got up from his cross-legged pose and stretched. He could almost feel the phantom pain of the broken ribs he suffered from the band kid's well-placed elbow. He imagined that this would be the same pain the man on the boat would have felt before he bled to death. Victor shrugged it off. The man was now in Hell where he belonged.

Chapter 32

Jack now knew death on an intimate level. His entire abdomen burned as he struggled to come out of his latest nightmare. He felt nauseous. The nocturnal demon he faced every night had a twisted sense of humor and Jack was tired of playing its deadly game. The only thing Jack could be happy about is that he kept waking up, period.

He struggled to get out of the lounge chair on his balcony. Although its sleek design was meant for a comfortable couple of hours in the sun, it was certainly not meant for a restful night of sleep. His tongue moved back and forth across his furry morning teeth. He could still taste the remnants of the bloody onion that had been put on his burger by mistake. But he also tasted something else. There was a residual taste of alcohol and Jack knew it was not the stale wine taste he usually experienced in the morning. There was also another element to his halitosis, but Jack could not put his finger on what it was. Whatever the missing flavor was, Jack did not care. He just wanted to brush his teeth and get rid of his hideous morning breath.

Once he had brushed three times and was minty fresh, he grabbed a glass of water and his journal, and fell into the recliner. He could not bear to put his body through more discomfort by sitting at his desk after having slept in the lounge chair. He did his best to describe all his physical pain as well as the God-awful taste in his mouth. He also did a spot check on his body to see where he felt the most pain. No ribs were broken, but the middle of his sternum argued vehemently as he gingerly probed it with his fingers.

Jack closed his eyes and tried to remember as much as he could about his last dream. His upper body began to sway back and forth, and Jack immediately remembered the boat. The undulating motion of the boat in his mind made him feel seasick and he opened his eyes to regain his bearings. He wrote the word boat in his journal.

He sat for an hour, reclining comfortably while trying to squeeze every memory of the past night from his brain. He was about to give up when he remembered the voice. He sat up so quickly in the recliner he knocked his side table over and sent a lamp and his glass of water flying. Tiny beads of perspiration appeared on his forehead and his hand trembled as he tried to put another entry in his journal. He was shaking so badly and putting such tremendous pressure on the pen that he almost tore the journal page.

After he collected himself, he leafed back through the few entries he had already made in his journal. The word voice was present in several of the accounts of his dreams and that could not be just a coincidence. Without even realizing he had still been writing, he looked down at the question he had just written. Who is this guy?

Jack got up and righted the side table. He picked up his empty glass and used some tissue to extract the spilled water from his carpet. He went into the kitchen, filled his glass, and stared at his freezer door. It was not long ago that Jack had heard the name Charlie and almost knocked himself unconscious by hitting his head on that door. He went back to his journal and wrote the name Charlie at the bottom of the page.

He paced his apartment and tried to recall any other details from his dream. The more time he spent trying to pull fragments of memories from his brain, the more those images turned into vapour and disappeared. He finally conceded to the fact he would not coax any more information from his memory and he thought about the poor man on the bus trying to decide if Jack had won or lost the fight that had caused his black eyes. He moved over the mirror and noticed his eyes were no longer bruised. Now he just carried the bags under his eyes from his fits of restless sleep.

As his thoughts turned back to the previous day, he replayed the bus ride in his head, and he remembered the girl with her dog. Had he not been pushed onto the bus by the others waiting to board, he would have surely followed them. He remembered the antique shop but since he had not really been paying much attention to the detour route, he had no idea where the shop was located or what the name was on the sign.

He went back to his journal and, on a new page, he wrote girl, dog, antique shop, underlined them three times and stared at those four words. He had no idea if they were connected to what was happening in his dreams but there had to be some relevance since he felt like he had seen them both before on separate occasions. Now they were together, and fate was begging him to find them.

Going to the office the day before was enough, so Jack decided to get out of his head space and venture into the city. He was more of a homebody but being in his apartment these days meant he either fell asleep and died a horrible death in his dreams or he tried to remember things he simply could not. He showered, dressed in some comfortable walking attire, and hit the pavement. He grabbed a coffee and bagel from the bakery that was a block from his apartment and began to walk. He had no direction and no destination in mind.

He followed some familiar streets but, as he got deeper into the heart of the city, he felt the urge to follow a few side streets he had never travelled. He knew no matter where he ended up, even if he felt lost, he could always hail a cab to get himself home. The streets he found were lovely. Large houses that had been some of the original city homes were settled amongst towering trees. The gardens were lush and were showing off their late June flowers. Children ran up and down the sidewalks from house to house without seeming frightened by any threat the city could impose.

He allowed himself to serpentine through the streets and arrived at the edge of the park he had never taken the time to visit. It was now early afternoon and the sun kissed everything it touched. He glanced around the park and noticed a few groups of people loitering by the picnic benches, unwilling to go back to work on such a beautiful day. Jack had the luxury of not having to go to work, so he parked himself on a bench shaded by a large oak tree and just breathed in the city atmosphere. Even though most of the infrastructure was a concrete jungle, the city made sure they maintained a few small pieces of a forest oasis.

The city was buzzing with activity. He could hear the clanging of the street cars as the wheels whined along the tracks. The sound of sirens was an expected background noise in a city this size and today was no different. Jack had lived in the city long enough to differentiate between the sounds of fire trucks, police cars and ambulances. The overlapping sounds blended in an almost symphonic vibration as Jack let the sounds of the city soothe him.

The flowers that were in bloom smelled divine and, although he had no idea what each flower was, he inhaled deeply. His eyes were closed as he savored the scents, but his enjoyment was suddenly interrupted when he opened his eyes and saw the dog he had seen yesterday. The dog sat directly in front of him, wagging his tail and panting. Jack would have sworn the dog was smiling. The sun reflected off his dog tag and Jack could see that his name was Norman. He tentatively reached out to pet the dog and was greeted with nothing but affection. Norman seemed to move into his hand and allowed Jack to scratch behind his ears.

He glanced at his watch three times and realized he had wasted the better part of an afternoon doing nothing but sitting on a park bench. Next time he would remember to bring breadcrumbs so he could at least feel useful feeding the pigeons. Norman's panting lessened the longer he sat and both Jack and Norman seemed very content to enjoy each other's company.

Jack heard her frantic cries for Norman before he looked up and saw a woman running in his direction. As she neared the bench, he stood up to greet her. Norman stood as well and looked incredibly pleased with himself as his gaze went from Jack to the woman and back again. Jack watched as she leaned over slightly, putting her hands on her knees, and tried to catch her breath. She stood upright after a few seconds and Jack reached out his hand to introduce himself. She missed the gesture as she bent down to admonish Norman for running away.

When Norman's tail was appropriately tucked between his legs, she stood up to face Jack. The two of them stood motionless for several seconds before she broke the silence and introduced herself. When their hands met, the simple handshake lingered as they looked at each other quizzically.

"Why do I feel like I know you?" Surprisingly, Charlotte said it first.

"I don't know, but I feel the same way." Jack realized their hands were still together and pulled his hand away, suddenly blushing like an adolescent.

Norman was enjoying the exchange when he caught the scent of something in air. The hair on the back of his neck stood straight up and his body became rigid. His growl was low at first, a sinister warning, and then he began to pace slightly to discern where the danger lay. His bark was low enough he did not draw unwanted attention and, as quickly as he had run in to the park, Norman glanced at Charlotte and took off towards the street knowing she would follow him.

The Waking Hours

Apologizing to Jack, Charlotte turned and was hot on the heels of her crazy new roommate. Jack seemed fixed in his place but slowly regained his composure. He was about to head in Charlotte's direction to help her chase Norman, but he froze when he heard the deep, hoarse voice say Go.

Chapter 33

Victor felt refreshed after his recent meditation, and his trip down memory lane was a bonus. Not very often did Victor allow himself to dwell on things from the past but this memory really helped shape Victor into who he had morphed into in his adulthood. Had he not been willing to take the life of the band kid, Victor's thoughts on death may never have evolved to the level where they were currently. He had left his apartment and was strolling through the park again when his cell phone rang.

His low voice growled, "Go."

The voice on the other end had asked if they were on a secure line and when Victor had assured them that they were, the voice continued. Saying nothing, Victor made mental notes with the details and he listened intently as he scanned the park. The job would be relatively simple, so Victor allowed his concentration to break slightly. He continued to walk as the man shared more information. Victor noticed several couples walking hand in hand. He saw a dog running out of the park being chased by a woman with long brown hair and, as Victor continued to walk, he passed by a man seemingly frozen in front of the bench behind him.

Victor glanced at the man as he passed by and almost tripped over his own feet as he walked. The man, who seemed to be staring at Victor very intently, had one green eye and one blue eye.

Chapter 34

Charlotte was feeling the pre-summer surge as the shop became busier each day. Customers would now take more time browsing in the store to spend time with Norman and he seemed capable enough to convince them to buy the things they never meant to buy at all. Charlotte was sure she had overhead a few people asking Norman if they should spend so lavishly and she could hear his chuff in approval. She would either have to put Norman on the payroll or start buying him some treats worthy of a top sales dog.

The shadows moved across the store as early afternoon passed into late afternoon. Usually, Norman could be found lounging in the filtered sunlight but today he seemed restless. He paced by the front window as if he were anticipating long lost relatives. When the door opened, Norman took his opportunity and bolted out of the shop. Charlotte yelled after him as she watched him jog along the sidewalk.

Apologizing to the latest customers, she ushered them back onto the sidewalk, locked the shop door and began to chase after Norman. For a dog of his speed and agility, he seemed to be running slowly enough so Charlotte could keep up with him. She could have sworn she saw him looking back over his shoulders to make sure Charlotte was keeping pace. Unlike the past few days, Norman headed straight for the park. His trepidation had vanished, and he followed the path deep into the park, picking up speed as he went.

Charlotte pushed herself to go as fast as she could. When she took a moment to scan the paths, she saw Norman sitting in front of a man who was alone on a bench. When she finally reached him, she was completely out of breath and bent over to take a moment to inhale deeply and slow her heart rate a bit.

When she had caught her breath, Charlotte leaned closer to the dog. As she strongly criticized his bad behavior, the dog responded appropriately by hanging his head. Realizing he was still wagging his tail, Norman quickly tucked it between his legs.

Charlotte stood up to greet the stranger and surprised herself by speaking first to make the introductions. Their hands met in a handshake and stayed there for longer than necessary. She knew him. She had no recollection how, but she knew this man. Their hands were still gripped as they stared at each other.

He pulled his hand away first and she could have sworn he was blushing. Charlotte's attention was pulled away from Jack when she heard Norman begin to growl. The hair on his back stood up and he was noticeably tense. He sniffed the air and, as he did, the hair on the back of Charlotte's neck stood up. She glanced around the park and saw a shadowed figure across the park, slowly approaching the spot where they were standing. Charlotte got the sense this man was the cause of the dog's tension. She felt it as much as he did.

Norman looked up at her as if to say, let's get out of here. and he began to jog towards the street, looking back to make sure Charlotte was following. Charlotte apologized to Jack and followed Norman out of the park. She had half-hoped that Jack would follow them, but he remained in the spot where he had been standing when they met. She had no idea why she wanted him to follow her but, now that they had met, she had every faith that she would see him again.

Norman's pace was somewhat frantic until they were a safe distance from the park, and he knew Charlotte was safe. Both Norman and Charlotte were panting when they reached the store. The closing hour had come and gone so Charlotte retrieved her things, set the alarm, and locked the shop for the day. Looking at Norman, she wondered why this furry creature had come into her life. He showed up out of the blue and did not appear to have any desire to leave. She knew she should call the animal rescue, but she had become so attached to Norman in such a short period of time that she could not imagine letting him go.

Their way home was a similar route to the previous night. Norman now avoided the park at all cost and Charlotte mused at how willing she was to follow Norman's lead. They had developed a very quick trust and she knew she was smart to rely on the dog's keen instincts. She tried to figure out why Norman was so willing to rush into the park earlier today and stop in front of a stranger, although the more Charlotte thought about him the less he seemed like a stranger.

Charlotte stopped in the middle of the sidewalk when she remembered the man she had seen so long ago, the man who caused her to blush when she saw him peering in the window of the store. His face seemed different somehow but, in her gut, she genuinely believed he was the same man as the one she had just met in the park.

Norman had continued along the sidewalk and stopped when he realized Charlotte had lagged. They were only separated by a few meters, but Norman closed the gap and sat in front of her, turning his head to one side as if to say, what is the hold up? Charlotte bent down in front of Norman and began to talk to him about the man in the park.

"You wanted me to meet him, didn't you?" asked Charlotte.

Norman tilted his head from side to side as if he understood everything she was saying. He let out a small bark of agreement.

"What are you up to, my furry little friend?" she asked.

Charlotte could have sworn he was trying to answer her questions. If she did not know better, she would have said he was smiling and plotting his next move. They continued their way home and Norman seemed content to not have to mark his territory tonight. Charlotte thought he was hungry since he was in such a hurry to get upstairs. When they reached the apartment, she noticed the red light flashing on her antiquated answering machine. It still worked and she refused to pay any more money to her phone company to have voice-messaging when her machine worked just fine. When she pressed the button on the machine to retrieve her message, she heard her Tillie's voice on the machine.

"Charlie, it's Gramma. I am worried about Max. He hasn't been to visit lately."

Her voice cut off and the message was over. Charlotte fell backwards onto the chair beside the machine. Her grandmother did not have a phone in her room and had not left her bed in months. For her to be able to make this call, she would have had to have gone to the front desk and had someone help her call. Charlotte got the number for the nursing home and phoned them immediately. The nurse who answered the phone had been on desk duty for the last seven hours and had not helped Charlotte's grandmother place any calls. In fact, the nurse could not remember the last time she had seen Gramma out of bed.

    Charlotte lost track of how long she had been sitting in the chair holding her phone in her hand. Norman was like a statue in front of her, watching as she came out of her small trance. He nudged her hand, and she began to pet his head as she came back to reality. She hung up her coat, put some kibble in Norman's bowl and pulled out Max's photo album again. She was not sure what she was looking for, but she knew there was something in this album that she was missing and if she had to stay up all night looking, that is what she would do.

~~

    Charlotte awoke to the shrill sound of her cell phone ringing. She looked at her alarm clock. It was 7:00 am. Not many people had her cell number, and nobody ever called this early. She picked up her phone and listened to the voice on the other end. Charlotte's lip began to quiver, and tears welled in the corners of her eyes as the nurse explained that her grandmother had died in her sleep sometime during the night. When the morning nurse went in to get her up and ready for the morning, they found her on the floor, miraculously out of her bed curled up in a nest of blankets she had created.

    Charlotte hung up the phone and sobbed. At least Tillie went peacefully in her sleep, but Charlotte never really had a chance to say goodbye. She cried until she had no more tears to cry. She had never felt more alone. She got out of bed and sat cross-legged on the floor, leaning back into the bed frame. Norman watched her with deep concern and stepped closer only when Charlotte's sobs had turned into short gasps for air. He turned around to sit beside her and nuzzled under her arm until she embraced the dog and began to cry again. Norman was now the closest thing she had to family and she held him as tight as she could. When he felt the time was right, Norman lifted his head to lick the tears from Charlotte's cheek.

Charlotte lost track of how long they had been sitting like that, but Norman remained vigilant. There was no reminder of his morning trip outside or his empty food dish, there was only friendship.

Chapter 35

Gunner leaned back in his kitchen chair. His stomach was full, but his mind was empty. The information charts on his white boards did nothing to help reveal any clues he may have missed. The names of the deceased stared at him, begging him to find out what happened to them, but Gunner could not come up with any connections between any of these murders.

Frustrated, he got up from the table, threw the pizza box in his refrigerator and grabbed his car keys. He needed to clear his mind and driving usually helped. He climbed into his unmarked car and drove through random streets, watching as the streetlights flickered against the impending darkness. When he had driven for several blocks, Gunner noticed the on-ramp to the Expressway and felt compelled to follow it. Traffic was still heavy but, for a city of its size, getting onto the highway and maneuvering the flow was easy compared to the earlier parts of the day.

He pushed the pedal to the floor and carefully wound his way through the lanes of traffic. He was speeding but his job gave him a get out of jail free card. Any patrol car seeing his vehicle would know who was behind the wheel and avoid him at all cost. Gunner turned on his radio and was happy to hear his favorite Canadian music icons blasting from his speakers. He had seen Rush in concert years ago and had always been a big fan of their music.

His car moved from lane to lane and he now knew where he wanted to go. Looking over his shoulder, Gunner cranked the wheel to the right and veered across several lanes to barely make the off-ramp ahead. Horns blared and Gunner could see a few finger gestures in the windshields of the cars behind him. He returned the inaudible expression and narrowly missed hitting the concrete divider that separated the highway from the ramp.

Although he was officially outside of his jurisdiction, Gunner was still familiar with these streets and knew all too well how to find the Division Office he was looking for. It was later than Gunner thought but police stations never closed so he parked his car in a reserved space and went inside. The man behind the desk seemed surprised to see someone coming in who was not in handcuffs or flanked by uniformed guards. Gunner flashed his credentials and introduced himself.

After he gave the desk-jockey a brief run down of what he was looking for, Gunner was buzzed into the squad room and was met halfway by Officer Murphy. Murphy was interested to hear what Gunner had to tell him and anxious to show him a file that had just come across his desk. Like Gunner, Murphy had several files on murders in his district, but most were bar fights gone wrong or drug and gang related killings. But this last file that Murphy was looking at lacked any sort of randomness and did not feel like an opportunity kill.

Murphy was happy to let Gunner peruse the file while he went to grab them both a coffee. As soon as he opened the file, Gunner knew that this murder was somehow connected to his cases. Angus McAllister had been killed while on his boat in the harbor. What struck Gunner was the method of his death. McAllister had been harpooned on his own boat and left to bleed to death. The shot was made with precision and accuracy and had hit one of McAllister's major arteries, making his death that much quicker.

As Gunner looked through the crime scene photos, he gasped slightly when he saw the photo of McAllister in the pool of his own blood. Beside the body were three diamonds, apparently written in McAllister's blood. Murphy had just come back into the office with the coffee when Gunner held up the picture.

"Have you looked at this?" Gunner was anxious to know what it meant.

"Yeah, we have been trying to figure out why someone would go to the trouble of discreetly killing a man and be able to walk away but go onto the deck of the boat to leave this message." Murphy was just as perplexed as Gunner.

Gunner told Murphy about the body on the roller coaster and the 111 that was carved into Keston's hand. Neither cop could figure out the relation between 111 and three diamonds, but both knew with every cop instinct they had there was a connection. Gunner felt like he was sitting at a very morbid slot machine and, every time three of something came up, there would be no prize, just another body.

Gunner gave Murphy his contact information and asked him to keep in touch if anything came up in this case or if he had any more bodies he thought might be connected. After shaking hands, Gunner left the office feeling like there was something on the tip of his tongue, but he just could not figure out what it was. He got back in his car and drove around for a few hours. Before Gunner even realized the time, the sun was pulling itself out of bed and announcing the start of a new day.

Not feeling the need to shower or change his clothes, Gunner headed straight for his office. As his car made the turn into the circular driveway, he could see the media positioning themselves just outside of the main doors. Tripods were set up, reporters began their opening remarks and hoped to catch an unsuspecting officer or two with a rapid-fire barrage of questions. This tactic was usually the best for getting rookies so rattled they inevitably said something they had no authority to say.

The window of silence had closed, and Gunner cursed under his breath. Someone in the department had leaked something to the wrong person and that wrong person alerted the media. And since the media responded to tips of this magnitude like Piranhas in a lake with fresh blood, Gunner knew this was not going to end well. He used the remote to open the gate, drove to the back of the building, and was buzzed in through the security door. He made his way to his office without having to deal with the feeding frenzy out front.

He could not help but think about his favorite band and the lyrics to their song Limelight. Somehow this throng of reporters represented the verse, All the world's indeed a stage and we are merely players, performers and portrayers, each another's audience, outside the gilded cage. Gunner knew he was now 'living in a fish-eye lens' and would eventually be 'caught in the camera eye'. He had hoped that Geddy Lee, actually Neil Peart, would be proud of the fact that he was slightly plagiarizing his lyrics, but in the most flattering way possible.

As he made his way to his office, he could not stop thinking about the three diamonds on the boat deck and what it could mean. It was still early so not many people had arrived to work and Gunner made the first pot of coffee of the day. While the pot filled, Gunner took off his coat and turned on his computer. Murphy had told him that the files on McAllister would be emailed to him and Gunner heard the familiar tone that meant he had new mail. He printed everything that Murphy had sent and was still drawn to the three diamonds.

    He opened the Google homepage and entered the phrase three diamonds into the search box. The first thing that came up was a website about the cards of life. Gunner knew it was not going to be what he was looking for, but he clicked on it anyway. The playing card, the three of diamonds, was meant to represent indecision and uncertainty. There was no way the person who killed Angus McAllister was indecisive or uncertain.

    Gunner typed in the name Angus McAllister and was given an endless list of people who were not remotely related to the latest victim. He typed in a few more phrases into the search engine and felt like he was spinning his wheels. He had even typed in, death by harpoon, and was shocked to see how much crap was delivered to his screen. In a last-ditch effort, Gunner typed diamond, nautical symbol and received pages and pages of information. Most of the definitions of the symbol were of current direction, but one jumped out at him. The diamond was the waterway marking symbol for danger.

Chapter 36

Jack stood frozen in his spot in the park. He knew he was in danger the minute he heard that voice. His fight or flight instinct was in overdrive and flight was the only option. The man that stood in front of him was no adversary, he was a threat. He was of similar height to Jack, and though Jack had mentally compared their weights, Jack knew he was no match for this guy.

The man was holding his cell phone to his ear and saying absolutely nothing. Jack looked up and immediately regretted it as the two locked eyes. Jack felt like the air had been sucked out of his lungs. The man paused briefly and seemed to lose his concentration for a moment. In his peripheral, Jack could see a couple approaching on the path and he improvised. He waved and nodded like he recognized the couple and approached them quickly, talking to them as he moved out of the way of the man now fading into the background. They were complete strangers to Jack, but they were his best chance of a quick escape.

The couple interacted with him, pretending like they knew him to avoid the embarrassing situation of admitting they did not recognize him. Thankfully, they kept walking as they talked, putting a greater distance between them and the waning figure that slowly diminished as he was left behind. When they were out of earshot, Jack apologized to the couple, citing that he thought he remembered them from a party and the three parted ways.

Jack tentatively looked over his shoulder, relieved to see that he had not been followed. His blood still felt cold as his rapid pulse pushed the ice through his veins. Jack had no tangible reason why he should have reacted the way he did, but he always trusted his gut. This time his gut told him to get out of there and he obeyed.

Jack hailed a cab as soon as he was out of the park. Once inside and safely behind the closed door, the taxi pulled away from the curb and the driver asked for Jack's destination. Jack had not given any thought to where he was headed. He did not want to go home, and he had no idea where to begin looking for Charlotte, so he relied on the driver's knowledge of the city.

Jack leaned slightly forward and said, "Take me to your favorite pub, but on the other side of the city."

The driver nodded and smiled. "I've got just the place."

The cab sped away from the park, breezing through a few yellow lights that made Jack tightly grip the interior door handles. He began to relax as he realized how adept this guy was at driving through the city. He let go of the handle and let himself sink into the back seat. The buildings went by in a blur. Each block looked like the ones they had already passed. Crowds moved in unison along the sidewalks and the homeless began to roll out their beds. They were staking their territory for the night on the grates that emitted heat from the subway below since the late-June nights still had a chill to them.

Jack was guessing the ride would take about thirty minutes to cross the city. He closed his eyes and replayed the previous few hours that had just unfolded. While sitting idly on a bench in a park that he had never been in, he had seen the mysterious dog that had stared at him from the courtyard beside his building, met a beautiful woman who seemed oddly familiar and come face to face with a man who could chill his blood in mere seconds. Jack went back to the beginning of the scene and replayed it from the dog arriving at his bench to meeting Charlotte.

"Holy shit!" Jack sat up in his seat, startling the driver to the point that he almost rear-ended the car in front of him.

Charlotte. He was almost positive that she was the woman from the first lucid dream he could remember and the one he had seen with the dog on his detoured bus route. Charlotte. That was the only thing he had to go on, and if he was playing by the Criminal Minds rules, it was a weak lead. He had no idea how he could have seen her in his dream and then seen her in his real life. It made no sense. She could not be the same woman.

Jack's mind was racing, and he needed a drink. Thankfully, the cab had just pulled up to the curb outside of a little pub that looked like it could have been a bookstore. Jack handed the driver some cash, thanked him and headed for the bar. He took a seat at the far end of the bar so he could see the entire pub. If he had been followed, which he was sure he had not, he could at least see the entire restaurant and keep an eye on the door. The bartender threw a coaster down in front of him and Jack ordered a Whisky Sour. Wine was not going to cut it tonight.

The bartender put the drink on the coaster and left Jack alone. A two-man band was playing some old seventies tunes on guitar and keyboard and the multiple conversations in the pub were almost drowning them out. Jack focused on the television above the bar and read the news feed along the bottom of the screen. Nothing really grabbed his attention until he saw the flock of reporters outside of a police station and was following the story along the news ticker feed. Jack had not realized he had been holding his drink in front of his lips without taking a drink. He dropped the glass on the bar as he took in the details of the alleged murders that were being investigated. The glass shattered and the Whiskey had become more soured than it had been a few minutes ago.

Jack was riveted to the screen. He tried to get the bartenders attention to turn up the volume, but the guy was too busy flirting with the girl at the other end of the bar to even notice Jack's broken glass. Jack left a ten-dollar bill on the bar, hoping that would be enough to cover the drink and the broken glass, and went outside to find another cab.

Once he was in the taxi and on his way home, he called his television provider to reactivate his service. He knew it could take anywhere from two to twenty-four hours, but he had never had to wait more than two on previous occasions. He had the cab driver drop him at the liquor store a block from his apartment. Jack paid the driver, shut the door, and stopped in front of the store. He knew that more booze was not going to help so he turned away from the door and went straight home. Pulling out his cell phone on the way, he ordered some Chinese take-out and went home to wait for his dinner.

He turned his television on and pressed the guide button three times. Nothing appeared on the screen apart from the contact information for Bell Canada. He was usually a patient man but tonight Jack obsessively turned

The Waking Hours

his television on and off until the buzzer sounded to announce the arrival of his dinner. Jack found his wallet, paid the delivery guy, and took his food to the kitchen. He had just filled his plate with a mixture of egg rolls, fried rice, and chicken chow mein when the television sprang to life in the other room. Jack grabbed his plate and his chopsticks and decided to eat in the recliner, so he had the best view of the screen.

He surfed the news channels until he found the same broadcast he had seen at the bar. The ticker was still active under the newscast and Jack's eyes darted up and down from the anchor to the ticker and back again. He picked at his dinner while the news hour came close to its end. He knew they would recap the day's top stories and, just as he was about to take a bite of his eggroll, the anchor touched on the stories of several homicides that had recently taken place. The eggroll fell back on to Jack's plate.

The recap only skirted around the details but did skim over the cause of death in each victim and the blood drained from Jack's face. He put his dinner on the side table and jumped up to grab his journal. He methodically went back to the beginning of his entries and noticed similarities between the murders and the physical side effects of his dreams. The bruise from the bullet hole, the chafing of his wrists, the nausea, and the bitter taste in his mouth, they were all far too relatable to be coincidental.

The six o'clock news ended, and Jack wanted to stay awake for the eleven o'clock news to get the whole story and see if they had any further updates. He had lost his appetite, so the remnants of his dinner were scraped back into the containers and put into the fridge. He went back to the recliner and channel surfed for a while, hoping something would be on that would hold his attention for four hours and keep him awake. A Criminal Minds rerun was on A&E and Jack hoped there would be a few more to follow. In the middle of the third episode, Jack nodded off before the late news broadcast ever began.

~~

He awoke feeling slightly uncomfortable and felt the curved wooden seat of a bar stool underneath him. When Jack looked around, he was no longer in his apartment. The first thing he did was raise his arms to make sure his wrists were not restrained. He moved his legs back and forth and realized he was not confined in any way. Once he regained his bearings,

Jack recognized the surroundings of the airport. The loudspeaker announced boarding calls for several flights and Jack could see passengers scrambling to get to their gates on time.

He soon realized he was once again a passenger in someone else's body when the man got up to stretch his legs. Jack noticed they walked with a slight limp and the man rubbed his right thigh several times. The man did not seem to notice Jack moving his own limbs but when the man moved, Jack moved with him. They sat back down to watch a bit of the baseball game that was on the big screen and enjoyed a nice cold beer. A few other patrons came and went. When he heard his boarding call, the man paid for their beer and headed for their departure gate. Jack remembered his host saying something to another man about his war injury and they were off to board their flight.

After take-off, the plane leveled out and the seatbelt sign was turned off. The man got up from his seat and he and Jack walked up and down the aisle. Jack was thankful that the man avoided the plane's tiny lavatory. Instead, they sat back down and ordered a drink. With his vodka and tonic in hand and headphones on, Jack and his host watched Good Morning Vietnam on his laptop. At least the guy had good taste in movies.

After an hour and a half of enjoying Robin Williams at his finest, and filling in the rest of the flight reading, the captain came over the loudspeaker announcing their descent to the Lynden Pindling International Airport. Jack's arm involuntarily reached to help shut off the laptop and pack it away for their landing. The plane glided onto the runway and taxied to the gate. Jack wondered when he would meet his demise in this dream but since the plane had not crashed and he had ruled out terrorism, he could not imagine what this dream had in store for him.

They disembarked, travelled with the herd to collect their luggage, and hailed a cab to take them to a hotel. Jack was certainly enjoying this dream much more than he had any of the others.

The drive from the airport to the hotel was lovely. The cab ride took about thirty minutes to get to their destination which Jack now knew was Atlantis. The Bougainvillea was in full bloom and the rest of the tropical foliage was stunning. Jack noted the lack of palm trees for such a lush climate but quickly became distracted as he watched the sun bend down to caress every living thing in its path.

The Waking Hours

When they reached their destination, they were given a key to a ground floor suite that had a private pool and hot tub. They changed out of travel clothes and into a pair of swim shorts, grabbed a cold beer from the mini bar and relaxed in the mid-day sun in the comfort of a lounge chair.

One beer turned into four and, although Jack was not digesting any of the beer himself, he was feeling the man's buzz and slight exhaustion. They leaned back in the lounge chair and in a matter of minutes, Jack's host was snoring. The rhythmic sound of his breathing made Jack tired and he seemed to drift off as well.

~~

Jack woke up with a start and realized he was back in his apartment. Because his dream was still fresh in his mind, he remembered a few fragments of what had happened during his sleep. He recalled a pool and a lounge chair and, as he ran his tongue over his teeth, the taste of stale beer contaminated his mouth. He felt flushed and his skin felt tender as if he had been sunburned. He pulled himself out of his recliner and went to the mirror in the bathroom. His cheeks were rosy, and he looked tanned. He popped the button on his jeans and unzipped his fly, letting his pants fall to the floor. His legs were red from mid-thigh to his feet, but the upper part of his thigh was winter white, like he had been tanning in shorts.

For the first time in a while, Jack had woken up with no real signs of trauma. He did a full inventory of his body just to make sure he had not overlooked anything but every part of him seemed normal. He headed into the living room to record his most recent dream in the journal. He slowly regressed back to the beginning of the dream, or what he could remember of the dream, and thought about Robin Williams for some reason. The thought of him made Jack smile as he remembered how entertained he was by all the voices Robin could do. Jack suddenly felt an icy chill stab at him as he remembered the voice in the park earlier in the day.

Chapter 37

Standing in the park still gripping his cell phone in his hand, Victor startled himself when he heard his own voice slightly panicking, asking again for the information about his next job. The call had ended, and Victor could not move. He had been so distracted by the man he had just seen in the park that he had not paid attention to all the specifics he had been given over the phone. He was sure he had retained all the important details and the rest he would have to improvise. The only thing Victor was thinking about now was the man who had been standing no more than three feet away from him, staring at him with his one blue eye and one green eye.

His gut recoiled with the knowledge there was much more to this guy. But Victor would never miss a phone call and in the short time he was listening to the call, the guy met up with some friends and disappeared from the park. Victor knew it was pointless to try and follow him. They would meet again. And when they did, the circumstances would be much different than they were today.

He tried to recall as much of the phone call as he could. It would have to be done to look like a heart attack and it would have to happen before the man had a chance to board his plane and leave the country. Victor could do this. He was a professional. But he was rattled and that was not a feeling that he was accustomed to. He pulled himself together and slowly made his way out of the park.

As he walked back to his apartment, he made a mental list of the things he would need and began to formulate his plan. When he had finally arrived home, he opened his wall safe and rifled through the collection of valid passports, choosing one that he had not used in a while. He also saw the small vile of Succinylcholine, purposely mislabeled as a form of insulin, and a couple of syringes. If his plan went well, all he would have to do is sit close enough to the target and quickly inject enough of the liquid into his drink. In a matter of minutes, every system in the man's body would become paralyzed and he would asphyxiate. There was no chance of him making his flight if he died in the terminal.

After Googling his latest mark, Victor changed into a more presentable wardrobe, put his falsified doctor's notes in his pocket and grabbed his messenger bag. Knowing he would be questioned about his medication and needles once they were scanned by security, Victor was prepared with his medical explanation. He was ready, or at least he thought he was.

He arrived at the airport and made his way to the ticket booth with the shortest line. Victor was trying to recall whether he was given the man's actual flight itinerary or if the information he got during the phone call was the approximate time he would be leaving. He did not really think it mattered. All he had to do was be in the same departure lounge at the same time, find the man and get the job done. With his ticket in hand, Victor made his way to security and surprisingly breezed through the check point. His brief explanation of his feigned diabetes seemed to be enough to allow him to continue to his boarding gate. He threw the strap of his messenger bag over his shoulder and went to find his target.

His search results had been quite effective, and Victor spotted the man within minutes of wandering through the departures area. Google had been quite accurate when they described the gaudiness of the man's wardrobe and he certainly stuck out like a clown at a funeral. He was sitting on a bar stool at a sports lounge and Victor grabbed the stool beside him. Victor said nothing but simply pointed at the man's beer and the bartender pulled the tap on the keg to pour Victor a pint of the same.

They sat in silence, both seemingly lost in the game, but Victor's mind was racing. He had to figure out a way to divert the man's attention so he could spray the drug into the man's beer. Just as Victor thought he had found a way, there was an announcement over the intercom system.

"This is a pre-boarding call for Martin Lancaster, a pre-boarding call for Mr. Martin Lancaster. Please go to your departure gate immediately."

The man got up, smiled at Victor, and patting his thigh he said, "old army injury, comes in handy".

He winked and left the bar, leaving Victor staring after him. The syringe weighed heavily in Victor's pocket when he realized he had not put the drug in the man's drink. He watched Martin Lancaster limp across the small terminal to the boarding gate and then he was gone.

Chapter 38

Although she knew she had to deal with the death of her grandmother, Charlotte's mind was churning with thoughts of Max. She remembered the last night she saw him, drenched in sweat, stringy wet hair hanging in his face and a look of pure joy on his face as he wailed away on his guitar. For that moment he was right in front of her and hours later he was gone. The search for Max had gone on for three years. Her parents had refused to give up hope, but they knew the outcome looked grim.

It was after the urging of a family friend that they finally came to terms with the fact that Max was gone and everyone, especially Charlotte, needed some sort of closure. They had his funeral with no body to bury, only a few things that represented seventeen years worth of memories that they chose to put in his coffin. Each family member chose three items that either belonged to Max or reminded them of him and that was how Max was finally laid to rest.

Charlotte remembered that day like it was yesterday. There was not a cloud in the sky, not even a wisp of a Cirrus cloud. The internment was at 2:00 pm in the same cemetery that cradled their ancestors and Charlotte recalled seeing their names on the tombstones as Max's coffin was taken to his final resting spot. The sun was high in the sky and the melodies of the birds were far too cheerful for this overwhelmingly somber occasion.

Charlotte had been in college for two years and was living with some girls from her program. Her parents wanted her to stay home and commute and Charlotte knew it was because they were afraid to lose her too, but she needed her independence.

She scanned the crowd as they gathered around the coffin, waiting for the Minister to begin, and every face she looked at mirrored the emptiness and despair that Charlotte felt. The prayers and the eulogy were touching, and all written with great emotion and affection for Max. As the casket was being lowered into the ground and the Minister was reciting the committal, Charlotte's memory stumbled on a fragment of an image she had not remembered before. There was something in the distance that caught her attention on the day of Max's funeral and, until now, she had not given it a second thought. It was only a small point of light, but it was noticeable enough that it drew Charlotte's attention from the ceremony.

      She sat back on her couch and immediately she was transported from the funeral service back to her apartment. Norman had been watching her with a great deal of curiosity and was happy that she was interacting with him again. But her brain was now working in overdrive. She was desperate to remember more of that moment, but it was fading away. She was sure someone had been watching the service from behind the large Oak tree that had towered over the grave sites on the other side of the road, but she had seen the matured faces of all of Max's friends at the internment. They had all turned into men over the last few years, but their faces still emulated the boyish good looks they had in their late teens. There was not a single person Charlotte could think of who had not attended the service but the more she thought about it, the more she was sure that someone had been standing behind that tree watching Max's coffin being lowered into the ground. Had she waited, she may have caught a glimpse of him, but she turned back to the service and missed the sun reflecting off the familiar gold ring on the man's finger as he walked away.

The Waking Hours

Chapter 39

Victor was frozen in his seat. The gold ring on his right hand felt too tight and he began to spin it around on his finger. He leaned back on the bar stool, putting his hands on the bar as if to brace himself. The brightness from the pocket lights in the bar reflected off the ring and created a rainbow of colors on the wall to his right. He always thought the ring had brought him luck but today he felt betrayed. He had missed his mark and, apart from trying to figure out how to follow Martin Lancaster onto a sold-out plane for which he had no ticket, he was going to face some serious consequences when his new boss discovered that Martin had, indeed, boarded his flight and was about to leave the country.

Victor continued to move the ring around on his finger using his right thumb. The dancing colors on the wall seemed to have a macabre feel to them and, as Victor tipped back the last of his pint, he realized his abstraction had made him unaware of the man trying to avoid the light Victor had unconsciously directed into his eyes. Victor nodded an apology and shoved his right hand into his pocket, extinguishing the reflection.

Victor's unease made him continue to fidget with the ring. It was the only piece of jewelry Victor owned and, for the last seventeen years, it represented his ability and his strength. He had to have it resized to fit his large hand, but it had never been off his finger since then. Leaving his hand in his pocket, He flagged down the bartender with his left hand and ordered another pint. He knew his phone would ring after his boss got word that Martin Lancaster had departed the airport alive and well and had arrived at his destination without incident. Barring an unforeseen malfunction with the plane and a subsequent crash landing, Victor was going to be in some serious shit.

The twenty-four-hour news station was playing silently on the television in the bar while soft strains of seventies rock played through the speakers at the bar. Victor sipped his beer as he watched the news ticker highlighting the day's stories. The screen flashed "breaking news" and Victor watched as the cop lights flashed and uniformed officers were moving quickly in all directions. The background was unfamiliar to Victor, but he knew it was a marina of some sort. There were boats on trailers in the background that had not even been put in the water for the season. Victor was having difficulty reading lips and the ticker was a few seconds behind the actual story. When the news feed finally caught up with the news, Victor's face grew suddenly pale.

The man in front of the camera wore camouflage hip-waders and was grinning like an idiot as he hung onto his fishing pole. Victor's eyes jumped from the man's face to the news feed and back like they were following an aggressive tennis match. The ticker described the man's latest fishing expedition and the catch he never thought he would make. In the background, Victor could see the gurney being wheeled up from the end of the dock by the fishing boat. The sheet covered whatever was on the stretcher so the news-watching public would not be horrified but Victor already knew what it was. Ted Baines had just surfaced, and Victor's day had just gotten a lot worse.

Chapter 40

Ted Baines had finally surfaced, literally and figuratively. Gunner was looking through the file that Murphy had sent to his tablet a few hours ago. The man had been tangled in some over-hanging branches that belonged to a partially submerged tree and was then snagged by a fishing hook, much to the shock of the man on the other end of the fishing pole. Although his body was grotesquely distorted and partially eaten by sea-dwellers, Baines was easily identified by a tattoo on his left shoulder. Alice Baines had been notified and had gone to the morgue to positively identify the bloated corpse.

Before he left his office to head home to his white boards, Gunner called to thank Murphy for keeping him in mind and sharing his information. Both had the same feeling that they were now looking for the same guy and each of them agreed to share information on any new cases that came across their desks.

Gunner was going to pick up some food on his way home, but the pictures of Ted Baines did much to mitigate his appetite. He drove far more quickly than he should have through his neighborhood and received some familiar stares from the neighbors who were tending to their lush, early summer gardens. And as he always did, he responded with two blasts of his police siren to let them know he was on official business, not that he gave a shit what they thought. His right front tire bounced up over the curb and he narrowly missed hitting the garage door as it was still making its way up into its tracks.

He put on a pot of coffee and opened the new file on his tablet. He erased the question mark after Ted Baines' name on the white board and replaced it with the word deceased. He transferred any other pertinent information and stood back to look at the cases in front of him. The coffee maker gurgled and sputtered in the background, signaling that the pot was almost ready to go. Gunner poured himself a cup, topped it off with a bit of

Grand Marnier and paced in his kitchen. The coffee would keep him awake and the liqueur would help to calm his increasing sense of dread. The longer they went without a lead, the colder these cases were going to get, and they were already bordering on tepid.

Once the media got hold of this new story, the feeding frenzy would escalate and reach a height Gunner could only imagine. He could already picture the cameras and reporters camped out in front of his house once they found out who was the lead investigator trying to piece together these murders. Gunner needed to find this guy, and fast. The last thing he wanted was a bunch of cameras shoved into his face every time he tried to leave his house or come back home. Freedom of the press was a pain the ass.

His eyes moved slowly across the information in front of him. There was something there, he felt it, but he did not know what the hell he was looking for. There were no patterns in the cause of death. There were no relationships between any of the deceased. But Gunner knew there was something there that he was not seeing. He slugged back a few more sips of coffee and refilled his cup. Each refill became less coffee and more Grand Marnier but it seemed to be helping his brain relax and think outside of the box. He ignored the obvious details and tried to look beyond what he saw. The only thing that seemed out of place were the three lines on Gord Keston's hand and the three diamonds left on the deck of the boat beside Angus McAllister. Gunner's limited Google searches on each of the marks had come up with a few meanings for each symbol but nothing that seemed to be related to either case.

Gunner continued to pace. It was the thing that kept his brain motivated when his instincts felt like they were failing him. There were no obvious messages in the murders themselves, but the key he needed to unlock the mystery was in the notes he had made. Gunner knew it as much as he knew his next coffee would be one hundred percent Grand Marnier.

Staring at the symbols only frustrated him. He paced for a while longer and once he had exhausted himself, he poured the rest of the straight liqueur down the sink. The only thing those two markings had in common is that each symbol appeared to be left as a trinity.

Chapter 41

Jack spun his pen in his fingers three times. He stared at his journal entries and recalled the details of the murders he had seen on the news. There were some similarities that begged further investigation, but Jack was stymied by his inability to want to scrutinize his dreams any further. Initially they were just dreams, but Jack was now sensing a much deeper level of meaning to the details he had written in his journal. He closed the cover of the book for the third time and got up from the desk. His need to be outside was overwhelming and he made his way on to his balcony.

Taking in large gulps of fresh air, Jack held fast to the railing and rocked back and forth. What once seemed like just a series of dreams now had a much more ominous undertone. He was hoping that the resemblance of his dream sequences to the particulars on the news was purely coincidental, but his gut told him otherwise. Somehow, Jack had vague details of these murders. He did not know how or why; he just knew he had to talk to someone and share his information before he went crazy.

Jack went back inside and logged on to his laptop. There was a profusion of articles relating to each of the murders and the name that kept jumping out at Jack was Carrick Doyle. He was referred to many times in the details of the investigations and Jack assumed he was the lead detective. He knew his story was unbelievable, but he had to find a way to make himself seem credible and not sound like a guy who was completely out of his mind. He could not just show up at Doyle's office without some sort of a script and a whole lot of confidence and, right now, Jack had neither of those things. Doyle would think Jack needed some serious psychiatric care and most likely push an unseen button, alerting a crew of burly officers who would swiftly remove Jack from his office.

Jack stared blankly at his laptop. He needed a plan, and he knew the answer was not going to magically appear on his monitor. He shut down his computer and sat in relative silence. There were muffled noises coming from the street and the constant drone of the highway in the distance, but his apartment remained muted. Jack pressed his finger to his forehead in a succession of threes willing himself to come up with a plan. His scant collection of photographs documenting his injuries and his disjointed journal entries were hardly what anyone would call evidence, but Jack had nothing else. He could not recall his dreams with much clarity, but every dream was leaving him with more residual memories than the last. He was happy he kept waking up each morning as himself and not succumbing to the tragedy he faced in each of his nightmares.

Jack wanted nothing more than to barge into Carrick Doyle's office, show him the journal and his pictures and have Doyle say, "this is the evidence we've been waiting for", but Jack knew that was a foolish pipe dream. He needed to give a more detailed documentation of what he could remember and give Doyle something to nibble on that would whet his appetite enough to make him interested in the second course.

He shifted in the dining room chair but could not get comfortable. He picked up his pen and his journal and moved over to let himself be swallowed by his recliner. He went back to the beginning of his entries and tried to elaborate on the sparse information he had entered but he could not, for the life of him, remember anything more about any of the dreams he had encountered.

Jack had no idea what time it was, but he was starting to feel the burden of exhaustion. The weight of his eyelids became heavier with each blink. He was beginning to think he was borderline narcoleptic. As much as he forced himself to open his eyes by jerking his head up, gravity eventually won the battle and Jack's chin came to rest on his chest.

~~

He instinctually knew the sounds of the downtown core in the prime of its night life. It was only from a very distant memory, but he still knew it. The thumping sound of bass notes was emitted from every club door as patrons came out to cool off and have a cigarette. Young couples, heavily marinated by the bar scene, clung to each other as they gave their futile efforts to appear sober. As he walked, Jack felt his legs moving in a strange and sultry way. His hand involuntarily went to his head and his fingers twisted through a cascade of long, carefully curled hair. As his legs continued to move in their sensuous manner, Jack caught a glimpse of himself in the reflection of a club window.

He had always wanted to use the phrase 'her legs went on for days' but as he gazed at his mirror image, he could honestly use those words. Jack was a woman, but not just any woman. Jack was sure that he was a prostitute. Her wardrobe left little to the imagination and Jack could feel the seam of her skin-tight skirt rubbing on her legs barely below her ample backside.

They moved like a jungle cat through the night, a predator in search of prey. Calculated movements meant to garner the attention of willing and available men were made at just the right time and Jack could not ignore the stares from the men lingering on the sidewalk. The legs continued to cross, walking like they were on a model runway in Versailles and the catcalls were fighting each other to be heard.

Jack felt exposed even though he could not be seen. He wanted nothing more than to pull a robe over this poor woman's body and shield her from what he knew was her reality. Thankfully, they continued past the bar crowd and kept walking. Jack could feel his calves beginning to burn from walking with her in heels. The putrid stench of stale urine was strong in the air and the sidewalks were littered with cigarette butts and roaches. Drunk men and women brushed past them on their way from one club to the next. The downtown night life was just as ugly as Jack remembered it to be, if not more grotesque.

They meandered their way past the bar scene and eventually found themselves in a more upscale neighborhood that was littered with proper pubs and not meat-markets. Jack instinctually felt that this was her regular territory. Her tension level fell, and their pace was much more relaxed. Small trees rooted in cement cast lovely evening shadows on the sidewalk. There was a slight breeze, and the movement of the air combined the smells of pub food with inexpensive cologne. She seemed comfortable enough to chat with a few bar patrons who she recognized and felt content enough to know that she would not have to be the one to make the first move.

They both saw him exit the pub and Jack knew she wanted to attract him by the immediate change in her body language. She waited until he saw her, and she knew by the look in his eyes that he would make the first move.

But he hesitated slightly. He seemed to be staring past her, lost in a memory. Not a word was spoken, he simply put his hand on her back and they walked down the street.

The hair on the back of Jack's neck stood up but she seemed oblivious to any danger. Jack knew this guy. Although he was in a dream and had no real sense of his reality, he knew this guy. He could feel the strong hand of the man now holding her elbow as he escorted her further away. There were still no words exchanged between them, but Jack could hear the underlying rage coming from this man and he knew his fate and her fate before they turned the corner into the alley.

When they were a safe distance from the street, the man's grip became tighter and he spun them around to face him. Jack was staring into the man's eyes with as much fear as she was. Time felt like it had stopped. Had the night been colder, Jack would have sworn their breath would have been frozen into tiny icicles in front of their face. The man slowly cocked his head from one side to the other, taking in every detail of her face, her hair, and her body. The lines on his forehead became more pronounced and Jack could have sworn that this heavyset man standing in front of him seemed disappointed. Not a word was spoken between them from meeting outside of the pub to standing face to face in the alley.

Jack thought the suffering would be unbearable, but her death was quick and perfunctory. The weight of the man's forearm pressed heavily into her larynx and Jack was happy she was spared from a more savage end to her life. Although she struggled and clawed at the man's forearm, she was no match for his strength. Jack could feel her oxygen supply slowly being depleted as she lost consciousness and finally succumbed to her death. Her limp body was slowly lowered to the pavement as if he were quietly laying her to rest. Jack continued to watch the man as he lingered, his gaze riveted to the dead woman's face. The giant leaned down and let his fingers graze her cheek. There was a melancholy look in his eyes that made Jack's blood suddenly feel like he had ice in his veins. There was no remorse emanating from this beast. He was not sure what the feeling was, but Jack knew that if he ever remembered this part of his dream, he would never forget it.

The man left the alley as quietly as he had entered it. The woman lay dead on the pavement and Jack remained a prisoner in her corpse. As in his last dream, Jack lingered for several minutes after her heart had stopped beating. He did not know where he was or who she was, he only knew that he had to try to leave some sort of message. Although she was lifeless, Jack was still miraculously able to move his arms and was able to use them as if he were fully conscious. He reached out to see what he could grab, found her purse lying beside her and fumbled through the contents until he found her lipstick. Jack drew three x's onto the pavement by her body and made a matching one on her left hand.

    Jack was becoming more aware in each of his dreams. His ability to leave physical clues was a welcomed progression from his helplessness in his past dreams. After lingering for longer than he anticipated, Jack could feel himself finally slipping out of the dream. He looked at the three x's on the pavement and saw the one he had put on the back of the woman's left hand. He wondered if that lipstick mark would be on his hand and still be intact when he hopefully woke up in his apartment, once again as himself.

Chapter 42

For the first time in his life, Victor did not feel like himself. He never missed a mark, he never failed at an assignment and he never misread the signs. He was not a drinker, but the couple of pints he had at the airport compelled him to head to a proper pub and have a few more. Victor paid his tab at the airport bar and made his way through the crowd in Departures to hail a cab. Since he rarely left his apartment for anything other than work, he relied on the cab driver to take him to a place somewhere downtown where he could drown his growing sense of failure. Victor stared out the side window of the cab as his thumb unconsciously spun the ring on his finger.

After thirty minutes of watching a countless number of headlights and taillights, Victor realized the cab had slowed and taken a moderately busy off-ramp. After a few crafty turns and questionable runs through yellow lights, the cab pulled up in front of a quaint pub in what Victor surmised to be an upscale neighborhood. There were no groups of young people littering the streets and the only sounds coming from the pub were the strains of old Irish tavern music. Victor paid his fare and stood on the sidewalk for long enough to canvass the neighborhood. The late June blooms on the trees were lovely but their scents were overwhelmed by the smells of corned beef and deep fryers. People came and went from the pub, but none seemed like they had been served more than their fair share. Victor went in and found a seat at the far end of the bar. He was not one to frequent bars often but when he did, he wanted to see the full bar and the people on the street outside. He ordered a pint of Kilkenny and leaned back in his seat.

The atmosphere in the pub was surprisingly soothing. Once his pint had been delivered, the bartender had read his customer well and left his newest patron alone. Victor let the bitter creaminess of the ale wash away what it could of the past few hours, but his glaring failure refused to be eradicated. He was distracted and he knew it. He could not get the girl from the park out of his mind and every move he made he seemed to be followed by one blue eye and one green eye. His hardened exterior gave the impression of success, but it was nothing more than a mask for a man who was falling apart on the inside.

He was startled by the ring of his cell phone. Since he had not had time to replace the disposable phone with another, there was only one person who had this number. Victor dropped the phone on the ground and crushed the face of it with his heel. He had no answers and no excuses so there was no point in engaging in a futile conversation in a very public place. He signaled the bartender and ordered another pint. The pub music temporarily silenced Victor's thoughts of failure but soon the music was extinguished by his inner voices and he became fixated on his thoughts of her. Her portrait was etched in his mind and, although he was still on his bar stool in the pub, Victor was back in the park and seeing her again for the first time.

He could see the floral patterns in the surrounding bushes and watched in slow motion as she kicked the leaves on the path. The waning sunlight caressed her hair, and she was lost in a moment of wantonness. Victor was unaware he had closed his eyes and been holding his breath as he recalled her free spirit in the park.

When he pulled himself from his reverie, he saw her. It was not the sunlight, but the warm glow from the streetlamps gently kissed gold flecks into her hair. She was standing outside of the pub and he could not take his eyes off her. Fate had somehow brought her to him, and Victor was suspended in time. His hand hovered in front of his lips, holding his pint of beer, but he was too distracted to drink. The entire scene in the bar became nothing more than a blurred background and she was the focal point in a stage spotlight. Victor threw some cash on the bar, drained what was left of his pint and made his way to the door.

He stood inside for several moments studying the contours of her face. For as much as he wanted this to be the girl, it was someone else. She was so close to what he remembered, but something was different. There was no innocence in her eyes. There was no purity in her demeanor. This woman was a fraud. He had been so absorbed in his memories that he had been deluded by a lookalike.

Victor took several deep breaths before he left the pub. His emotion began to bubble in his gut, but he had never let his mental state control him before and he was not going to start now. He regained his composure as they made eye contact. He knew instinctually that she was responding to him and he made his way to her. His hand cupped the small of her back and she was more than willing to be led away from the pub. Since there was no real exchange between them, anyone else on the street would have assumed that they either knew each other or had arranged to meet here. Her face was no stranger to this neighborhood and since she was not offensive in any way, people rarely paid attention to her. They walked in silence, but he could no longer look at her. She was an imposter.

When they turned into the alley, Victor aggressively spun her around, so they were face to face. Her eyes immediately began to register a look of panic and Victor paused to look at her, tilting his head from one side to the other. She looked so much like her. His brow furrowed as he concentrated on the smallest nuance of her facial profile. Once he had convinced himself that this was not the girl, he slammed his forearm into her throat. Even though she made a feeble attempt to fight him, her weight was no match for his and he waited patiently until she was no longer breathing. He slowly let gravity help him put her on the ground and tried to imagine what her dead eyes were seeing now.

He kneeled, looking at the face of the dead woman. His fingers grazed her cheek, wishing so much that she had been the right one. He felt no remorse, only disappointment. He stared at her face for several minutes before he was brought back to reality by the sound of approaching footsteps. Victor slipped away from the body and quietly left the alley in the opposite direction of how he entered it. When he was obscured by the evening shadows, he turned to look at her one last time. The crowd of people moved past the entrance to the alley without even glancing in his direction. He knew it would be a while before she was found and that would give Victor plenty of time to get back to the safety of his apartment. He needed to punish himself for his failure and impulsiveness and he needed the guidance of his meditation.

Victor walked home, not wanting any other people to see his face. He wandered aimlessly, distracted by what had just happened and unable to pay attention to his surroundings to gauge exactly where he was. He began to wind through the streets until something was familiar and it began to lead him in the direction of home. He had no idea how long he had been walking

The Waking Hours

but he could feel a slight burn in his calf muscles and the night traffic had subsided to the point that he could hear the streetlights humming. The city was eerily quiet, and it left Victor alone with his thoughts.

He had been careless. Usually, he was methodical about not being seen anywhere near any of the crime scenes he left behind but his passion for killing this girl far outweighed his logic and it worried him. The subdued sounds of the residential neighborhoods did nothing to assuage his feeling of dread. His usual confidence had soured and left him with a bitter taste in his mouth. The fact that he was wandering the streets in the early hours of morning rather than being in his controlled environment only added to his sense of unease. Victor knew that if someone startled him, he would jump out of his skin and he hated the feeling of being that out of control.

Slowly the scenery in front of him morphed into something much more familiar and he found his way home. The guard on duty was leaning back in his chair, feet on his desk and snoring loudly. Not wanting to alert the guard to his late arrival, Victor quietly passed the desk and entered the stairwell. He climbed the steps to the first floor and boarded the elevator there so the sounding bell of the elevator's arrival did not wake the guard.

Once he was back in the safety of his apartment, Victor stripped out of his clothes and sat naked on the floor of his living room. No light seeped into the room from anywhere and Victor allowed himself to be bathed in the darkness, hoping it would take him back to that root cellar so many years ago.

Chapter 43

Charlotte needed to take more control of her life. Her grandmother was gone, she had no real family left apart from a few distant relatives she never heard from and she could not get Max out of her mind. She had let Anna manage the antique store for a few days so she could mourn her grandmother and get her head together. There was no funeral since there were no real family members to appease. Charlotte had her grandmother cremated and had not yet been able to bring herself to pick up the remains from the funeral home.

Norman had, on several occasions, voiced his concern for her by uttering a few well-placed barks that were quiet but understood. Charlotte put on her Beethoven CD, poured herself a small glass of Sherry and invited Norman onto the couch. They sat silently together and let the strains of piano and violin wash over them. Charlotte closed her eyes and lost herself in the latest concerto. She let the Sherry linger on her tongue and felt it burn as it went down her throat. She let the music transport her and, as the intensity of the music increased, Charlotte's sadness became slowly distorted. With the help of a few more sips of Sherry and the more aggressive tone in the music, her sadness turned into frustration.

Norman remained on the couch while Charlotte got up to fill her glass. She stood at the dry sink, her eyes closed and her head moving like a conductor's baton. She continued to sip the Sherry and Norman watched with great interest as she seemed to be having a very voluntary, very controlled seizure. As the symphony came to its crescendo, Charlotte's arms were now conducting the invisible orchestra and the Sherry was struggling to keep its place in the glass. The music was forceful and when the room fell silent once again, Charlotte was furious. Norman sensed the change in her mood and remained vigil on the couch.

All she wanted to do was scream. Her life had been a series of unfortunate events and she was finally giving herself permission to be angry.

The Waking Hours

Her parents were dead, her grandmother was now dead, and the authorities had given up years ago trying to figure out if Max was dead or alive. But that was going to change, and it was going to change today. With the courage of a couple ounces of Sherry and her new resolve to strengthen her backbone, Charlotte gathered all the information she had collected over the years about Max's disappearance and got ready to head to the police station. She wanted his case reopened, today!

After letting Norman outside to do his business, Charlotte fed him and explained where she was going. Norman seemed content to let her go on her own, so she collected her files and left the apartment. The bus ride downtown gave her time to regain control of her emotions but she held on to some of the antagonism so she would not allow herself to be told there was nothing they could do and be politely ushered out of the detachment.

As the bus meandered its way through the streets, Charlotte's determination never wavered. She could hear her mother's favorite phrase in her mind "she wouldn't say shit if her mouth was full of it" and she felt slightly empowered by her mother's silly idiom. Charlotte was going to say shit today, and she was going to be heard.

She pulled the chain to signal the bus to pull over at the next stop and she gathered her files and her courage. The brakes squealed slightly, and the bus stopped, allowing Charlotte and a few other passengers to disembark. The police station was only a block from the bus stop and Charlotte was climbing the steps to the precinct in a few short minutes. The day sergeant acknowledged her while she finished her phone call and asked how she could help.

"I'd like to speak to the officer in charge of your cold cases", Charlotte said as she shuffled her feet slightly.

The woman behind the desk did not speak to Charlotte but merely picked up her phone and dialed an extension. She muttered a few words which Charlotte was sure were some sort of code and hung up the phone.

"Officer Kennedy will be out in a jiffy." She attempted a smile, picked up the phone again and pretended to make a call so she would not have to make small talk.

Charlotte's weight continued to shift from one foot to the other. Police officers came and went, some were escorting some questionable looking characters in shackles. Charlotte moved over to the bench against the wall and waited for Officer Kennedy. Seconds turned into minutes and the minutes accumulated to almost an hour. She knew she should not press her luck by being pushy, but her anger level was starting to rise again. After what seemed like an eternity, a man in a pair of wrinkled khakis and a button-down shirt approached her.

She stood up from the bench, "Officer Kennedy?"

"Nope, Gunner. Why are you here?"

After quickly rebounding from the man's terse introduction, Charlotte did her best to sum up the story of her brother's disappearance and practically demanded that his case be reopened. Although she was trying to hold it together, she was visibly shaking and doing everything she could to not cry. Charlotte knew this guy could read her body language and he eased her back on to the bench and got her a glass of water. He sat beside her and listened as she continued to talk about what he would eventually read in the files.

When she got to the end of her story, Charlotte took a deep breath and exhaled years of heartache. And then the tears came. The poor guy on the bench beside her looked like he was trying to find the closest escape route. He got her some tissues and excused himself. Charlotte did the ugly cry for a few minutes and slowly gained control of her breathing. The sobs subsided. The staccato bursts of breathing became less labored and she was once again in control of her emotion.

The somewhat irritable officer returned, wrote down Charlotte's contact information on the inside of the file she had given him and promised that someone would be in touch. He put his hand under her elbow, helped her get up from the bench and escorted her to the door. Her time was up, and Charlotte felt like she had blown her chance by getting so emotional.

She fought tears all the way home. The bus ride seemed twice as long as it had been to get downtown, and it gave her too much time to reflect. This guy, Gunner, was going to throw her file into a pile on his desk and not even give it a second glance. Her determination had been trumped by the ways of the real world and Max was going to be forgotten again. Before the bus had a chance to pull over at her stop, Charlotte was sobbing again.

When the bus slowed to its stop by Charlotte's building, she could barely see to get down the steps. Her swollen eyes betrayed her as she tried to follow the sidewalk. She continued to wipe the mutinous tears as they welled in the corners of her eyes and steadily escaped down her cheeks. Her apartment building was only a block and a half from the bus stop and as much as she knew she needed to be with Norman, Charlotte knew there was only one way to distract herself from her looming bout of depression.

The little market stood on the corner of the block and stuck out like a sore thumb. In a neighborhood of high rises and shiny new storefronts, the family run grocery store was a throw-back to the fifties. The striped green and white awning was fully extended to protect the fresh produce from the elements. The display in the large picture window was filled with rounds of cheese, packages meant to look like meat wrapped in butcher's paper and twine and an array of other specialty items that would surprise anyone who had not shopped there before. Charlotte heard the bell sound as she entered the store and kept her head down to avoid eye contact. She knew her eyes were red and swollen and she did her best to pick up all the items she needed without directly looking at anyone in the store.

When her basket contained the items she required, she grabbed a crusty French loaf and made her way to the counter. The woman working the cash register looked briefly at Charlotte and knew there was no small talk needed. She quickly rang Charlotte's items through, waited patiently as Charlotte used her Apple Pay and nodded briefly as Charlotte left the store.

Knowing he would read her emotion immediately Charlotte was prepared for Norman to shadow her every move. She put the groceries on the counter and took Norman outside for his afternoon pee. He was disinterested in doing anything other than relieving himself and he left the sniffing of the area for another time. He was right back at Charlotte's side and the two went back up to the apartment.

Charlotte began to unpack her groceries and found her Dutch Oven. After putting a few teaspoons of bacon fat into the pot, she began to chop her onions and garlic. The only way for Charlotte to really lose herself and forget about her afternoon of misery was to make soup. She put the onions and garlic in the pot and watched them jump feverishly in reaction to the hot bacon fat. The aromatic smells in the kitchen were already making Charlotte feel better. Norman lay in the doorway, watching as Charlotte conducted her new orchestra of ingredients. Once the onions had begun to soften, Charlotte deglazed the pot with a bit of Sherry and added her chopped pears. She took the remains of her earlier frustration out on an innocent head of cauliflower, viciously tearing it to pieces and adding it to the pot. She added a few chopped potatoes and chicken stock and covered the pot to let it come to a boil.

  While the soup was on a low boil, she toasted some walnuts for a garnish and crumbled some Stilton for the soup. The clock read 5:01 pm and Charlotte poured herself a glass of wine. She left the pot and moved over to stare out of the balcony door. She could see her reflection in the glass and was shocked by how physically exhausted she looked. Norman sat at her feet and even he knew that her physical appearance was no match for her emotional exhaustion.

  When the soup was finished, Charlotte made sure Norman had his dinner as well and the two ate in silence. She knew tomorrow she would return to the antique store and delve back into her reality. She needed a distraction, and the store was now the only one she had. She enjoyed her dinner and her glass of wine. She looked at her phone a few times, but she knew it was futile to expect a call from the overly critical officer she had met earlier, and she spent the rest of the night trying to forget about her experience at the police station and the man named Gunner.

Chapter 44

Jack decided to do some more digging into Carrick Doyle and found out the man only answers to the name Gunner. An hour earlier, Jack had awoken in his apartment with nothing more than a sore throat and very strained calf muscles. He had a vague memory of walking around downtown in some extremely uncomfortable shoes and feeling like he wanted nothing more than to cover himself up. He had jotted these things down in his diary and was back at his laptop, getting the dirt on this guy named Gunner. The more Jack looked through recent articles, the more he realized that Gunner was the guy he needed to talk to about his dreams.

As he was entering some new words into a search engine, Jack was distracted by something on the back of his left hand. He held it up and moved it around in the light. He could see a faint X on his hand in a light shade of pink. It was almost invisible, but Jack reached for his phone to see if he could capture it in a picture. He got the camera as close as he could without the image being too blurry and tried a shot with no flash and one with a flash. He flipped through the images and realized that the last one with the flash captured an extremely vague outline, but it was there. He had no idea if this mark had anything to do with his latest dream but if he were a gambling man, he would have put money on it. Jack would need to print this new picture for his journal and catalogue it with the rest of his evidence.

He turned off the laptop and went back to the beginning of his journal. If he had not experienced the aftermath of each of these dreams, he would have believed these entries to be the diatribe of a lunatic. Thankfully, he had begun documenting his signs of physical trauma during his waking hours to give his stories a bit more credibility but convincing someone of that would be a stretch.

Because his first few entries were so ambiguous, Jack passed by them quickly. He realized he was smiling as he read his accounts of the woman he had seen at the beginning of this absurd journey he was on and he remembered their brief meeting in the park. He vowed to spend more time trying to find her after all this lunacy was over. And the dog, he really wanted to find that dog.

Jack put his journal, his photographs, the green towel, and all his hope into his messenger bag and hung it on the back of his shoddy recliner. He knew he needed to make a good impression with this Gunner guy, so he took a hot shower, shaved, and dressed in clothes that made him look relatively sane. Once he had made himself presentable, Jack called the police station and asked to speak to Carrick Doyle.

"Who?" The day sergeant was being a dick.

"I'm sorry. I'd like to speak to Gunner." Jack knew the officer knew damned well who Carrick Doyle was, but he did not want to voice his annoyance.

"He don't take calls. You can come down here and take a chance. He's either in, or he's out."

The line went dead, and Jack hung up his phone. He took a deep breath and exhaled his apprehension about the step he was about to take. It was a bold move, but one Jack would have to make eventually and certainly one that would potentially help the police find the man behind the murders. He threw his messenger bag over his shoulder and casually glanced back at his apartment. The clay figurines were rooted in their place. The foam in the recliner still clung to the chair for dear life and the dust particles danced in the sunlight streaming into the living room. Jack took a few extra moments to take it all in. For some reason, he did not think he would be back here for a while, but he did not know why. He left the apartment, turned the lock three times, and embarked on his crusade.

The bus ride seemed to take forever but Jack finally signaled his stop and exited the bus. The police station was a block away and Jack was frozen in his place. He was sure he was doing the right thing, but the seed of doubt was planted. His civic duty forced his hand, and he put one foot in front of the other until he reached the steps of the police station. He climbed the steps one at a time, pausing after reaching the next level. For some reason he

The Waking Hours

felt like he was turning himself in instead of helping an investigation. He got to the top step and pushed open the door.

The day sergeant looked just as unimpressed to see Jack as he sounded on the phone. Jack strode with confidence to the desk and asked to speak to Gunner. His hands inadvertently clutched his messenger bag as the man behind the desk punched in an extension number. Jack could feel his brow dampen as he attempted to appear as casual as possible.

"Have a seat." The guy behind the desk did not even bother to look at Jack as he dismissed him from the desk.

After what felt like an eternity, Jack saw Gunner approaching. He had seen enough of his pictures on the internet to know who he was. Jack stood and stretched out his hand.

Gunner looked at his hand and back at Jack's face without extending his hand, "What can I do for ya?"

Jack's words began fighting each other to get out of his mouth first. Gunner put his hand up to stop Jack's babbling. Jack took a deep breath and began again. He told Gunner about his dreams and physical indications that he had somehow been there. He was about to pull out his journal when Gunner grabbed him by the elbow and escorted him out of the lobby and down the hall to his office. Once inside, Jack sat down and pulled out his documentation and his pictures to back up his stories. He felt like he had been talking for hours but Gunner seemed riveted to what he was saying so Jack kept going.

Jack talked about each of the dreams he had been able to remember and referenced his journal for more details. He showed what few pictures he had and as he did Jack noticed that Gunner's body language had changed slightly. Where he had seemed disinterested and was sitting back in his chair at first, he was now leaning on his desk and staring intently at the pictures and back at Jack. Jack pulled out the tissue from the back of his journal.

"I don't know what this is, but it was under my fingernail after one of my dreams," said Jack.

Jack had come to the end of his narrative. He was convinced that his information could help catch the person, or people, the police were looking for. He expelled a loud sigh, leaned back in his chair, and waited for Gunner to say something. As they waited in silence, a knock on Gunner's door interrupted the quiet and a young officer threw a new file on Gunner's desk. With no apology, Gunner ignored Jack and began to skim through the new file. Jack watched as Gunner looked from the file and back to Jack several times. Gunner put the file down and stared at Jack, saying nothing. Jack was convinced their meeting was over and Gunner had written him off as being insane.

Chapter 45

The more Gunner studied this guy, the more he thought this guy could just be certifiably insane or, quite possibly, the killer. Gunner could not believe his luck when Officer Jarred walked in with the file on the latest murder in the city. A prostitute had been strangled the night before and the crime scene investigators had found three pink x's on the pavement beside the girl's body. And here was this guy sitting in front of him, with a journal full of vague details about the other murders, now with a faint pink X on his hand.

Gunner was not a betting man but, if he were, he would bet five bucks that this guy had something to do with all these murders. There was no way in Hell Gunner was going to let him loose on the street without checking every detail about him while they had him in their custody. Gunner, quite out of character, excused himself for a moment and left Jack alone in his office.

Gunner and Officer Jarred exchanged a few words outside and both law officers entered Gunner's office and stared at Jack. Officer Jarred was the first to make a move and Jack suddenly sensed that something was horribly wrong. As he stood from his seat, Jarred's hands were on Jack before he could turn around and Jack heard the handcuffs engage before he felt the metal on his wrist. Jack did not put up a fight.

"You understand that this is just a precautionary step," Gunner spoke with great clarity. "You are not under arrest, yet. We would just like to have more time to ask you some questions. Obviously, there is something going on here."

Officer Jarred escorted Jack out of Gunner's office. Jack's messenger bag with his journal and his photographs remained with Gunner and Jack was led to a holding cell somewhere on the other side of the precinct. Before being put in the cell, Jack was stripped of all his personal possessions, had his mug shot taken and fingerprints documented. He felt like a criminal. Thankfully, the cell he was in was unoccupied so he did not have to worry about the nature of any character he would have encountered in his personal space. Jack was given a meal at 5:30 pm and was left on his own for the rest of the night.

~~

Gunner sent the unknown sample from under Jack's nails to have it examined by forensics. He then packed his files, grabbed Jack's messenger bag, and headed for home shortly after Jack had been detained. There was something to this guy. Gunner's instincts were lighting up like a Christmas tree. Somehow Gunner knew Jack was not the killer but having him behind bars for the night would make Gunner feel better. If something happened through the night and another body ended up in the morgue, Gunner would know that his intuition had been right and that somehow Jack could be the key to this whole investigation.

He sped through his neighborhood and hit the sirens twice. His neighbors looked as unimpressed as they had been the last time he came home, but Gunner didn't give a shit. He was trying to catch a killer, or killers, and that far outweighed the look of disdain he received from the people with whom he shared some geography. He missed the curb this time and skillfully pulled the car into the garage. The door came down behind him and Gunner collected the files and Jack's messenger bag and made his way to his makeshift office. He was eager to compare Jack's notes from each of his dreams to the notations that he had made on his white board. He retrieved Jack's journal from his bag and began to compare notes.

The first case Gunner had received was a John Doe - shot in the head at point blank range. Jack's file only had a few notes about his first dream and no photographs to go with it. Jack's description of his bruised forehead and subsequent headache were consistent with John Doe's cause of death.

The next case on Gunner's list were the two kids killed in the park. Jack's files made no mention of their deaths at all so Gunner quickly skimmed Jack's next entry while glancing up at his board. The second hit that Gunner had on his board was Peter Mahon. Peter had suffered a horrible death by asphyxiation after ingesting a poisonous substance that Gunner surmised to be chlorine gas. Once again, Jack's notes were in accordance with what Gunner would assume would be the side effects of inhaling a poisonous gas. Jack listed nausea and extreme abdominal pain as his waking symptoms after this dream. He also had made a point to document the horrendous smell of his breath. There were two words written on the side of this entry that made no sense to Gunner, but he knew they would have some relevance to what was going on. The words 'voice' and 'Charlie' stared back at Gunner as if they should mean something, but they did not, not at this point.

    Gunner moved on to his next case on the white board, Adam, the university kid killed outside of his house. As with the park murders, Jack had no corresponding journal entry. Gunner was becoming more and more convinced that these two murders had nothing to do with the more professional murders, but he was not ruling anything out just yet. Gunner looked at his notes on Gord Keston, the man put on display on the roller coaster. When he looked back to Jack's journal expecting it to be the next entry, Gunner found Jack's notes were about waking up soaking wet and in possession of a strange green towel with the letter "B". Gunner made the connection when he looked up at the last entry on his white board. Ted Baines had been recovered weeks later but his drowning could certainly explain Jack's waking up drenched. He pulled the towel out of Jack's bag and hung it on the corner of the white board that had Ted Baines' information. He was sure the towel was somehow connected to Baines' drowning but could not fathom how Jack could physically bring an item out of a dream.

    Gunner moved forward in the journal to find the details that reflected Keston's murder. Jack's notes were more detailed about this dream than any of the previous dreams and the photographs were a fantastic way to solidify his testimony.

    As he made his way through the rest of the journal entries, Gunner was torn. All these entries could certainly mean that Jack was, indeed, having very lucid dreams but it could also mean that Jack was committing these murders in a fugue state and only remembering the aftermath and not the actual murders. But Jack hardly seemed like a killer and willingly bringing himself and his journal into the precinct helped his defense significantly.

Gunner made it to the last entry about sore calf muscles and the dim photograph of the back of Jack's left hand. He could barely make out the faint X on the back of Jack's hand and suddenly remembered the latest file that had been given to him while Jack was sitting in his office. Gunner grabbed the file and read about the prostitute who had been found dead in an alley in an upscale neighborhood. She had been strangled. The thing that grabbed and held Gunner's attention were the three pink X's beside her body, apparently written in a shade of her lipstick. Gunner sat back in his chair and laced his hands behind his head. All he could think to himself was, "what the fuck?"

Gunner went back to the beginning of the journal and started making notes of his own. This was far beyond what he was able to grasp this late at night, but he could not seem to shut his brain down. He made his own version of a flow-chart and began writing questions that he wanted to ask Jack in the morning. If Jack did not kill any of these people, there were a lot of unanswered questions that Gunner hoped they could find an explanation for, even if they were not easy answers.

Gunner went back to the latest file. He looked at the crime scene photos and took in all the small details. The girl's face was partially covered by her long hair but something about her seemed familiar. Gunner turned the file over to see her mug shot and could have sworn she was the same girl who had been in the precinct earlier. Their facial structure, eye color, the length and color of their hair were almost identical. But the dead girl was Sally Michaels and the girl that Gunner had spoken to earlier was Charlotte Beckett. Gunner stared at the file for longer than he should have but it was too coincidental that this dead woman was a doppelganger for the woman wanting to reopen her brother's cold case. And Gunner did not believe in coincidences.

His eyes burned as he pored over the files and the journal incessantly. He knew he was losing the battle against unconsciousness, but he refused to give in. The shrill sound of his phone woke him at 5:30 am.

The Waking Hours

The voice of the desk sergeant said, "Sir, you gotta get down here and see this for yourself. This guy, Jack, he's hyperventilating, and he looks like he's been used for target practice."

Chapter 46

Victor missed target practice. He was not sure why his meditation had taken him to that time in his life, but he found himself wrapped in his memories of gun clubs and archery ranges. He was a frequent face at both places but had not been for years. Since his fake identification had come into question on one of his visits, he had never gone back.

His apartment was still bathed in darkness and Victor felt marginally calmed after his rumination. He still felt a nagging sense of failure, so he tried to focus on the future and not the past but the remnants of the past night with the look-alike girl still invaded his memory. He had been deceived. He thought the universe had rewarded him but instead he had become a victim of the trickery of fate. He had been on the cusp of rightfully claiming what he felt was his, but it was dangled in front of him like a cheap toy and suddenly pulled away.

Victor slipped out of his Zen state. His feeling of agitation came back slowly and started to build. He knew it was only a matter of time before his current mood morphed into consummate rage and he would need to satiate his urge.

He could see the light crackling in the corner of the room, like a thunderstorm was getting ready to send a bolt of lightning into the horizon. Victor could smell the electricity and he pictured the massive bolt exploding through the ceiling and into the floor in the corner of his living room. The bolt was so powerful that it fractured into several smaller arcs of lightning that slowly moved towards Victor. Suddenly he was surrounded by light and he could feel the electric current running through his body. As quickly as it came, the light was gone but the burning smell remained. Apart from a few pinpoints of light, Victor was once again in the dark.

His rage was so intense it startled him. His obsession with the girl and his recent failure to kill Martin Lancaster had weakened him and he hated that feeling. His breathing was labored, and his face was beaded with sweat. Victor knew he had to pull himself together and formulate a plan. His urge to be at his warehouse was strong and he knew he needed to get ready for the girl. Her death was going to be sweet torture for him and pure Hell for her and he had much planning to do before he welcomed her to the warehouse and to her final moments on this Earth.

He gathered the few items he needed from the apartment and went to the basement. His car was just as he left it and he removed the canvas cover, folded it neatly and opened the trunk. A few tools were neatly stored in a plastic travel bin and Victor put the cover on top of them. The trunk closed without much sound and Victor climbed into the driver's seat. The car came to life as he revved the engine, and he pushed the button on his remote control to lift the garage door.

Within minutes, he was on the highway and cruising at an average speed, so he did not attract any attention to himself. The off-ramp lay just ahead, and Victor steered the car to the right and began to head North. His warehouse was another thirty minutes from the city and he drove in absolute silence apart from the sound of the vehicles around him. He stayed to the right in case he felt threatened and wanted to exit the highway in a hurry.

The further North Victor got, the more the traffic thinned. When he was ten minutes from his exit, Victor shared the road with only one other vehicle that was ahead of him and travelling at a much faster speed. After watching its taillights wane in the distance, Victor looked ahead to his right and saw him. On the side of the highway, thumb in the air, a hitchhiker was about eighty yards ahead and Victor immediately took his foot off the gas. The man stood out like a beacon under a sputtering streetlamp. His was the only car on the highway and this man, Victor was sure, was fate's way of giving him back his confidence.

His car pulled smoothly onto the shoulder of the road and stopped about twenty feet past the solitary traveler. Victor watched him in his rear-view mirror as the man jogged towards the passenger door. The door opened and Victor's mood became suddenly elevated. He did not smile, but merely nodded as the man lowered himself into the passenger seat.

Breathing heavily, the hitchhiker said, "Thanks so much, man. I think you were my last hope tonight and it would have been a long walk."

Victor simply nodded and, as soon as the door was closed, he put his foot down on the accelerator. Both Victor and his new passenger were pushed back into their seats as the man struggled to put on his seat belt.

"I'm not sure where you're headed, but I'm just going North. I just need to get out of the city, you know?" The rider soon realized that Victor was not going to make small talk and he turned his head towards the side window to watch the world go by.

Victor stared ahead and realized that his exit was coming up sooner than he thought. He let the car slow down slightly and began to pull the car to the right. His passenger looked perplexed as he realized his journey North was quickly turning into a journey East. As the man leaned closer to Victor and opened his mouth to speak, Victor slammed his fist into the man's temple. He watched, and listened, as the man's skull connected with the glass and bounced back. The sound was like a basketball slamming into the backboard. The man's chin met his chest, and he was unconscious.

Victor maneuvered the car along the familiar dirt roads as the man's breath rattled in his nose and mouth. It was disturbing Victor's usually silent drive, but it would not be long before they were at the warehouse. He could see the smoke ahead and knew the occupants of the farmhouse were burning again. It seemed to Victor that every time he drove by, they were burning something and as he got closer to their property, he could see the flames licking the latest pieces of furniture and random junk on the pile. Scattered pieces of ash blew past the car as Victor drove by their driveway and he could smell the fetid stench of burning rubber and wood mixed. They were nowhere to be seen, as Victor anticipated, so nobody even knew Victor was in the area.

After several more kilometers, Victor's driveway appeared, and he turned the wheel to the left a little more aggressively than he meant to causing his passenger's skull to collide with the passenger window once again. The blow was not as hard as the first time, but it helped to convince Victor that his quarry was still passed out. Gravel flew in random patterns behind the car as Victor picked up his speed and fishtailed down the driveway. He knew this road well and knew that no other vehicles would be on it so he could drive as quickly as he desired. When he saw the warehouse

The Waking Hours

looming ahead, Victor opened the garage door with his remote and pulled into the parking bay. The door quietly closed behind him.

Without wanting his guest to awaken before Victor had a chance to restrain him, he pulled the man from the car and threw him over his shoulder in a fireman's carry. The man issued no sound apart from his now labored breathing as his diaphragm was resting on Victor's shoulder. Victor made his way into his hidden chamber and sat the man on the floor against the wall. He lowered the shackles from their position and secured both of the man's wrists in the metal cuffs. With the flick of a switch, the sound of the pulley engine roared to life and chains were pulled into the machine. With every link of chain that was consumed by the machine, the man's body slowly inched off the floor. The jerking motion and the sound of the machine promptly brought the man back to consciousness as his arms were pulled above his head and he was being drawn up from the floor with significant force.

His scream came as no surprise to Victor, but the shrill cry would never escape the four walls that contained him. Victor waited until the man was fully upright with his arms stretched well over his head. He turned off the machine and watched as the man made a vain attempt to free his arms. Before the man could ascertain that his legs were free, Victor quickly grabbed his right leg, putting his ankle into Victor's home-made boot shackle. Without the use of his right leg for leverage, his left leg was useless, so Victor had no trouble shackling the left leg.

Victor stood back and admired his work. This was the first time he had used his newest invention and he was pleased thus far. The man was held in place with each of his limbs in a manacle stretching him out to look like a giant X. The man had not made a sound since the first scream. He stared intently at Victor, almost resigned to the fact that he knew he was going to die. Victor stared back for a few moments and got close enough to the man to look him in the eyes. The two brown eyes met his gaze and a single tear slid down the man's cheek.

Victor did not want to hear this man plead for his life so he left the room to change his clothes and get the tools he would need. He stripped out of his day clothes and hung them in the locker. He gowned himself like a surgeon and went to his bow rack. He picked up his compound bow and seven arrows and headed back to see how his guest was doing. When he entered the room, the man took one look at Victor's mask and his eyes became riveted on the bow. He noticed the stream of urine as the man wet his pants and then passed out.

Victor would have had much more fun had the man remained conscious. He did not know how long the kid would take to wake up and Victor's appetite for death was bordering on irrational. He placed the arrow shaft on the arrow rest and raised the bow. He pulled the arrow back until his hand was beside his jaw, just below his ear. He enjoyed feeling the tension of the bow. Victor was pleased to see the man begin to regain some of his cognizance and he released his grip on the arrow, watching it go through the man's abdomen and stick into the wall.

The man's scream hung in the air and finally fell to the ground as the first sign of blood began to seep into his shirt. Victor loaded the next arrow and took aim. The second arrow hit the other side of the abdomen but must have hit an artery. Blood rushed from the wound, saturating his clothing, and began to pool around the man's shackled foot. Victor knew his prey would be dead soon from the loss of blood so he fired as many arrows as he could while the man still had any strength to struggle. The last two arrows went into his chest, one into each pectoral muscle and the dead man's head hung in defeat.

Victor removed his mask and sat down to admire his work. He had not lost his touch at all. He had just hit a slight bump in his road. He was in no rush to dispose of the body. He was sure he would come back to look at his success a few times before the night was over. He got up from the chair and moved in front of the man, careful not to step in the pools of blood. Victor wanted to see his eyes one more time, so he grabbed a handful of the man's hair and lifted his head up. Staring back at Victor was one blue eye and one green eye.

Victor let go of the hair and watched the man's head drop back onto his chest. He abruptly changed his plans. He wanted this man's body out of his warehouse and as far away from him as possible. He grabbed two of his large tarps and laid them on the floor. One by one, he pulled the arrows out of the man's body, releasing him from the wall. He removed the boot shackles and let the machine lower the body back onto the floor. Victor removed the handcuffs and dragged the man's body onto the tarp, tossing the arrows beside him.

The Waking Hours

After he had tightly wrapped the hitchhiker in the tarps, Victor carried him back to the car and threw him in the trunk. He was not worried about fingerprints or anyone being able to trace the tarp or the arrows to Victor. They were both very standard items that could be purchased in any sporting goods store. Victor turned off all the lights in the warehouse and backed the car out of the parking bay. The moonless night was dark, but the sky was littered with stars. Victor watched the garage door close. He would have to come back soon to clean up his mess, but it would not be tonight.

Chapter 47

Gunner ignored the mess on his dining room table and quickly shook the cobwebs from his brain. He was anxious to get to the station to see what had happened to Jack while he was locked in his cell. He grabbed his keys and jumped into his car. He had no concerns about how early it was, so he flipped on the lights and the sirens as he backed out of his garage. His car jumped the curb and the tires screeched as he shifted the car into drive and took off down the road. He was sure half the neighborhood was now awake as well, but he had more important things to care about.

Since the traffic had not really begun, Gunner made it to the precinct in record time. His stride was long and meaningful as he passed the night guard without so much as a wave. As he reached the entrance to the holding cell area, he held up his badge and was buzzed in. Jack was in the end cell, so Gunner had to go around the corner before he saw him. Jack was drenched in sweat and his breathing had slowed from his earlier hyperventilating to almost normal. He was tenderly rubbing his wrists and Gunner noticed his shirt was slightly opened. When he was facing Jack head on from the other side of the bars, Jack opened his shirt so Gunner could get a look at his latest wounds. There were seven bruises, each about 4 millimeters in diameter, five on his abdomen and one on either side of his chest.

Gunner signaled the guard to open the cell door. As soon as he heard the lock disengage, Gunner entered the cell to get a better look at Jack's wounds. He was no forensic expert, but Gunner had seen enough holes in bodies to know that these marks were made with an arrow and not a bullet. Nothing looked cauterized and there was a slight X to indicate the tip of an arrow had penetrated the skin. Gunner pulled out his iPhone and took some pictures to add to Jack's journal.

The Waking Hours

"Do you remember anything?" Gunner hoped Jack's clarity would be better than some of his other dreams.

"It's like it always is, I seem to enter the dream in the middle." Jack rubbed each wrist three times. "From where I start remembering, I was already cuffed and standing up and I couldn't move my feet." He paused and said, "I think I left something behind."

Gunner listened and made mental notes as Jack described as many details as he could. The killer never spoke and was completely covered in a gown and mask. Jack had no idea where he was. The only thing he could remember was a very sterile white room and the feeling of intense pain in his stomach. His hand moved gently over his lacerations three times as he spoke. When Jack finished speaking, Gunner held up his phone so Jack could see the picture of his wounds.

"I'm not an authority on this stuff, but it looks like this guy used a bow and arrow." Gunner noted Jack's reaction to the image on Gunner's cell phone as he realized the sadistic bastard had created a smiley face with the positioning of his shots.

Jack slumped back onto the cot and Gunner noticed Jack pulling the sides of his shirt together three times. Gunner now had more of an understanding of the clues left behind at the crime scenes. Jack suffered from OCD and did things in a succession of threes. Gunner left the holding cell and locked Jack back in, now for his safety more than Gunner's original worry that Jack was the killer. Since each cell had a small camera in the corner, Gunner was eager to watch the surveillance video of Jack's cell the previous night to watch what exactly happened. All the video equipment was in the back corner of the evidence room for safe keeping. After signing himself in and showing his badge, Gunner made his way to the back and told the officer at the desk what video he was looking for. Within minutes, Gunner was sitting at a desk watching Jack as he slept in the cell. Apart from a few slight movements of Jack turning from side to side on the cot, nothing seemed out of the ordinary, so he forwarded through the boring stuff.

Without warning, Jack sat upright on the bed. Gunner's eyes grew wide, his head moved closer to the monitor and he was captivated by what he saw on the screen. Jack's eyes remained closed, like he was still asleep, and Gunner watched as Jack's head flung to the right, seemed to connect with something solid and his chin fell to his chest. Jack's body remained upright and sat this way for more than twenty minutes. His body swayed slightly and reminded Gunner of watching someone sleep in a moving car. Gunner's eyes were glued to the screen, not wanting to miss a moment of this macabre show.

After what felt like an eternity to Gunner, Jack's body slumped forward and seemed to swing back and forth. Jack remained asleep. After another seven or eight minutes, Jack's body sat upright again but his chin was still on his chest. His arms slowly moved upwards and came to rest, fully extended like he was stretching while he yawned. Gunner almost jumped out of his seat as Jack's head snapped up to a normal position. Jack's eyes remained closed, but Gunner sensed that he was petrified. He could not see it clearly from the poor quality of the video, but Gunner could swear he could see Jack's eyes moving frantically under his eyelids.

The show continued and Gunner watched as Jack went, almost mechanically, from a sitting to a standing position. Jack's arms remained in the air and his legs were now splayed. He stood in the middle of his cell, still asleep, and waited for his new torture to begin. Gunner was captivated by what he was seeing. As the video continued, Jack's body began to react to the arrows being shot into this abdomen. His body twitched and bent slightly forward in reaction to the pain from the first shot. Since Jack's body in the cell still had his shirt on, there were no immediate signs of trauma, but Gunner would stake his life on the fact that Jack's wounds were somehow physically materializing under his shirt as they happened.

Gunner knew that the second shot was the fatal blow. The arrow must have hit a major artery because Jack's body became morbidly inanimate after only a second of being hit. Somehow Jack seemed to hang from the shackles in his dream while remaining upright in the cell. Gunner had no idea how this was happening, but he was watching it with his own two eyes. Jack's body scarcely moved as the last five arrows were shot into his torso, but Gunner knew the velocity of the shot would make the corpse react with the impact.

The Waking Hours

Moments after Gunner figured the last arrow was shot, Jack's body twitched seven times and then moved slowly downwards and, once again, was sitting on the side of the cot in his cell. His arms remained above his head and ultimately were lowered down to his sides. Jack was slumped down on the side of his bed, still alive in his cell but dead in his dream.

Gunner did not think he had blinked once during the last ten minutes of watching Jack's dream. He had just witnessed something he would have never thought possible. Just as he was about to stop the video, Gunner noticed Jack's right hand begin to spasm. The rest of Jack's body remained listless, but his right hand moved erratically until it was down beside his right thigh. Jack's fingers made irregular motions on the cot and his hand lifted to his torso. With a quick movement, Jack's index finger seemed to draw a line on his stomach. The convulsive action happened two more times and Gunner now knew what Jack meant when he said he thought he had left something behind. True to his OCD nature, Jack had tried to leave three marks as a message for whomever would eventually figure out what the Hell was going on.

Just as Gunner was about to get up, Jack's head lifted and, although he still seemed to be asleep, his eyes were wide open. Gunner turned the video off and leaned back in his chair. He knew he needed to get back to his house to go through each of the recent murder files with a fine-toothed comb, but he could not leave Jack behind. Somehow, Jack was a key to this whole thing and leaving him in a cell would not benefit either one of them. Gunner copied the video so he could later show it to Jack and went to fill out the necessary paperwork to release Jack into his custody. Jack was going to spend a few nights with Gunner, whether he liked it or not.

When Gunner approached Jack with the idea of going home with him, he was met with much less resistance than he expected. Jack seemed relieved to know that he was not crazy and someone else believed what was happening. Jack wanted to get to the bottom of this as much as Gunner did and Gunner was keen to see what may happen next.

It was only seven in the morning but before they left the precinct, Gunner buzzed the office to see if any new bodies had turned up. So far, there had been no new reports. Any other police officer would have thought that was a blessing, but Gunner was disappointed he did not have a corpse to tie into Jack's latest dream. He grabbed one last file from his desk then he and Jack left together and made their way to Gunner's house.

It was still early but Gunner could see his neighbors through their windows as he passed by in the cruiser. Most of the houses had their lights on to battle the blackness of the sky. Gunner was guessing they had been awake for a few hours since he blasted the sirens when he left the house. Jack did not seem to notice Gunner smiling as they pulled into his driveway.

They entered the house and Jack was immediately drawn to the white boards in Gunner's kitchen. He stood in front of the first board taking in all the details that were written under each case name. John Doe had been shot at point blank range. Subconsciously, Jack's right index finger made three small circles on his forehead as he continued reading Gunner's notes. He also noticed the green towel hanging on one of the boards.

When he got to the end of the last file Jack turned to face Gunner and asked, "How the Hell is this possible?"

Jack could sense that Gunner was apprehensive, and he could see Gunner's right hand slightly twitching above the holster on his belt that held his revolver. His finger was ready to flip the release and draw that weapon in a second if it were required. Jack could not blame him for being suspicious. He stood unmoving and Gunner's hand finally relaxed by his side.

Gunner opened the fridge door as he responded to Jack, "I have no fuckin' idea, but I need to eat. Want some bacon and eggs?"

Jack nodded, subconsciously rubbing his wounds, and sat down as Gunner whipped up some breakfast. They ate in silence, both concentrating on the information Gunner had been compiling. The only noise interrupting their reticence was the sound of the wind picking up and a few raindrops pelting off the shingles. The sky was black, and the tops of the trees moved in frenzied patterns as the storm blew closer to the house. The rain became heavy and the flashes of lightning cast eerie shadows on the walls of Gunner's kitchen. Gunner was the first to break the dead air.

The Waking Hours

"I brought home the recording of you in the cell last night. I want you to watch it to see if it triggers any more memories."

Jack shoved the last piece of bacon in his mouth and said, "I'll do anything at this point if you think it can help."

Gunner picked up the plates, put them in the kitchen sink and pointed Jack to the living room. Thunder rumbled in the distance as Gunner loaded the disc into his DVD player. The television came to life and instantly Jack was watching himself sleeping on the cot in his cell. The rain was heavier now, and Jack could hear the drops pinging on the aluminum overhang at the front of Gunner's house. Neither of them spoke a word. They both watched as Jack slept soundly in his jail cell. Once again, Gunner forwarded the video to the time that he knew the action started.

The turbulence of the impending storm had increased, and the rumble of the thunder was beginning to shake the house. Both men were still focused on the recording of Jack sleeping. Thunder sounded again like it was directly above the house and the first bolt of lightning struck just as the video showed Jack's body forcefully going into a standing position from the cot in the cell. It was like watching Frankenstein come to life. Gunner and Jack were both startled by the crack of lightning hitting so close but thankfully the power remained on and they continued to watch the animation Jack was performing while asleep. Jack struggled to remember even a small detail from last night that he had not told Gunner already, but he could not recall anything else.

Gunner switched off the TV, looked at Jack and said, "I want you to stay here for a couple of nights. I will set up a camera here and you can sleep on the couch. Let's see if we can figure out what the Hell is going on and catch this bastard."

Gunner's land line rang, and he went to the kitchen to answer it. After only a few seconds he hung up and turned to find Jack staring at the white boards again and leafing through the files on the table. Jack picked up the file that Gunner had brought with him. From what Jack could tell, it had nothing to do with the recent murders. It was a case about a teenage boy who had disappeared well over a decade ago. Gunner had just hung up the phone and Jack was about to question him about the relevance of the missing kid when Gunner spoke first.

"We gotta go. They found a body wrapped in a tarp in the ravine across town. I don't have any more details yet, but this could be our guy."

Gunner grabbed his coat and headed for the garage with Jack following close behind, still holding on to the file. The car rocketed out of the garage as Gunner switched on the lights and the siren.

Gunner looked at Jack with a sly smile and said, "The neighbors love this!"

"I'll bet," Jack said dubiously.

Jack's attention was not on Gunner's antics. His thoughts were focused on the crime scene they were headed to and the file he held in his hands. As Gunner raced the cruiser along the expressway, Jack read about the disappearance of Maxwell Anderson Beckett. Gunner glanced over and noticed Jack was skimming the notes.

"His sister came into the station today asking us to reopen the investigation, Charlotte something or other," said Gunner.

Jack's head snapped to the left as he said, "Did you just say Charlotte?"

Jack's words tumbled over each other to get out of his mouth as he told Gunner about meeting Charlotte in the park and being ninety-nine percent sure that she was the girl from the first dream he had recorded. As he was talking incessantly, Gunner had pulled his cell phone out of his pocket to call the station. In less than a minute, the day sergeant was patching Gunner's cell through to Charlotte's phone. As the phone started to ring on the other end, Gunner looked at Jack and said, "I don't believe in coincidences."

Chapter 48

Since she had Anna coming in to cover her shift at the store, Charlotte slept in and woke at nine to find Norman sitting beside her bed, staring intently at her cell phone on the nightstand. His nostrils flared and Charlotte could have sworn his head moved forward a few times, like he was willing the phone to ring. When it eventually did, Charlotte practically jumped out of her skin. Norman sat back and seemed pleased with himself as Charlotte picked it up.

Gunner's curt tone on the other end of the call was much more of a shock than Norman somehow being able to will the phone to ring in the first place. He did not give much pause for Charlotte to speak so she listened, got in a few 'uh-huhs' when he took a breath and then the line went dead without even giving Charlotte a chance to say goodbye.

She looked at Norman and said, "I don't know how you did that, but thank you."

She wanted to be at the police station when Gunner got back. She did not care if she sat there for hours so she skipped her shower, threw her hair into a bun, and pulled on some jeans and a light shirt. Charlotte was sure Norman would be able to wait to relieve himself on the way downtown, so she got herself ready, packed the few items Gunner had asked her to bring and took some food for Norman. She had no idea how long she was going to be there, and she did not want Norman to go hungry. For the first time in a while, Charlotte left the apartment with a smile on her face.

Although the walk would have only taken thirty minutes, Charlotte wanted to get there as soon as she could. Gunner had said he was on his way to a crime scene and may be a while, but Charlotte was unconcerned. She hailed a cab and she and Norman got in and headed downtown. Norman did not display the usual canine behavior of wanting to stick his head out the window. Instead, he sat in the middle of the back seat and focused intently through the windshield as the cab driver adeptly maneuvered through the traffic. Charlotte could swear Norman was leaning into the turns as the cab changed lanes.

They pulled up in front of the police station shortly after ten and took a seat in the waiting room after Charlotte explained she was waiting for Gunner. Norman sat at Charlotte's feet, waiting to protect her should the need arise.

Hours went by and Charlotte and Norman watched what seemed more like a reality television show than reality. Charlotte knew she had led a sheltered life but watching the diversity of people come and go from the station was mind boggling. She had once toyed with the idea of writing a book and this place would give her much fodder for character ideas.

Her train of thought was derailed as the mood in the station was instantly altered. The air felt like it had dropped ten degrees and Charlotte knew Gunner was back. Even the hair on the back of Norman's neck stood up as he felt the change in the mood as well. Charlotte gathered her things, holding the family photo album close to her, and waited to be summoned into his office. She could see him conversing with another man and once their brief conversation ended, she saw Gunner heading in her direction. She stood up, clutching the album, and Norman stood on all fours beside her.

"Hope you haven't been here too long." Gunner spoke rather gently as he pointed in the direction of his office.

Charlotte only shook her head, unsure of what to say, and she and Norman followed him into his office. She sat down and Norman sat beside her. They both watched him as Gunner moved around the desk and sat down to face her. Leaning forward, he laced his fingers together and rested his chin on his hands. Gunner stared at Charlotte for a few seconds, not sure where to start. He had not even begun to speak when Norman's head went up and he began to sniff the air. The dog did not seem agitated at all, but he was up on all fours and moving around the office trying to locate the source of whatever scent he had found. Gunner just assumed that the dog was smelling remnants from the lunchroom down the hall.

The Waking Hours

Charlotte watched Norman sniff the perimeter of the room and before she had realized the office door had been left ajar Norman had opened the door with his nose and was now in a canter halfway down the hall.

"Norman!" Charlotte called after him and chased him down the hall.

When she reached the door that Norman had entered, she stopped in her tracks. Norman was sitting at the feet of the man she had met in the park. Norman's tail was wagging, and Charlotte felt the blood rush to her cheeks. She was embarrassed to have such an adolescent reaction to seeing him again and before either of them could speak, Gunner was behind her.

"I believe the three of you have met before," said Gunner.

Jack stood up and introduced himself properly, "I'm Jack Brandon, we met in the park."

"Charlotte Beckett. And this is Norman," she pointed at the dog as she spoke.

Jack reached out to shake her hand. Charlotte did the same and when their hands met, the touch lingered longer than a standard greeting. Gunner watched the exchange and looked over at the dog. He could swear the dog was nodding. The four of them went back to Gunner's office and this time he closed the door.

"I'm confused. Do you know something about my brother?" Charlotte asked Jack.

Jack responded, "No. At least I don't think so but I'm not sure about anything anymore."

Gunner could see the look of puzzlement on Charlotte's face, so he took control of the conversation. He watched her facial expressions change from confusion to disbelief as he detailed the first murder and what had happened to Jack in his first dream. Jack's hand subconsciously went to his forehead three times, making a circular motion each time.

Charlotte interrupted Gunner and looked at Jack, "Wait, if you were in a dream and not really you, then how and why did I see you in my reality?"

"That is a very good question," said Jack.

When Gunner moved on to the young couple who were murdered in the park, Charlotte began to shake. Her memory of being so close to that crime scene still haunted her.

Her voice was a whisper, "I was in the park that night."

"What?" Gunner and Jack said at the same time.

"You may think I'm crazy, but I swear whoever killed those kids had been following me first. I had been walking home from work, like I always do through the park, and something startled me. Norman wasn't in my life at that point."

Jack and Gunner were both riveted.

Charlotte continued, "The park had gone completely silent, even the birds stopped chirping. I got out of there as fast as I could and kept checking to see if I had been followed."

"There's something you need to see," Gunner said.

Gunner looked around his office and realized the files were all still at his house.

"We need to take a road trip. Are you willing to come to my house? Norman is welcome," said Gunner.

The Waking Hours

Gunner flipped on the cherries and the sirens again and sped off down the expressway. Charlotte and Norman sat in the back seat and Norman seemed thrilled by the noise and the lights. Once again, he sat in the middle of the seat so he could see everything that was going on around him. There was not much conversation in the car. Jack was trying to figure out how he and Charlotte had been able to see each other and Charlotte was trying to think of anything other than that night in the park.

When they reached Gunner's house, Norman sniffed as much as he could before they went inside. He seemed content that no danger lurked in the shadows and found a spot on the kitchen floor as Charlotte and Jack settled into the chairs. Gunner had gone through the files and pulled the one he wanted Charlotte to see, dropping it on the table in front of her.

When Charlotte opened the file, she did a double-take. The picture attached to the file looked just like her. She was about to ask who the girl was, but Gunner spoke first.

"Sally Michaels," he said. "She was a prostitute in the Beaches. Like I said to Jack, I do not believe in coincidences. The two of you look like identical twins."

As she continued to stare at the picture of Sally Michaels, Charlotte listened as Gunner told her about all the murders and Jack's subsequent dreams until it ended with the homicide this morning and the man wrapped in a tarp. Gunner had known that the body they found this morning was the same one from Jack's dream. The unknown man's torso had shown the same marks as Jack had on his abdomen and had the three lines drawn in blood that Jack had left behind.

When Charlotte began to question the validity of Jack being at the crime scene in his dream, Jack turned to her and opened his shirt. Charlotte could see the faint bruises on Jack's stomach and chest, and she slumped backwards into her chair in disbelief. As her eyes went from the files to the white boards, the green towel caught and held her attention and she quickly sat upright. She could see the embroidered letter B on the bottom of the towel, and she could barely breathe. Charlotte could hardly make her words loud enough for Gunner and Jack to hear them.

"Where.........where did you get that towel?" she asked as she pointed to it.

Gunner stared at her for a minute and could see the blood had drained from her face. Jack was staring at her as well and Norman had moved over to sit beside her. Sensing her agitation, Norman put his head in her lap and she unwittingly began to pat his head for comfort.

Charlotte almost whispered her next words, "I had a dream that Max had shown up on the doorstep of my childhood home with a strange man who was soaking wet. I gave the stranger that towel."

Jack was now the one having trouble speaking, "A young girl gave that towel to me in my dream."

"That was me," said Charlotte.

"And I was with Max?" asked Jack.

"Yes," answered Charlotte. A single tear carved its way down her cheek.

Gunner was speechless for the first time in decades and for a few minutes nobody said a word. Each of them was lost in their thoughts and trying to figure out how any of this was possible. Gunner went to the cupboard and grabbed a bottle of red wine and three glasses. This was going to be an interesting afternoon and a little libation would certainly help to calm everyone's nerves. Charlotte and Jack willingly accepted the drink and sipped in silence. Charlotte was still patting Norman and realized he had not eaten yet today. She asked Gunner for a bowl and poured his kibble in, letting him enjoy his dinner in the corner of the kitchen.

"May I," Charlotte asked Jack, pointing at his journal.

"Be my guest," Jack responded.

Charlotte picked up the journal and started from the beginning as she paced the kitchen. Gunner and Jack were still sitting at the kitchen table, each still lost in their thoughts. Charlotte flipped through the pages of Jack's journal and froze as her eyes focused on the word Jack had written in the margin of the page. She took the book over to Jack and pointed at the word.

"Why did you write this?" she asked, still feeling short of breath.

"I remembered that name from one of my dreams," Jack replied. "Why? Do you know him?"

Charlotte responded through tears, "Max used to call me Charlie when we were kids."

Charlotte sat down and took a gulp of her wine. She told Jack and Gunner about the day she had walked home from work and heard someone whisper the name Charlie but there had been nobody near her when she heard it. Jack responded with his story about hearing the name Charlie again when he had been in his kitchen. Gunner reacted by getting up and grabbing his bottle of single malt Scotch and three tumblers. Wine was not going to cut it today.

Since Charlotte was not a big drinker, she stuck to the wine while the men swirled their Scotch in their glasses. Gunner mentioned the video of Jack's dream the previous night and Charlotte wanted nothing more than to watch it. The three of them, followed by Norman, went into the living room and Gunner turned on the show. Gunner and Jack watched with slight interest to see if there was anything they had missed but Charlotte and Norman were engrossed in the show. There was no lightning this time when Jack came to life but the reaction from Norman and Charlotte was just the same. She marveled at how Jack's body had seemingly become a marionette in his sleep. Norman's head turned from side to side each time Jack's body moved.

When the recording ended, Charlotte noticed Jack's fingers caressing his wounds in patterns of three. She had noted earlier when she was looking at the whiteboards that some clues were left behind in patterns of threes and she asked Jack about it. He explained his obsessive quirk and seemed to be embarrassed by it, but Gunner quickly interjected and told Jack that he was convinced those clues would eventually help to tie all the murders together.

Gunner had gone to the kitchen to fill his tumbler and grabbed Max's file on his way out. He sat in his armchair and leafed through the limited information as Charlotte and Jack made small talk. The case was so cold that Gunner did not know where to begin. Max's disappearance had happened seventeen years ago. For all Gunner knew, the kid could have run away and was now living in Vancouver.

He read the physical description of Max and almost spilled his Scotch as he lifted the file closer to his face. He looked at the file and then he looked at Jack. His eyes went back and forth a few times before Charlotte and Jack took notice and stopped making idle chitchat.

Gunner said, "Remember when I said I don't believe in coincidences?"

Charlotte, Jack, and Norman all nodded.

Gunner looked at Jack and said, "You and Max both have one blue eye and one green eye. This just gets weirder by the minute."

Charlotte had been too shy to really make eye contact with Jack but now she stared into his eyes like she was trying to bore a hole in the back of his head. Jack could feel all the eyes in the room on him and he began to fidget in his seat. He took a long haul of the Scotch.

"That has to mean something, doesn't it?" Jack's question was directed at Charlotte.

"I hope so," she said.

As Gunner looked at Charlotte sitting across from him, he knew she was in danger. If this was the guy Charlotte ran from in the park, he could still be looking for her and now killing girls who remind him of Charlotte until he finds her. Gunner's house was going to be busier than it ever had been, and he insisted that Charlotte and Norman stay with him as well. There was no hesitation in her acceptance and Norman showed his gratitude by putting his head in Gunner's lap. Gunner told her he would escort her to her apartment tomorrow to get the things she would need for the next few days and showed her to the spare bedroom downstairs. Jack would take the couch.

Gunner also began to make a list of the things he would need to record Jack while he slept. Since he had already had a few drinks, he called the station and requested the equipment be delivered to his house. He ordered pizza for everyone and they spent the rest of the afternoon and early evening going over the files and trying to find a pattern or anything that could tie the murders together. They were not all trained detectives but, including Norman, four sets of eyes were better than one.

Chapter 49

Victor was more than curious about the different sets of eyes in his victims. He could not explain to himself how it was possible, but he was certainly going to be more diligent about paying attention the next time he took a life. It was almost like someone else was in there, watching him, robbing him of his moment to be the only person there when his prey finally succumbed to his whim.

He had not replaced his cell phone since the Martin Lancaster fiasco. He did not want another paid job that played by anyone else's rules but his need to kill was intense. He felt an electric charge running through his veins and all his senses were heightened. He could think about nothing more than the girl from the park. His want had turned to need, and that need was primal. He needed to hunt.

He had been at his warehouse for several hours, cleaning the mess he had made the evening prior. He had made sure his return was inconspicuous by driving back in the middle of the night. Now, looking at all the tools he had on hand only made his urge to kill that much stronger. He packed a few items into his trunk and locked the warehouse.

It was still early, and dusk was just introducing itself today so he assumed his departure would go unnoticed as well. His car made the familiar right turn onto the dirt road and he sped along towards the highway. Victor could see the billows of smoke coming from the neighboring barn, but the plumes were much larger and much darker than Victor had ever seen them. He was so busy staring at the smoke that Victor did not immediately register the flashing lights on the road ahead. There were a few cars ahead of him, already stopped, and he could see a car slowly coming up behind him. The police had blocked the road down to one lane to control the safety of the cars passing and Victor was trapped.

Until now, nobody had seen Victor or his car, so he felt a slight panic, but he was not sure why. He had nothing to hide, now, and he was not

The Waking Hours

doing anything to draw attention to himself, but his car was something people would remember. There were not many shiny white 1976 Cadillac Deville's on the road these days and Victor was hoping there were not too many car buffs on the road at this time of the morning. His body shifted uneasily on his red leather seats.

Traffic had now stopped completely so Victor had a chance to see what was going on. The neighbors had added one too many pieces of old furniture to their burn pile and the wind had shifted, sending sparks into their barn. Victor watched the flames lick the walls of the barn as the fire department tried to get it under control. The water from the fire hose did its best to battle the blaze and the monstrous inferno was putting up a good fight. Victor could hear the glass exploding from the windows as the flames continued to macerate the old wooden structure.

When the police officer who was directing traffic deemed it safe to pass, the cars ahead began to move, and Victor put the Cadillac back into drive. The line was slow moving and when Victor reached the cop holding the traffic sign, he could see the man admiring his car. They made eye contact, although briefly, and Victor could see the officer's surprise at the size of the man in the driver's seat. Victor quickly looked back to the road and drove past. He had begun to sweat and wanted nothing more than to get back to his apartment and cover up his car in the basement of his apartment building.

For the remainder of his drive, Victor could think of nothing more than the numerous ways he would use to torture the girl from the park before he let her die. He could understand how some killers would feel sexually aroused by the thought of taking a life but, for Victor, it had nothing to do with sex. Murder was simply about power and the ability to take the most important thing from another human being, life.

Lately, Victor's thoughts had often turned to his own mortality. He was convinced that he was going to be on this earth for a long time because of the number of divine breaths he had inhaled as his victims exhaled for the last time. Victor knew that part of their dying energy was absorbed by him. He always felt invigorated afterwards and attributed the surge of emotion to the passing of energy from their death to his life.

He had been so lost in his daydreams of killing and energy that Victor had not realized that he was on the highway. Daylight had won the battle over the dusk and the sky had become much brighter. Victor could still see traces of the thick, black smoke from the barn in his rear-view mirror as he drove towards his apartment. Traffic was steadily increasing as the daily commuters joined the struggle to fight the traffic to make it to work on time. Victor did not have to be anywhere at a particular time, but he did want to get his car off the road. The delay at the barn cost him thirty minutes of time and he could have missed most of the morning commuter traffic. He could see the looks of the drivers passing him as they admired his car. The Cadillac was in pristine condition and stood out from the myriad number of newer cars on the road.

Victor saw his exit approaching sooner than he realized and he pulled the car to the right without checking his blind spot. He heard the horn before he felt the black Mazda graze the back quarter panel of the Caddy. The driver of the Mazda had pulled too hard on his steering wheel, over-corrected and bounced off the guardrail on the right. The black car then ricocheted back into traffic and collided with several other cars. Victor put his foot down on the gas pedal and fled the scene of the accident. There was no license plate on the car so he would not have to worry about the cops tracking him down, but the Cadillac would be out of commission now that it had been seen and been involved in a collision. He would have to ditch the car and come up with a back-up plan.

The West side of the city had an abandoned building in the middle of nowhere that Victor had passed many times. He was not sure if it had already been slated for demolition but, if it had, he was going to expedite the process. He kept to the quieter streets as much as possible to avoid any more eyes seeing his car. He pulled under the covered parking area with the passenger side of the car as close to the wall as he could and shut off the engine. He gathered his tools from the trunk, shoved them into his backpack and pulled his pistol from its holster under his jacket. The heat of the day was steadily increasing but Victor required the jacket to conceal the weapon. When he was more than twenty feet from the car, Victor took his shooter's stance and aimed at the back of the Cadillac. The first bullet sounded as if it hit the body of the car. Victor could not smell the gas, but he knew he had successfully hit the gas tank when he could see the liquid slowly pooling below the trunk. He found a shaded area and waited for about fifteen minutes.

The Waking Hours

He glanced around before he pulled the pistol out one last time. The vapor to air ratio should have been enough to spark the gas into a fire so Victor raised his arm and fired his second shot onto the pavement by the puddle of gas. He waited to see if his aim had been successful and was satisfied when he saw the orange glow lapping at the gas pool. The spark from the bullet hitting the concrete was enough to ignite the vapor so Victor picked up his bag and continued to walk away from the car. The explosion was not immediate. It took a few minutes for the flames to feed on the gas and become hot enough to affect the gas tank, but the resulting blast would be enough to destroy the car and anything Victor may have left behind. Fingerprints were not an issue since Victor was not in any system that would make him identifiable, so he strolled away from his car and made the long trip home. Victor entered the wooded area just to the East of the lone building that was now becoming a victim to the flames that had enveloped Victor's car. As he entered the cover of the trees, the birds stopped chirping and there were no discernable animal sounds in the dense cover of the bush. The only noise in the woods was the snapping twigs under Victor's feet as he walked along the path. Victor's thumb subconsciously spun the gold ring on his finger for the entire journey.

The overhanging branches had added some time to Victor's walk home. Once he made it back to civilization and meandered the back streets, the walk to his apartment had taken just under five hours. Victor was drenched in sweat by the time he climbed the stairs to let himself into the lobby and his finger was raw from spinning his ring. He ignored the guard on duty and went straight to the elevator. Once he was back in his apartment, Victor stripped out of his clothes and took a shower. The cold water felt like small daggers piercing his hot skin, but it made him feel rejuvenated.

Since he had not eaten in the last twenty-four hours, he stood in the kitchen and scarfed down some cold leftovers. When he felt satiated, he sat down cross-legged on his living room floor. He wanted nothing more than to meditate and he hoped that some guiding spirit would lead him to where he could find the girl.

His visions during this meditation were unfamiliar and haunting. The girl was not in any of them. Instead, Victor saw the image of a man and a boy. Although Victor was sure the two were not related by blood, he knew they were connected. The details of their faces were distorted, and Victor strained in his reality to see them in their ambiguity. If Victor could have watched himself meditating, he would have seen that he was using his thumb to spin the ring around on his finger in a very agitated manner.

The images of the man and boy disappeared, and his vision was now focused on a small side street lined with trees. His eyes were closed but his head moved back and forth, as if he were looking up and down the street for something, or someone. It was an artsy community and each of the shops that lined the street had an eclectic awning or window display, making them stand out from each of the other shops on the street. He did not know what he would find there, but Victor knew he had to find this row of shops.

His vision faded and, as he was about to come out of his meditation, he heard the name Charlie and unexpectedly he pictured the girl. He could feel his heart rate increase, but his agitation lessened, and his thumb stopped moving the ring. He inhaled deeply and released his breath in a loud exhalation.

"Charlie," Victor spoke the name aloud and startled himself.

Victor was wide awake now and felt more focused than ever. He did not know where those shops were, but he knew it was his best chance at finding her. He stretched his legs before getting up from the floor and immediately went to his laptop. He typed a few key words into Google and tried to pinpoint the area of the city that he may be able to find this row of stores. He narrowed it down to a few different areas, jotted down the addresses and dressed for his newest quest.

Once outside, Victor hailed a cab and climbed in the back seat. Victor gave the driver the first address and they sped off down the street, narrowly missing a few red lights. He seemed pleased that the driver felt his sense of urgency and the speed of the ride would get them there sooner. Victor watched the neighborhoods as they raced by, eager to see if this first address would be the right one.

The Waking Hours

The driver turned off the main arteries and into some of the more diverse communities. The first address was not like Victor's vision at all. He was disappointed but he knew they would eventually find the spot he was looking for. There were two more hamlets on Victor's list and the cabby skillfully made his way back to the wider streets and accelerated around the traffic to find the next area on Victor's agenda. It was closer to what he had seen but still not exactly what he had received in his vision.

The third time was a charm and Victor's eyes grew bigger as they cruised down the tree-lined street. Something about this place was familiar and he asked the cabby to pull over. Victor threw some bills through the window and asked the driver to wait for a few minutes. The cabby counted the wad of cash and said, "You got it."

Victor lifted his head and smelled the air, like a dog catching a scent of an animal. He looked up and down the street and knew that she had been on this street. He walked in the direction he felt compelled to go, taking the time to look in each of the store windows as he went. When he reached the display in the antique store window, he stopped. This was it. He knew it, he felt it. He opened the door to the shop and expected to see her there. Instead, Victor was greeted by a petite blonde woman wearing a nametag that told him her name was Anna.

Victor spoke first before she could give him the sales preamble, "Do you have a guy named Charlie who works here?"

"No, we don't have any guys who work here. The owner's name is Charlotte," she replied.

"Does she go by the name Charlie?" Victor asked, hopeful that it was a nickname.

"Not that I know of," she said.

Victor turned towards the door. He took a moment to look back at the counter and tried to picture her there. Charlotte, he thought to himself. This was her store. And now Victor knew where to find her. Without saying a word, he left the store and got back into the waiting taxi.

"Is this it?" the driver asked.

"Nope, this isn't it," Victor lied.

Victor gave the cab driver an address close to his home address and began to formulate a plan in his head on the drive back. He was excited. He could almost imagine what it felt like to be a kid at Christmas, anticipating the opening of his present and his present would be Charlotte. His plan was unformed as to how he would get her but all of that would come to him. At least he knew where to find her, but he did not think he could wait that long. His urge to kill was too strong and he wanted to be able to control his urges, not be so hungry for death because, when he found her, he wanted to take his time with her. He needed to hunt tonight.

Chapter 50

Gunner knew they were on a hunt for a psychopath and the unusual method they were using to track a killer did not escape him. The surveillance equipment had arrived at his house in the early evening and he had set it up in the living room to face the couch. He put microphones close to where Jack's head would be so they could pick up any sounds Jack might make during his dream. The effects of the Scotch and the pizza had taken their toll and they were all exhausted.

Jack lay down on the couch, pulled a blanket over himself and tried to sleep. It was difficult with three sets of eyes staring intently at him as he drifted off, but the Scotch won the battle and soon Jack was breathing the heavy sighs of sleep. Charlotte watched for as long as she could, and her head eventually fell back into the wing-back chair she had been sitting in. Gunner lasted thirty minutes longer than Charlotte had and soon he was asleep in the matching chair. Norman was the only one still watching Jack as he slept. Every twitch Jack made, Norman leaned forward, ready for any evasive action he may have to manage. As Jack lay still on the couch, Norman eventually let himself fall asleep as well. If Jack made any sudden movement, Norman was sure he would sense it immediately and spring into action.

Morning came and Gunner was the first to wake up. Jack was lying on the couch in the same position he fell asleep in and Charlotte was snoring slightly in the chair beside him. Norman opened his eyes and wagged his tail at Gunner. Jack was still asleep, and Gunner got up to get a closer look at him. Jack did not show any physical signs of trauma and Gunner was almost disappointed. He was leaning over, getting close to Jack's face when Jack opened his eyes and yelled slightly. Waking up with a man hovering over his face was not something he had prepared for and it startled him. His yell woke Charlotte and the three other pairs of eyes in the room were all trained on Jack. They watched as he removed the blanket, lifted his sleeves, checked his chest, and even took off his socks to check his ankles. There were no marks on him at all and he did not remember dreaming about anything.

Gunner put on a pot of coffee and they all watched the video from the night before. Jack had not moved. If Gunner studied sleep patterns, he would have said Jack had the perfect night's sleep. Charlotte was bored by the video and went into the kitchen to make breakfast. She easily found all the things she needed and whipped up a batch of scrambled eggs, some bacon, and some toast. Gunner came in to move all the files from the table and the three of them ate breakfast at the kitchen table while Norman ate his breakfast in the corner.

It was late morning and Gunner had watched the video multiple times, convinced something had happened that they missed. When he had surrendered to the fact that Jack had gone nowhere, he drove Charlotte and Jack to their apartments to collect some things.

Now that they seemed to travel everywhere together, Jack, Gunner, Charlotte, and Norman all got into the elevator and headed up to Charlotte's apartment. After Charlotte had disengaged the lock, Gunner went in first with his service revolver in his hand. He did a quick sweep of the apartment while Jack and Norman stood ready to defend her in the hallway. Gunner gave the thumbs up and the three of them followed him into the apartment and shut the door.

Gunner's cell phone rang seconds after they had entered Charlotte's apartment. While not much was said on Gunner's end, Jack knew that some important information was being fed into Gunner's ear by the stern look on his face.

While Gunner was busy on his phone, Jack took a few moments to look at the pictures on the walls and the personal items Charlotte had on display. The apartment was tastefully decorated and extremely comfortable. As Jack went to the sliding door to look at her view, he noticed Norman in the corner of the room gathering a few of his things as well and leaving them in a pile for Charlotte to pack. Jack realized that Norman was much smarter than the average dog.

Charlotte emerged from her bedroom with a small carry-on bag. She noticed Norman's pile of toys on the floor and added them to her bag. Jack was dying to see where Charlotte slept but he felt uncomfortable about asking to see her bedroom. He did not know her that well and it seemed intrusive. He would have to settle for the snapshot he had in his mind about her quaint living room. Gunner was at the door waiting for them and peered through the peep hole before opening the door and making sure the hallway was empty.

As they left the apartment, Gunner looked at Jack and said, "You're not gonna believe this, but what you had wrapped in that tissue was a piece of Gord Keston's skin. It must have lodged under your nail when you made those marks on his hand."

Jack looked bewildered and said, "I'm glad the three of you are here to witness this because I still don't believe this is real."

They went through the same routine at Jack's apartment, but Jack was much more self-conscious about his living space, especially when the door opened, and his decrepit brown recliner was the first thing everyone saw. Charlotte could sense his embarrassment.

"Don't worry, mine was hiding in the bedroom," her hand grazed his upper arm to let him know she understood.

"At least it looks comfortable," said Gunner, nodding in the direction of the chair.

Jack smiled at them and hurried to gather the things he would need for the next few days. Charlotte did the same thing Jack had done and scanned Jack's apartment to see how he lived. She noticed the very strategically placed clay figurines and walked over to the sliding door to see his view. She saw the park below and the bench on which Jack first saw Norman. Jack still had not told Charlotte about that day. It was another implausible part of Jack's story that may require some wine to become believable.

When Jack emerged from his bedroom, Gunner was at Jack's front door. He did the scan of the hallway and the four of them were on their way. Gunner stopped at a grocery store and the four did some shopping. When one of the store clerks pointed at the dog, Gunner was quick to flash his badge and said, "service dog". Norman walked much more proudly than when he had first entered the store. Since Charlotte loved to cook, she and Norman were left in charge of the food shopping and the boys gathered the necessary accompaniments like wine, beer, and munchies.

Gunner pulled out his credit card and said the department would pick up the tab since Charlotte and Jack, and Norman, were assisting with an ongoing investigation. They all climbed back into the cruiser and headed back to Gunner's house. The conversation went back to the murders and Jack's dreams. Charlotte still could not understand how Jack was able to physically leave clues behind if he were not actually there. Nobody had a persuasive explanation as to how it was happening and suddenly Gunner sat up in his seat as he drove.

"I wonder if you are physically able to take something tangible into your dream and leave it behind at the crime scene," Gunner's words spilled out of his mouth.

"I guess it's worth a try," said Jack as he shrugged. "What did you have in mind?"

"I'm not sure yet, but we'll see what I have at the house, maybe something to remind the killer about one of the other murders. That would send a message," said Gunner.

"As long as it doesn't give him any tie to where we are now, I'm scared enough as it is," said Charlotte.

Norman could sense her unease and moved beside her, laying down on the back seat and putting his head in her lap. She stroked his head and ears, knowing if Norman could speak, he would tell her that he would protect her from everything.

Gunner pulled the car into the garage and they loaded their personal items and the bags of groceries into the house. Charlotte put away the groceries while Gunner went through any evidence he had from any of the crime scenes. He was keen to try a little experiment with Jack, hoping Jack would dream tonight so they could test his theory. He took one of the photos that forensics had taken at the first crime scene and showed it to Jack. Jack looked at the familiar single gunshot wound to the temple and his hand went to his forehead, making his usual three small circles.

"I want you to put this in your pocket before you go to sleep," said Gunner, "and see if you are able to leave it behind if anything happens to you tonight."

Jack nodded and tucked the photo into his pocket. He doubted he would be able to do it, but it was worth a shot. If they could catch this guy maybe Jack could go back to a normal life, at least as normal as he had been living and he would be forever grateful.

Since they skipped lunch, Charlotte figured an early dinner was not a bad idea. She took out the pork tenderloin and cut it into medallions, sprinkling them with salt and pepper and setting them aside. She began to work on her mushroom sauce and when Gunner smelled the onions cooking, he poured glasses of wine for everyone. Jack and Gunner came into the kitchen and chatted more about the most recent murder while Charlotte whipped up dinner. With the pan deglazed and the sauce reducing, Charlotte continued to make the rest of the preparations for dinner. The house smelled better than it had in years and Gunner realized he was happy to have company. He pushed the files aside and was surprised that he was more interested in getting to know Jack and Charlotte on a personal level than he was in looking at any more files.

Jack was the first to tell Gunner a bit more about himself. He skimmed over much of his past and quickly talked about his parents having passed on. He talked briefly about his real estate career, if he could call it that, and finally mentioned seeing Norman on the park bench below his balcony.

Charlotte spun around from the countertop she was using to make a salad, stared at Jack, and said, "Are you sure it was Norman?"

Jack nodded, "As sure as I am that he is sitting right here."

Norman seemed to be following the conversation and nodding in agreement with everything they were saying. Charlotte turned her sauce down to simmer, checked on the pork in the oven and proceeded to tell her story. She mentioned the antique store and could see Jack remembering the bits of his dream when he saw her in the store. She skipped over Max, since they both already knew the story, told them about her parents being killed in a car accident and her grandmother's Alzheimer's and recent passing and then she told them about finding Norman outside of her store. Gunner and Jack looked at each other and back at Charlotte. They had both assumed that Norman had been with Charlotte since he was a puppy. She explained how he had assertively led her away from the park on one of their walks and how he had insisted she go into the park the day she met Jack. All three humans were now staring intently at the dog. Norman smiled at them and met each one of their stares with a happy face and a wagging tail.

Jack asked Charlotte more questions about the day she met Norman. She explained how he seemed to be waiting outside the store for her to arrive and how he bolted into the store when she unlocked the door and made himself at home. Jack and Gunner were both listening to Charlotte but both staring at the dog. Neither would have been surprised if Norman started speaking to tell his own version of the story.

Charlotte pulled the pork from the oven and plated dinner for everyone. Gunner and Jack cleared off the kitchen table and set it with cutlery and napkins. Gunner topped up the wine glasses and they sat down to eat. Gunner did not want to talk about his life, so they went back to discussing the cases and the plan for Jack to try to leave the picture behind if he was able. Gunner also went over some extremely strict rules for Charlotte and Norman. They were not to leave the house unaccompanied since Gunner felt she was in danger. She and Norman both nodded in agreement.

As dusk progressed into night, Charlotte and Jack tidied the kitchen as Gunner got the camera ready. As much as he was hoping the murders had stopped, he knew they were in for some sort of show tonight and his gut was never wrong.

Jack did not want to lie on the couch with two people and a dog staring at him while he tried to force himself to sleep so the wine continued flowing as much as the conversation did. After a few more glasses of wine and some much-needed laughter, Charlotte, Jack, and Gunner were all feeling the pull of sleep. Charlotte and Gunner went to the kitchen to make some coffee so they could try to stay awake and when they returned to the living room, Jack was asleep on the couch.

Gunner started the video and he and Charlotte sipped their coffee, not knowing what to expect. They shared a quiet conversation and endured endless moments of silence watching Jack as his chest moved steadily up and down and his body lay completely still. Seconds turned into minutes, and minutes turned into hours. When Jack began to twitch on the couch, both Charlotte and Gunner were sound asleep.

Norman lay on the floor beside Charlotte's chair. He faded in and out of sleep but was much more alert than the others. His ears perked up as he saw Jack's arms begin to move. His head lifted as Jack's movements became more animated and he began to bark in short, quiet staccato bursts as Jack stood up from the couch. His bark was loud enough to wake Gunner and Charlotte but not loud enough to interrupt Jack's dream.

Gunner and Charlotte both woke at the same time and could not take their eyes off Jack. His arms were moving in strange patterns and he was standing on his toes instead of flat on his feet. Gunner got up to make sure the camera was still filming, and Charlotte remained sitting, stunned at what she was seeing. Gunner quietly sat back in his chair and he and Charlotte watched as Jack seemed to be acting out some macabre scene. He pursed his lips and moved his hand back and forth. When Charlotte finally figured out what he was doing she leaned over and whispered to Gunner.

"It looks like he is applying lipstick," she said.

Gunner got up from his seat and went into the kitchen. He dialed the number for the station and waited for someone to pick up.

The voice on the other end of the phone was cut off as Gunner spoke, "We need to increase police presence in the red-light district. I think my guy is going after another hooker."

Gunner hung up the phone and went back to his chair to watch the rest of the show. Jack remained on his toes and reminded Gunner of a marionette who had been hung up in a closet to wait for the next performance. Jack's body was suddenly thrown backwards onto the couch and Charlotte had to put her hand over her mouth to suppress her gasp. She and Gunner both sat on the edge of their chairs and Norman was now sitting up watching the show as well.

Jack's body was somehow being physically pushed backwards into the couch. Gunner and Charlotte watched as the cushions took more of the weight of his body as he struggled against his unseen attacker. Charlotte glanced over at Gunner and she could see he was inching his way off his chair and closer to Jack. She did not immediately see what he was looking at but, as she looked back at Jack, she could see the bruises surprisingly appearing on his neck. Jack's breathing had become quite labored and Charlotte was beginning to worry. She could sense Gunner's apprehension as well which did not alleviate her concern.

In the aftermath of the dream, there was a whisper that came in a timbre much lower than Jack's normal voice. It simply said, "I'm coming for you Charlotte."

Jack's body slumped down on the couch and Charlotte turned to Gunner. Usually, she was not one to curse but now all she could say was, "Holy Shit." Gunner was speechless.

Charlotte focused on the slow rise and fall of his chest. Jack was still breathing. While appearing to be sound asleep, his hands began to move again in random patterns. Neither Charlotte nor Gunner could figure out what he was doing, and, after a few moments of fidgeting, Jack stayed at rest on the couch and gave the impression that he was in a deep, peaceful sleep.

Chapter 51

Victor knew he should sleep but his need for death far outweighed his need for rest. Real hunters never slept while they were in their blinds. They remained vigilant, always waiting for the right moment to strike. Victor excelled at hunting. He was patient and careful not to warn his prey of his presence and made sure the kill was clean and efficient.

Victor needed to kill tonight solely for the opportunity to clear his mental path so he could focus on Charlotte. After he had quelled his insatiable need, Charlotte's death would be sweet torture and he would be able to take his time. He crossed the living room and peered behind the black-out curtains. Night was rapidly approaching, and Victor needed to meditate before going out. He was certain he would receive another vision that would guide him to tonight's victim.

After sitting cross-legged on the floor, Victor chanted in a whisper until he was able to surrender to the darkness. The black canvas behind his eye lids became awash with color and, with his eyes still closed, he began to move his head back and forth trying to recognize the location he had received in his latest vision. His conceptions were never detailed enough to be able to read any signs, but he could always recognize the surroundings and pinpoint where he was meant to be.

Once he had a location, he brought himself out of his trance and prepared for his evening. He put on a fresh pair of black jeans, holstered his gun under his black leather jacket, put on his black Doc Martin's and left the apartment with a new sense of purpose. Death was his forte and tonight he was going to regain his sense of control.

Once outside his building, he hailed a cab and gave an approximate address of where he wanted to go. He knew it would not be precise, but it would get him close enough to finding the target he was destined to acquire. The cab sped off through the streets and pulled over in a seedy part of town.

"You sure you wanna get out here?" the cabbie asked.

Victor said nothing and slipped the driver a twenty. He left the cab and watched the car speed off into the distance. For the neighborhood he was in, the night was eerily silent. He should have been hearing the bass beats from the clubs but, as he strained to hear the noise, he was met with stillness. The hunt was on. Victor relied on his tracking instincts and made his way through the streets to find her. He had seen her face in his visions. He knew she was not Charlotte, but she was her match in every way.

He continued to move through the streets and eventually emerged onto a congested avenue. Girls crowded the corners in hopes of acquiring a date for the next few hours and Victor scanned the horde, hoping to catch a glimpse of her. His eyes travelled over the collection of women until he finally saw her. She stood on the opposite corner, her long brown hair cascading down her back. She was quieter than most of the girls and did not seem overly eager to catch the attention of any passing men. Victor went straight to her.

She had seen him coming and began applying a fresh coat of lipstick. As she was tossing her hair behind her, Victor was suddenly in front of her. She looked startled but simply nodded as he showed her a wad of cash. He led her away and they walked together for a few blocks before he made sure there were no onlookers and he guided her into a narrow alley. He could sense her immediate alarm and pushed her backwards into the side of a dumpster. His hands tightly wrapped around her neck and he watched as she struggled for air. Her feeble attempts to push him away only made him tighten his grip and he felt her body begin to lose its fight.

Victor leaned forward and stared into her brown eyes. Although she was not Charlotte, her death would gratify him for the time being.

The sound of his own voice surprised him, "I'm coming for you, Charlotte."

He felt the life leaving her body and, as he prepared himself to receive his gift, he noticed her eyes change color. Victor was now staring into what looked like a hologram of one green eye and one blue eye and he could have sworn he was looking into a man's face. Victor stared into those eyes for longer than he wanted to, and they seemed to match his gaze. Victor slowly lowered the dead girl to the ground and waved his hand over her face to see if the eyes would follow the movement, but they remained fixated on Victor's face.

Victor stood up, angry that his moment had been compromised again. He bent over slightly, and his right hand pointed at the eyes that were still staring so intently at him.

"I don't know who you are, but I'm going to keep killing you, and killing you, and killing you," said Victor, moving his hand closer to the girls face with every threat.

He knew he sounded like a petulant child and he admonished himself for lingering at the crime scene and allowing the strange pair of eyes to bother him to the extent that they did. He left the alley undetected and continuously mumbled to himself as he left the sketchy part of the city behind him. His thumb vigorously spun the gold ring around on his right hand as he walked. Had he been sitting in his apartment right now, Victor was certain he would be rocking back and forth in the darkness, trying to regain his sense of competence. He felt like the young boy that had been sent to the root cellar for the first time and was scared to death.

~~

Victor was at least two blocks away from the dead girl when he felt the urge to go back. When he got there, she was just as dead as she had been when he left her, but her eyes were back to the brown color they had been before Victor strangled her. As he was about to leave, he noticed the photo on the ground beside her. When he focused on the picture, he realized it was a photo of the man he had shot in the head several weeks ago.

Chapter 52

Gunner waited to see if Jack would become animated again, but the cadence of his breathing signified that the dream had ended. Gunner knew he would be getting a call about another body, but his mind was currently focused on Jack. Charlotte had gone into the kitchen to make a fresh pot of coffee and Gunner got up to get a closer look at Jack's injuries. The bruising on his neck was indicative of strangulation. If his eyes had been open, Gunner was confident that he would see signs of petechial hemorrhaging from the asphyxiation.

As Gunner's eyes roamed over Jack's body, he noticed that the photo was missing from Jack's pocket. The crime scene photo from the first murder was nowhere to be seen. Gunner looked on the couch and the floor, assuming it could have fallen out of Jack's pocket during his physical struggles but there was nothing. The picture had disappeared.

It was just after 5:00 am and still dark outside when Jack began to wake up. Gunner backed away and sat back in his chair. As Jack's eyelids fluttered open, he saw Charlotte coming back into the room. When he had blinked the rest of the sleep from his eyes, Jack was faced by three sets of eyes staring quizzically at him.

"Did it work," asked Jack. His voice was hoarse, and his throat was burning.

"Check your pocket," Gunner replied.

Jack's hand went to his shirt pocket and he realized the photograph was no longer there. His hand went to his throat three times before his hand gently massaged his neck.

"I remember seeing him this time," Jack croaked, "Not specific details but I can picture him in my head."

Gunner immediately grabbed his notepad, "What do you remember about him?"

Jack spoke quickly so it was still fresh in his mind, "He was average height, bigger belly, and dark hair."

Gunner scribbled down everything Jack said about the killer. Since he could not remember and specific details about his face, a composite sketch would be impossible. At least Gunner could put out a BOLO with the few details Jack did remember.

Gunner looked up to see if Jack was waiting for him to stop writing. Jack was pale and seemed almost catatonic. His eyes did not blink, and Jack stared through Gunner.

"Jack!" Gunner sounded alarmed.

Jack shook his head from side to side, looked at Gunner and said, "The voice."

Charlotte had been silent since she had heard the physical description of the man but now leaned forward and barely whispered, "the one from the park?"

Jack could only nod. Charlotte was now as pale as Jack. Now three sets of eyes were trained on Charlotte.

Gunner's hand could not write fast enough. He urged Jack to remember everything he could from the dream before he told him what Jack had said while he was sleeping. Jack wracked his brain. He knew the man had spoken but he could not remember what he had said.

Jack looked at Gunner and said, "Whatever it was that he said, it felt like he was talking directly to me."

Norman left his place beside Charlotte and sat down in front of Jack. Several times, Norman pushed his head forward like he was pointing at something. When Jack did not get his message, Norman gently put his paw on Jack's right hand. Jack looked down at the paw on his hand and then at his own fingers.

"The ring." Jack looked inquisitively at Norman, wondering how the dog could know so much.

"He has a gold ring on his right hand, not like a wedding band but something like a signet ring." said Jack

Charlotte felt like all her energy had been drained but she got up from her chair and went into the kitchen. She brought back some photos and handed them to Jack. He flipped through the pictures of Max, not sure why Charlotte had brought them.

"Look at his right hand, Jack," said Charlotte.

Jack looked closer at the photos and saw the ring on a young Max's hand. Charlotte told Jack the story of the Mustang and Jack could see the hurt in her eyes.

"Charlotte, I wish I could say one way or the other that it is the same ring, but I can't," said Jack, "and I don't want to give you false hope."

With everything that had been happening since Gunner started investigating these cases, he would put money on the fact that somehow this killer was wearing the same goddamned ring, but he would keep that to himself for now. The cold case file that Gunner had on Max had just become much warmer.
When Norman finally removed his paw from Jack's hand, Jack noticed something under his fingernail. He was about to pick it out when Gunner saw what he was doing and yelled, "Don't touch it!" Gunner went to get his evidence kit. He grabbed a set of tweezers, picked the substance from under Jack's nail and put it into an evidence bag, marking the date and sealing the bag. He wanted to get it analyzed immediately.

The Waking Hours

Gunner hooked the surveillance camera into his sixty-inch screen television and the four of them watched Jack's sleep from the night before, fast-forwarding through the moments when Jack only slept. Since Gunner and Charlotte had drifted off sometime during the night, they missed the beginning of Jack's dream sequence. Jack watched with more disbelief than any of the others since he was watching his own body go from slumberous to completely animated while he slept. He watched his arm move in strange patterns and Charlotte could see that he was puzzled as to what he was doing.

"We think you are applying lipstick," she said. "We think he killed another....."

"Hooker," Gunner chimed in. He knew Charlotte could not bring herself to say it.

They continued to watch as Jack's body was thrown backwards onto the couch. The indent on the back cushion made Jack's hand rub his neck three times. The video continued and Jack, Charlotte and Gunner all began to talk about the scene they had just watched. Jack tried to remember more of the dream and Charlotte and Gunner urged him to remember everything he could. They had taken their focus from the recording and Norman's bark made all three of them look in his direction. Norman was still watching the recording and Jack's arm had begun to move in the video. His erratic pattern was confusing but soon they saw his hand move up to his chest.

"This must be when you left the photo behind," said Gunner.

Jack's hand unwittingly went to his chest three times, looking for the photo that had been there when he went to sleep. He could not fathom how he could take an object from reality and leave it in his dream, but somehow the photo had vanished from existence.

It was still early in the morning and they were all exhausted from their lack of sleep. Charlotte figured everyone needed a good breakfast and went into the kitchen to start preparation. Jack needed a hot shower and an Aleve, so he made his way to the upstairs bathroom. Gunner needed to check in with the station to see if there were any new murders reported so he went down the hall to his office.

Charlotte watched Norman as she prepared breakfast. He had been quite agitated since they had watched Jack sleeping. Charlotte thought perhaps he was adjusting to their temporary living arrangement or he sensed some nocturnal creature around the house. Norman was not growling but he was making noise, nonetheless. Charlotte peered out the kitchen window and could not see anything in the darkness. The closest streetlamp cast soft light at the corner of the property, but Charlotte could not make out any shapes in that dim glow. He paced the floor from the kitchen to the living room and back. Charlotte finally let Norman out at the front of the house where the lawn was surrounded by a fence and she returned to the kitchen to finish making breakfast.

Within minutes of Norman being let out, he began frantically barking. Gunner could hear the dog from his office and was surprised Charlotte had not gone to tend to him. Gunner left his office to go to the front door to let Norman back in the house and as soon as the door opened, Norman bolted past Gunner and into the kitchen. Gunner followed him and watched as Norman ran out of the open kitchen door.

Gunner noticed the frame on the door had been cracked when his kitchen door had been forced open. Jack had heard the commotion after he shut off the shower and ran downstairs in his towel. When he reached the kitchen, Gunner was making sure his revolver was loaded and Norman's bark was fading as he took off down the street. Jack glanced at the stove and noticed the eggs and bacon were still cooking on the stove, but Charlotte had vanished.

Chapter 53

Victor lumbered away from the crime scene with the photo in his hand. The implications of that photo being at this crime scene had grave undertones and Victor began to sweat.

When he finally got back to his apartment, Victor turned on his computer and began to watch the media reports on all the murders. The same name kept appearing as the investigating officer. He knew he needed to find Carrick Doyle to find the girl. He no longer had the advantage of walking into her shop and taking her. Every fiber of his being told him that. Victor knew finding Doyle was not as simple as typing his name into Google. Doyle's personal information would not be readily available on an internet search. Victor needed to meditate and ask for the information he required.

He stripped out of his clothes and got into his meditation position on the floor. It was still night so there was no chance of any light seeping through the black-out curtains. Victor pinched his thumbs to his index fingers and began to breathe deeply. His head and his upper body began to move in circles and the chant started low and rose in volume as Victor's body moved more quickly. His torso soon looked like it had been caught in a vortex and his chant became a mumbled mess of sounds. Victor shouted out a loud sigh and his arms stretched out as his elbow fell forward on to his knees. Sweaty and spent, Victor made a mental note of his destination.

He got up from the floor and entered the address he had received in his vision into his phone's address book. For the first time in any of his visions, Victor had seen the street name and number and knew Charlotte was with Doyle at his house. Victor knew it would be tough to kidnap her from a cop's house, but he knew it could be done and he was ballsy enough to do it.

He showered and got into a fresh change of clothes. With a destination in mind, Victor needed a vehicle since he had torched his precious Cadillac. He did not want to rent a vehicle with any of his fake identities and he figured a stolen vehicle in this city was trivial with everything else that was going on these days.

He left his apartment and was several blocks away when he found an unlocked car parked on the street. Before he went to the trouble of pulling off the casing to hot-wire the car, Victor tipped down the visor of the driver's seat and the keys fell into his lap. He started the engine and sped off before anyone noticed the car was missing.

The address of Doyle's house was unfamiliar to Victor but that was not a concern. He knew he would be pulled in the general direction of where he needed to be, and he would eventually find the house he was looking for. Victor found the street about an hour later and drove by Doyle's house several times. The lights were on in the living room and Victor could barely make out the shapes in the house through the thin veil of curtains.

It was just before 3:00 am and no lights were on in any of the other houses. He parked one hundred yards down the street and walked to the edge of the fence at the back of Doyle's house. Although the lights were on, the house seemed unnaturally silent. Victor stood on the sidewalk staring at the small window. He lifted his head to smell the air. She was in there. He knew it. Her scent lingered in his nasal passages and he began to spin the gold ring around on his finger to calm himself. Every nerve ending in his body felt like it was electrified, and he wanted nothing more than to break down the front door and find her, but she was in a cop's house and that cop was wired to shoot first and ask questions later. Victor had to be smart.

While there was no movement inside the house and the surrounding neighborhood slept, Victor circled the house several times to study the doors and windows. He needed to know all the access points before daylight, so he was ready to take her when the opportunity presented itself. The outside lights were already on and no other lights were triggered as he made his way around the house and the dense brush between houses gave him great cover. He knew the dog would be with her and the cop, but he did not know if anyone else was in the house.

With the sun still hidden under the blanket of the horizon, Victor strained to see anything from any vantage point he could. For a cop's house, everything was remarkably accessible and there were no hidden alarms. This cop must be as cocky as the reports made him out to be for him not to have a

The Waking Hours

better security system. From the front of the house, Victor could discern three bodies in the living room. He assumed, at this hour, the dog would be asleep on the floor. Of all the occupants, Victor was most concerned about how to circumvent the dog.

Just as that thought had crossed his mind, the dog barked, and Victor thought he had been made. He moved into the bushes and out of the sight line of the living room. The dog's bark had alerted the people in the room and soon two of the three figures were moving. Victor watched as they began to engage in conversation and he stealthily moved around to the back of the house.

His vantage point was not as great from his current position, but he could still see two of the three of them moving around the living room with the dog. After some time had passed, all three of the people were now in his line of sight and Victor could not understand why they were all now awake at 3:30 in the morning. From where he currently stood, it looked like they were watching television.

Eventually the television was turned off and Victor watched as one of the men left the living room, followed by the other. Charlotte came towards him into the kitchen and Victor was close enough to get a good look at her. She glided around the kitchen as she began to cook. He wanted so much just to take her now, but he did not know where the dog was.

Straining his eyes, Victor could barely make out the dog in the hallway. He seemed to be pacing and Victor was sure the furry little bastard knew he was close. Victor watched as Charlotte left the kitchen and made her way to the front of the house with the dog beside her. Victor could see the door open and, when Charlotte returned to the kitchen, the dog was nowhere to be seen. Victor waited until he was convinced Charlotte was alone and he made his move.

Putting his extra weight into it, the door was no match for Victor's shoulder. He leaned into the door, the frame cracked, and the door swung open. He could see the look of panic in Charlotte's eyes as he grabbed her arm, punched her in the head and carried her out of the kitchen. She had been cooking breakfast and thoroughly unprepared for an attack, so she had not even thought to scream. Once his fist connected with her head, Charlotte was unconscious. Victor threw her over his shoulder and moved quickly through the bushes to the stolen car. He could hear the dog barking wildly in the front yard and hear his nails scratching the fence as he tried to jump high enough to clear its height. Victor had dumped Charlotte in the back seat before the dog had time to process which direction they went. He left the lights off, punched the gas and raced out of Doyle's neighborhood unseen.

Victor knew the police presence was going to be coming soon and the search for Charlotte would be intense. When word got out that Charlotte was taken from under Doyle's nose, he knew Doyle would send everyone in the force out to look for whoever took her, and Victor had to be long gone by then. His saving grace was that nobody had seen the type of car he was driving, and he still had a couple of hours before the sun came up. The sky was already lighter, so Victor knew he had to make the best of his time and get out of town before every cop in the city was on patrol looking for him.

The stolen car's gas gauge showed a tank that was half full and that was plenty of fuel to get Victor to the warehouse. He had his own supply there to fill the car up to make the journey back after he had finished with Charlotte. He glanced in the rear-view mirror several times to remind himself that she was in his possession while he also checked for any approaching car lights. He appeared to have the road to himself and pushed down on the accelerator, confident that he would not be pulled over at this hour of the morning.

As he made the familiar exit off the highway, daylight was becoming more noticeable. Charlotte had not moved since they left Doyle's house and Victor was hoping the blow to her head had not been fatal. He had not even thought to check for a pulse when he put her in the car, but he did not want to waste precious time getting away from the cop's house.

The dirt road was dry, and plumes of dust billowed behind the car. Victor drove past the piece of land that used to house the old barn before it burned down. No smoke was in the air from any burn piles and the black skeleton of the barn stood out against the light blue of the early morning sky. To Victor, that bony structure of the old barn felt like death was welcoming him home. As he watched the burnt frame fade into the distance, Victor could see Charlotte beginning to move in the back seat. He was only half a kilometer from his driveway, and he knew she would not regain enough strength by then to put up any sort of a fight.

Once down the driveway, Victor made sure Charlotte was only semi-conscious before he got out of the car and entered the security code into the alarm panel on the wall. He had forgotten to remove his remote car door opener from the Cadillac before setting it on fire. The door chugged open and Victor drove the car into the parking bay.

"Welcome to Hell," he said.

When the garage door had closed, he got out and opened the door to the back seat. Charlotte still lay on the seat like a rag doll, moaning in her drowsiness. Victor grabbed her from the car and threw her over his shoulder, slamming the door shut with his foot. Charlotte swung like a pendulum as Victor carried her across the warehouse to the room he had prepared especially for her. He was eager to get started but he wanted to make sure tonight was perfect for him. There would be no excitement that would cause him to make mistakes. While she was still listless, Victor needed to meditate. She was going nowhere and could be heard by nobody, so he left her alone, enslaved in her death room.

His meditation was terse. Knowing that she was under his discipline was a great distraction for Victor and he had difficulty controlling his thoughts enough to be able to concentrate on finding his focal point. Each time he thought he was entering his spiritual realm, the thought of Charlotte confined in her room brought his mind back to reality and he wanted nothing more than to walk into that room and kill her instantly. But she was his Mona Lisa. He wanted to take time to make sure her death was painted in the exact way he had pictured it on the canvas in his mind so many times. Victor slowed his breathing and quieted his mind. He would need all his concentration for what was about to happen.

Chapter 54

"How the Hell could this happen?" Jack's voice was an octave higher than usual.

Gunner had been on the phone to the station before the words were out of Jack's mouth. Jack could see something in Gunner's other hand but could not make out what it was. Gunner's arms were madly flailing as he requested every car in the city to respond. When he ended the call, Gunner threw something on the table and ran out of his kitchen chasing Norman down the street.

Jack went over to the table to see what Gunner had been holding. It was the crime scene photo he had left at the most recent murder. Jack trembled as he picked up the picture and turned it over. On the back were two words, 'she's mine'.

Jack resisted the urge to gag, quickly dressed and followed Gunner out the door. After a few minutes of running, Gunner's neighborhood was filled with the sound of sirens and every house within a one-kilometer radius reflected the red and blue lights from the cruisers. Uniformed officers banged on every door hoping to get any information about the person who took Charlotte, but nobody had seen anything. They had either still been in bed or it was too dark to see anything on the street.

Gunner's inner dialogue was ugly, and he knew the whispers would be coming from every cop in the station. He could neither deny nor defend the fact that Charlotte had been taken from right under his nose. He berated himself with every pounding step of his loafers on the pavement and the sound of the rolling expletives fell on Jack's ears as Jack stayed well behind, knowing that Gunner was one step away from shooting anything if it moved in the wrong direction.

Gunner and Jack could see Norman stopped on the sidewalk about thirty meters ahead of them. He was panting and he looked horribly defeated. Gunner knew Norman had lost Charlotte's scent after the car had rocketed out of the neighborhood. When Jack reached the dog, he bent down and consoled Norman.

The forensics unit had arrived on the scene and while two of the team went to Gunner's house, the other two joined Gunner and Jack on the street. There were marks on the pavement left by the car as it peeled away from its parking spot. Hopefully, the forensics team would be able to determine the size of the tire by its tread pattern and narrow down the list of vehicles with those tires. Gunner was sure there would be a report coming in of a recently stolen vehicle and only hoped the tire size matched the description of the car.

Once the uniformed officers had finished polling the houses in the neighborhood, they began to collect in the street close to where the forensic team was measuring and photographing the scene. Their idle banter was distracting Gunner from his thoughts and he was about to tell them all to shut the fuck up until he overheard one of the young officers and it piqued his attention.

"At least this feels more like police work than attending a car fire," said the young officer, "and such a waste of a beautiful old car."

The hair on the back of Gunner's neck stood up and he did not know why. He replied, "what kind of car was it?"

The kid answered, "a '76 Cadillac Deville. The frame looks like it would have been in mint condition before the torch job. White exterior and red leather seats, what's left of them, anyway."

Gunner grabbed the note pad from his jacket pocket and began to take notes about the car and where it was found. As he was jotting down the information, another young officer chimed into the conversation.

"I think I saw that same car just north of the city. I was playing traffic cop at a structure fire and a strange looking guy was driving that same car."

Jack and Gunner looked at each other and back at the young cop. He had veered off his story about the car and was telling his fellow officers about the idiots who burned down their barn because they were so stupid. He was in mid-sentence when Gunner interrupted him.

"Tell me more about this strange looking guy," Gunner asked. He could see Jack leaning more into the conversation.

"If he stepped out of the car, I would guess he would be about five-foot-ten. Brown hair, brown eyes and he wore black. Everything was black," the officer said. "The thing I remember the most was the skin on his face. It was quite pock-marked."

Jack almost stuttered when he asked, "Did he say anything to you? Did he speak at all?"

"Nope," said the young cop, "just nodded at me and drove off."

"It's him," said Jack. His voice was barely a whisper.

Gunner took the young cop aside and gave him specific instructions to get back to the station immediately and have the police sketch artists do a composite drawing of the man he saw in the Cadillac. Gunner also got the officer to give him an approximate address of the barn. If it were a rural area, there could not be too many properties out there so it should help narrow their search.

Gunner turned to look at Jack and said, "You need to go to sleep. She'll have more of a chance of survival if your dream takes you to her and you can help her even in the slightest way."

"And what if I wake up somewhere else?" Jack was almost yelling. "What if I can't find her?"

The Waking Hours

"Jack, you said it yourself, she's been in your dreams since you started having them. My gut tells me that you'll find her, and my gut is never wrong," said Gunner. "It's time to save Charlie."

When Gunner spoke those last five words, Jack knew he was right. Every one of his dreams had been tied to either Charlotte, Max, or this asshole who Jack now wanted to kill personally. Jack knew there was no way he would be able to sleep on his own, so he accepted two of Gunner's sleeping pills and washed it down with some Scotch. His adrenaline was still pumping vigorously through his body and he was not sure his heart rate would slow enough for him to be able to sleep.

The effects of the Temazepam came more quickly than Jack anticipated. He sat down on the couch and allowed his grogginess to envelope him. Norman was lying on the floor staring at Jack. Somehow the dog felt the gravity of the situation and Jack wished he could take Norman into his dream with him. Gunner was on his cell phone barking more orders at more cops and Jack noticed that Gunner's outline was becoming blurry. Jack lay down on the couch and let the sleeping pill work its magic. Soon the room was spinning, and Jack was sucked into the vortex of slumber.

Gunner finished his call and turned on the camera. Jack lay comatose on the couch and Gunner knew he had not had enough time to begin dreaming so he went into the kitchen to make a few more calls, not wanting to wake Jack from his sleep. Gunner knew time was not on their side. Charlotte's life was in his hands and he had to get things moving quickly. He put in a call to the traffic division and within minutes, the traffic helicopter was in the air and headed north of the city to scout the area.

As Gunner expected, the report of a stolen Nissan had come into the station earlier in the morning. The tire marks on the street were the same type of tire that the Nissan was equipped with, so Gunner put out a BOLO on the car as well as the driver. The clock ticked and Gunner paced in his kitchen. He was furious with himself. He admonished himself for the oversight in leaving Charlotte alone, assuming nobody would have the balls to break into an alarm-protected police officer's house so boldly. Gunner had no idea that his alarm had been remotely disconnected.

He poured some coffee into a mug and put it in his microwave. Even though the mere thirty seconds should have gone by quickly, Gunner was impatient and yelled "come on" through the small window as he watched the mug spin around inside. His irritation was evident and, as he thought more about the case, he realized his concern lay more with getting Charlotte back safely than catching the sonofabitch who took her.

As he brought the mug to his lips, he could hear Jack moving in the other room. He crossed over into the doorway from the kitchen to the living room and saw Jack sitting cross-legged on the couch. Jack's arms were out to his sides and he was making a guttural sound in the back of his throat. If Gunner did not know he was sound asleep, he would have sworn that Jack was meditating.

The Waking Hours

Chapter 55

Meditating usually brought back Victor's laser focus but as he sat in the Lotus position and emerged from his hypnotic state he felt disconnected from his body. He could not pinpoint a specific problem, but he did not feel like himself. He kept his eyes closed, taking a few moments to continue his deep breathing to see if he could collect himself but the disjointed feeling still haunted him. He rolled his head from side to side, shook his arms out at his sides but nothing he did could ease his sense of anxiety. His breathing relaxed him slightly, but Victor knew that this was not a good sign.

He opened his eyes and stood from his Lotus position, stretching every part of his body. The response from his joints and muscles felt awkward and Victor felt unbalanced. He walked to his storage lockers to begin collecting the tools he would need, and his slight stagger made him feel like he had been drinking. Victor lumbered over to the lockers and opened the one he had been saving. Looking at the many blades inside the locker made Victor begin to feel better but now he felt like he was being watched.

He spun around to look across the warehouse and found nothing. There were no eyes watching him and no other bodies in the building besides his and Charlotte's. Just the mere thought of her made Victor's pulse increase. He stripped out of his street clothes and got into his white coveralls. His safety goggles hung from a hook in the locker and he tucked those into his pocket. The blades were all neatly stored on a board that Victor removed from the wall of the locker. Each of the blades reflected the harsh florescent ceiling lights and the patterns created a macabre dance on the walls.

"The dance of death," grumbled Victor.

He was ready. He had done his due diligence in stalking and capturing his prey. He had enjoyed the hunt but now it was time for the kill. Victor opened the door to the small room and found Charlotte conscious again. The bruising was evident, and her left eye was swollen shut. Her head lifted as Victor entered the room and her breath seemed to catch in her throat when she saw him again. There had been no time to register who burst through the door at Gunner's house since it happened so quickly. But Victor knew immediately that she recognized him, and he watched as the first tear slide down her cheek.

Victor put the blades down on the table behind him and turned to face Charlotte. She was gently weeping now, and Victor waited for the begging to happen, but she never spoke a word. Her gaze met and kept his and she refused to look away. Victor was moderately unnerved. He was more equipped to handle people begging for their lives than he was a defiant and challenging quarry, but she refused to look away.

Victor was intrigued by her tenacity. Perhaps he had misjudged the timid girl he had seen in the park. This was going to be much more fun than Victor had anticipated, and he enjoyed their little staring contest. Her tears had stopped, and her fixed stare had gone from fear to hatred. He could feel the rage emanating from every pore in her body. Victor absorbed that seething hatred with pleasure. He felt the strength coming from it.

As Victor turned to get started, he heard the words as plain as day, "I'm coming for you, Charlie!"

Victor spun around and looked in all four corners of the room. The door was closed, and they were alone. He was sure he had heard the words but where had they come from? Her lips had not moved so she was not the narrator. Victor moved closer to her and stopped when his face was only inches from hers. His foul breath settled on her face and he could see her pull her head back slightly to put more distance between them. Her eyes blinked rapidly but when she looked at his face again and they locked eyes, she smiled.

"Jack." she whispered.

Victor was the one to pull his head away from her this time. He stood up, put his hands on his hips and turned away from her. The mirror

The Waking Hours

stood on the desk in the corner. He was going to set it up so she could watch herself die but instead he lifted the mirror to his face. When Victor saw his reflection in the mirror, he gasped. Staring back from his own reflection was one blue eye and one green eye. Victor forgot about the girl and continued to watch the eyes move in his mirror image. He had no idea how long he stared at himself in the mirror, but the white room had faded into the background and everything except the eyes faded to black.

Chapter 56

Black. When Jack awoke in his dream, his eyes tried to scan the room, but everything was black. He was seated cross-legged with his arms outstretched. He could only assume his hands were bound and he was somehow shackled to the floor. After several minutes of deep, rhythmic breathing, Jack's body was involuntarily moved to a standing position. He felt his arms stretch above his head and fall in an arc to gently touch the floor. Jack's vision suddenly went from black to stark white and he let his gaze travel over his surroundings. He was in a large, open space. Everything was hospital white and there were a few sections of lockers that Jack could see just ahead. He could also see many white doors that led to other rooms in the building, but Jack could not recognize anything in this place.

Unlike any of his other dreams, Jack felt alarmingly weak and powerless. He did not seem to have the freedom of movement of any of his limbs and was merely along for the ride. They moved across the floor towards the lockers. His host body began to move its arms and Jack realized this person was taking off clothing. Jack had not even thought about whose body he was possessing and suddenly felt very self-conscious about seeing the naked body with the assumption it was Charlotte. There were no mirrors and the host quickly dressed in another outfit, so Jack was spared the embarrassment.

They collected a few items from the locker that Jack could not quite make out and they moved across the open space towards one of the white doors. The door opened and they turned to the left, placing the board on the small white table. The items that were taken out of the locker now become more visible and Jack realized it was a small board filled with many sizes of blades. As the host body turned to face the other way, Jack saw Charlotte sitting on the floor. Her hands were bound, and she looked like she had been hit with a two-by-four. He wanted to reach out to her, to take her into his arms but he was immobile.

The Waking Hours

Jack could feel the rage now radiating between the two people in the room. He watched as Charlotte held the gaze of the man who was about to take her life and he was amazed by her strength. Jack was trying to conjure up as much energy as he could, feeding off the seething hatred in the room and as the man turned, Jack screamed, hoping Charlotte would be able to hear him.

"I'm coming for you, Charlie."

The words echoed in Jack's head and he did not know if his cry had been heard until the man spun around to stare at Charlotte. Jack's host sunk lower to the ground and got within a couple of inches of Charlotte's face. Jack did not know what the man's next move was going to be, but he could not sit idly by and not try something. Charlotte was doing everything she could to turn her face away from the man and Jack willed her to look up at him, just for a second, because he knew what she would see.

When their eyes met, Jack was silently cheering. He knew she had seen him, knew he was here to help, and when she said his name, Jack knew he had just bought them some time.

Chapter 57

Gunner knew they were running out of time. The longer Charlotte was missing, the less chance they had of finding her alive. He had been watching Jack's movements during his dream and something seemed off. If Jack had woken up in Charlotte's body, Gunner could only assume she had been restrained but Jack was moving freely and seemed to be undressing and dressing himself.

Gunner went back into the kitchen to make a few more calls and grab some more coffee. He could hear a low growl coming from Norman and the dog would not take his eyes off Jack. The hair on the scruff of Norman's neck had been standing up since Jack had become animated. Gunner took that as a bad sign.

He went back into the living room and sat down to watch Jack. There was no report back from the traffic helicopter and the composite sketch had been sent out to all the departments to watch out for the guy that had been seen in the '76 Deville. Gunner had just raised his mug to his mouth when Jack blurted out, "I'm coming for you, Charlie."

Gunner jumped back in his seat and coffee spilled down the front of his shirt and all over the arm of the chair. He silently cursed Jack but did not want to yell out loud for fear of waking Jack out of his dream. Gunner remained in the chair, watching Jack as he slept. Jack's movements became fewer and further apart until he was motionless on the couch. His eyes were open, and he seemed to be staring at nothing.

Gunner's cell rang and he moved quickly into the kitchen before answering. The voice on the other end talked for about thirty seconds and the call was ended. Gunner ran into the living room to wake Jack.

"Jack, we found the warehouse," Gunner yelled.

There was no movement from Jack and no reaction.

The Waking Hours

"Jack, we think we found him," Gunner was shaking Jack's shoulder as he spoke.

The slow rise and fall of Jack's chest still indicated that he was in a deep sleep and Gunner knew the Temazepam and the Scotch had really knocked him out. Gunner tried a few more police tactics to wake Jack, but he was out for the count.

Gunner looked at Norman and said, "I don't normally do this."

    Gunner picked Jack up off the couch in a fireman's carry and hauled him out to the cruiser. He opened the door to the back seat and dumped him in, hoping he landed squarely on the seat and did not hit his head on the door. There were no thuds, so Gunner tucked Jack's legs into the back and closed the door. Norman was waiting beside Gunner and eagerly jumped into the passenger seat. When Gunner hit the lights and the sirens, Norman's front legs bounced up and down on the front seat ready for action.

    The car backed quickly out of the driveway and jumped the curb again. Gunner put down the passenger window and Norman stuck his head out. There were a few people on the sidewalk and Norman howled at them on the way by. It was his siren, and he wanted the people to know he was on official business.

    The car sped along the expressway and took the off-ramp to follow the highway north. Gunner knew that the cops were already on the scene, but they were given explicit instructions not to enter the building without Gunner. He followed the directions and turned onto the dirt road. The sirens were off, but the lights were still flashing so any slow-moving cars would pull off to the shoulder and let him pass. They drove by the burned-out barn and knew they were going in the right direction. There was an unmarked car parked at the end of the driveway to the warehouse, so Gunner knew where to turn. He turned off the lights and cruised quietly towards the building.

    When they reached the warehouse, Gunner could see the full tactical teams in ready position. There were battering rams for the doors, night-vision goggles, smoke bombs in case they needed them, and each team was on high alert with rifles ready to fire. Gunner wanted to take this guy alive and everyone was made fully aware of his plan. He did not want some trigger-happy kid taking this guy down in a hail of bullets.

Gunner geared up in the bullet proof vest he had in the trunk and moved around to the passenger window. Norman was anxious to get out of the car and help and, for the first time since they had met, Gunner treated Norman like a dog.

"Stay," said Gunner and pointed at Norman so the dog knew he meant business.

Norman sat back on the seat and hung his head. Gunner felt guilty but he did not want Norman alerting anyone to the police presence outside the warehouse. Gunner slipped in his earpiece and began to communicate with each of the teams positioned outside the warehouse. They were all ready to go when Gunner gave the order. He reminded them again that he wanted the girl and the kidnapper ALIVE.

The team at the front went in first. They hit the door with the ram and threw the smoke bomb in through the small opening of the door. When they heard nothing, they moved one by one through the door with their rifles pointing in all directions. Through their gas masks, they saw no movement. With a few fingers pointing in different directions, the squad leader sent the team in smaller groups to check all the doors. They got word that the team from the back was inside as well.

Like a cluster of spiders, men dressed in black scurried around the shocking white interior of the building looking for any sign of Charlotte. They found the stolen Nissan and sent word to Gunner. He knew they had found the right place, but he had not yet heard if Charlotte had been found alive.

The teams had one door left to check and, since the rest of the building had been cleared, Gunner wanted to be there when they opened the room. He stealthily moved through the building to meet up with the team. He could hear the man's voice through the door and Gunner's blood ran cold. He now knew why Jack had been so affected by it. In the moment it took Gunner to register the voice, the entire building was cast into sudden darkness.

The Waking Hours

Gunner pulled his pistol and stood ready to fire. The night vision light on his face shield activated and he could make out the shapes of the officers surrounding him. He was happy he made the choice to put that face shield on before he entered the building.

The door in front of him was knocked open and Gunner stood looking at the man on the other side of the door. In his peripheral, he could make out Charlotte in a ball on the floor, gagged but still breathing. The monster was holding a knife at shoulder level. The blade was pointed at Charlotte and he could not see all the people shrouded in darkness standing outside the door.

The man's deep voiced growled as he spat out the words, "It's time for Victor to create his masterpiece, you Bitch."

Victor took one step forward and struggled to keep control of his knife. With his night-vision light, and through the arcing beams of flashlights, Gunner could see the man physically trying to push his arm in a downward motion, but it seemed to be suspended in mid-air. Without warning, the florescent lights began to burn brightly once again and startled everyone in the building. Before Gunner could make a move, Norman ran past him into the room and jumped in the air just as the man regained control of the knife and pushed it in Charlotte's direction. The knife connected and the dog yelped as he fell to the floor with a thud. As Norman lay motionless on the white tiles, his blond hair slowly became saturated with the blood from his stab wound. Charlotte turned towards the dog and began to sob. Gunner could almost see Jack struggling to gain control of Victor's body. Victor took one more step towards Charlotte and Gunner fired his gun twice, each shot hitting Victor above his knee on each leg. He fell to the floor and dropped the knife.

Gunner signaled the tactical team to apprehend the suspect and get him out of the room. When the officers moved in, Victor was looking down at his legs and focusing on the blood. Victor had never seen his own blood and when the realization of his own mortality had set in, he passed out.

~~

Jack was still passed out in the back of Gunner's car when Gunner emerged from the building holding Norman. The ambulance had arrived to take Charlotte to the closest hospital and Gunner knew he had to get Norman to a vet, and fast. Gunner lay Norman gently on the front seat, quickly glanced at Jack in the back seat and noticed the blood on Jack's pants. Gunner yelled for two officers to take Jack out of the back seat and put him in the ambulance with Charlotte. He had not noticed the gold ring that Jack was clenching in his hand before he was taken out of the car. Gunner called the station to get the address of the nearest vet and sped off down the dirt road.

Chapter 58

Jack waited for Charlotte as she got ready to turn over the keys for the Antique shop to Anna. She stood silently in the middle of the store, wordlessly saying goodbye to a life that she would look back on with great fondness because she had a feeling that the store had just become a part of her past. She circled around, letting her eyes cast a quick glance on all the antiquities that had been a part of her life for so long. Jack gave her the time she needed and stood inside at the front window surveying the street. His suspicious nature would always eat at him, but the world seemed much less threatening now. He moved to the front windowpane and felt the child-like urge to exhale his hot breath onto the cooling glass. As the air formed a cloud on the window, the outline of a heart appeared. Charlotte had noiselessly approached behind him and smiled at the appearance of the wish she had made so many months ago. She slipped her hand into his and they left the Antique shop, both filled with hope and not sadness. For Charlotte, this was not an ending, it was a beginning.

Gunner waited outside for them. He was happy to see his new friends in much better health than the last time he had seen them. Charlotte still had vague traces of her bruises and Jack's wounds were so superficial that he had not needed to be admitted to the hospital which gave him time to spend every moment by Charlotte's side. The sun was shining, and bright light reflected off the Mustang. The gold ring now found itself comfortably fitted onto Jack's finger. Charlotte thought that Max would have wanted it that way and she knew it was Max's energy associated with the ring and not Victor's. She had not even seen the ring on Victor until he had passed out from his gunshot wounds and she shuddered when she realized she had almost been killed by the same man who had murdered her brother seventeen years ago. At least now she had the closure she had so desired and she could move on knowing that Max was still around in spirit.

Gunner drove them to their new building and helped them bring in the last of their belongings. They toasted to their future and enjoyed a lovely dinner that Charlotte was more than happy to cook. Gunner left earlier than usual to allow them to settle into their new life together.

Ensconced in the comfort of their new apartment, neither one of them ever wanted to see true darkness again. Jack wrapped his hand around Charlotte's as he extinguished the last of the candle flames, but the steady glow of the nightlights still cast a dim light around the room as the shadows peered out from their hiding places. Norman was curled up on Jack's old recliner which Norman had claimed for himself, still heavily medicated and recovering from his injury. He seemed embarrassed to still be saddled with the plastic bucket on his head that dogs were made to wear after surgery, but he wore his shame well. Jack took one last tentative glance around the living room, making sure nothing was out of place. The night was on their terms now. His lips slowly grazed Charlotte's cheek and, for the first time in a long time, Jack looked forward to his waking hours.

The End

About the Author

Susan M. Nairn lives in a quaint town in the heart of Muskoka, Ontario. Her passion for words began as a child and her love of writing poems turned into short stories and eventually writing novels. The Waking Hours is the first in the RELATIVE series. She is currently writing the second in the series called One Eleven while madly documenting ideas for the following four books in the series: Dark Room, Root Cellar, Gemini, and Abbey In The Oakwood.

You can also follow her at www.susanmnairnauthor.ca

Manufactured by Amazon.ca
Bolton, ON